TOKEN CREEK

ERWIN DAVID RIEDNER

Waubesa Press
The quality fiction imprint
of Badger Books Inc.

© Copyright 1998 by Erwin David Riedner
Published by Badger Books Inc./Waubesa Press
Edited by J. Allen Kirsch
Printed by Documation of Eau Claire, Wis.

First Edition

Hardcover: ISBN 1-878569-55-4
Softcover: ISBN 1-878569-57-0

Badger Books Inc.
P.O. Box 192, Oregon, WI 53575
Toll-free phone: (800) 928-2372
Web site: http://www.badgerbooks.com
E-Mail: books@badgerbooks.com

For Susan

Token Creek

The title for these stories, *Token Creek*, is taken from the name of an unincorporated crossroads village set on the rich dark topsoil of Dane County in southern Wisconsin, in the Midwest. A creek called Token Creek purls through and by, every day. The majority of the episodes originate in and around the village. The stories are arranged in the order I remember hearing them. There should be no doubt that the events described here did take place, to one degree or another, to real people.

E.D.R.

These things seem small and indistinguishable,
Like far-off mountains turned into clouds.

Demetrius — A Midsummer Night's Dream

Stories

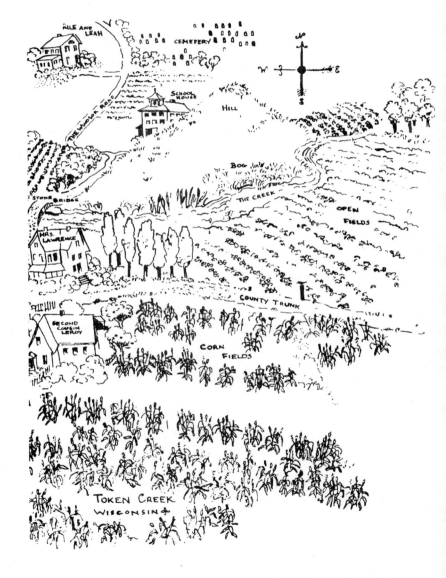

Artist — Edda Jakab

Iowa man shoots, kills unusual 14-tine doe

DEER, from Page 1A

animal was a doe. "It is unusual to find a doe with antlers, but what makes this particularly unusual is that the antlers had hardened and grown so big," Hainfield said.

More research will be required to determine whether the antlers are of record size for a doe. Other than state officials, probably no one keeps records on doe antlers, said Jack Reneau, director of big game records for the Boone and Crockett Club, a Montana-based organization that keeps track of record antlers and horns.

"We have no antlers on record that have been from a doe," he said.

Although Reneau hears of one or two antlered does a year in the United States, their antlers have been in the velvet growing stage and have never been as large as those on the doe Weymiller shot. Velvet is like a skin that covers antlers and supplies blood so they can grow.

Weymiller will have to wait about 60 days for the antlers to dry before they can be officially scored.

Hainfield said it takes a second boost of testosterone to drop the velvet and harden the antlers — and that second boost is rare for does.

Harpers Ferry

★ DES MOINES

0 Miles 200

"There are a number of reasons a doe could have enough testosterone to grow and harden the antlers," he said.

One explanation would be that a deer had both male and female reproductive organs — but Weymiller's deer was strictly female. Another reason is a deer's body might simply produce extra testosterone. And when a deer has twins, one male and one female, in the uterus, the two fetuses can share hormones, Hainfield said, resulting in a female with additional testosterone.

W

Just in tim
the holida

Under the Knife

The band is playing somewhere ...
And somewhere children shout ....

Junior sat watching the Regulator clock on the wall above the classroom, peering up at it over the top of his book. He held the book with both hands, his elbows on his desk. He was slouching just enough to keep his face nearly hidden behind the book, giving the impression of reading, that he was absorbed in his work. If he stared without blinking, he could see the big hand of the clock moving slowly upward — he could see time moving. He didn't dare keep his eyes on the big clock for too long though, in case Miss Liptrap might notice his wishing the minutes away, imagining he were already outside, in the sunshine.

Junior glanced down to read a few words, then raised his eyes again to check the progress of the clock. The big hand was practically on the XII — not much longer now.

Others in the room were aware that the hour was

approaching: amid the hush from in back of him tiny sounds were arising, new noises, rustlings. Books were shifted so they could be quickly closed, papers were stealthily brought together, pencils were eased into holders. Directly in front of him, in the head seat, he saw Emma carefully place a sheaf of exercise papers into her desk.

Somewhere off to the side there was a quick clatter, then a small movement of clothing — someone had dropped a crayon and immediately picked it up.

Quite suddenly the teacher moved her chair backward and stood straight up. She gazed over the classroom, stifling further preparations. The hush returned, only broken by an occasional squeak of a desk, or by a small shoe momentarily dragging on the wooden floor, or a cough. A whisper started from the back of the room but stopped sharply as Miss Liptrap's eyes searched for the source of the inappropriate hissing.

Junior held his breath. Any second now the teacher would reach out for her engraved brass handbell. Junior began to slide himself erect in his seat, ready to stand. He waited. The long hand of the clock touched the center of the XII.

But the teacher made no move. The clock's arrow-tipped hand continued to move across the number. Junior let his book down, watching her. Miss Liptrap remained standing, looking out over her classroom. She made no gesture, no glance even, toward the handbell. What was wrong? Why was she making them wait like that?

The great hand of the Regulator was nearly past the number. What was the teacher doing? There were stirrings in the room; there were more whispers.

Children were looking at the clock. Some one cleared his throat, as if puzzled, or to remind the teacher of the time. There were sounds of fidgeting and tappings.

Then she spoke.

"I know it's nice outside."

By now Junior was stewing. Correct, Miss Liptrap. It was nice out. It was, it was. Very nice — sunny and warm, and getting warmer. That's why they wanted her to let them out. That was the point. Somewhere in the room some one sighed. Workbooks were put on desks. Noises grew. Kids were definitely putting things away.

"Since it is so pleasant outside, finally, I want us to enjoy the good weather today. So, I have a surprise for you," the teacher announced.

Such words were unexpected. The movements in the room stopped dead still. All heads were turned up and forward; all eyes were on the stern figure in front of them. Junior softly closed his book and placed it into his desk.

"Instead of coming back in for lunch, we are going to have the afternoon off from school. In fact, I'm going to let you eat outside. We'll have a picnic. What do you think?"

"Yeah. Yes. Wonderful. Good golly! The whole afternoon?" There were cheers of approbation. There was chattering and laughing. This was unheard of.

A school day afternoon outside? Kids began making plans; some stood up.

"Wait, wait," the teacher commanded. Partial quiet returned, but there was a background of whispers and movements; there were still expressions of amazement.

"There are blankets in my car. We'll spread them out by the baseball field. We'll eat an early lunch there. When we are finished eating, and only when we are finished, we will choose sides for a baseball game."

More cheers of approbation. There were thank-yous; children were now standing. Some applauded. Imagine, an entire half day of school outside. Over the growing hubbub, Miss Liptrap appointed three of the older ones to go to her car for the blankets.

"Wait now, wait, boys and girls. Wait. I haven't dismissed you yet. I have one more thing to tell you. Sit down, if you please."

The teacher waited while they calmed down. They sat and were soon quiet.

"Emma's... " here she paused, " ...and Junior's second cousin, Mr. LeRoy Armstrong, will provide us with Kool-Aid for the picnic. He has promised to have it here before eleven, which means he should be at the field right now, setting out thermos bottles. And, after our picnic, Mr. LeRoy Armstrong has generously agreed to be the chief umpire for our baseball game."

The announcement caused more chattering and whispers. Emma turned around to look at Junior.

"Oh my gosh," she said to him, wide-eyed.

"Quiet please, quiet," called Miss Liptrap. "Now, those whom I have assigned to help with the blankets will come with me to the car. Emma, you and Joanne will bring the kitchen box. The rest of you may get your lunch boxes and go to the field, one row at a time, as usual, no running."

Miss Liptrap pronounced this last command with firmness and authority.

The children quickly settled down. Miss Liptrap

nodded toward the first row. Now everyone in the first row, the row nearest the window, stood and moved toward the door in the back of the room. As the last pupil of the row passed the end of the second row, the children there stood, turned, and followed the first line. The next rows stood and moved out in the same way. Finally the last row, row five, Emma's row, stood and began to leave. Emma brought up the rear of the entire school, with her brother Junior just ahead of her. Such was the burden of intelligence.

There was tumult in the hall as children grabbed for jackets and sweaters; there was commotion at the door as the liberated mob squeezed toward the outside. There was thundering on the wooden steps as they raced down, screaming for joy as they met the bright sun and clear air. With boisterous relief, with lunch pails swinging, the crowd ran, jumped, skipped. Arms were waving; fingers were pointing toward the sky; ears heard new birds singing, noses inhaled the perfume of spring and earth, and all dashed in exuberance toward the green expanses of the baseball field.

Mr. Second Cousin LeRoy Armstrong was indeed at the picnic site, as Miss Liptrap had promised. When the children burst onto the field, they found the rotund sportsman flushed with excitement as he unloaded the last of five, very large thermos bottles from the trunk of his car. He had already set out a wooden table and had placed several folding chairs on the first base side of the diamond, the side toward the schoolhouse. Now he was puffing toward the table with the last thermos, anxious to complete his assignment in time for the late-morning festivities.

Second Cousin LeRoy Armstrong had dressed himself carefully for his role as chief umpire in the upcoming contest. Besides an oversized red cap with a long bill, he sported a black-and-white striped referee's jacket, worn over an orange plaid work shirt. His trousers were dark green, with many pockets, some clearly containing baseballs. The bulging trousers were quite short, although they fit nicely over the top of his impressive stomach. Covering his thick calves were heavy white socks, fit into a pair of high-topped tennis shoes, black and white, and a fine match to his official's jacket. The trousers were so short that when Junior first saw his relative, he thought the white socks were leggings.

Awed curiosity drew the children to Mr. Second Cousin LeRoy Armstrong.

They stood around him. He was a sight to see. It was then that Mr. Second Cousin LeRoy made his declaration.

"Now, I don't intend to show favorites in this ball game," he said in his booming tenor, and as the school stood having a look at him.

"Emma and Junior Armstrong, you will very definitely, no question about it, have to be on different teams. I wouldn't want people saying I made an unfair call for one team, just because we're related."

Miss Liptrap agreed with this suggestion. It was reasonable, she said.

She then added that the baseball game would not start until everyone had eaten and thoroughly cleaned up. There could be no eating and ball playing at the same time. So everyone should prepare to eat. Second Cousin LeRoy nodded his agreement. He was as hungry as... no, hungrier than, a bear.

Miss Liptrap continued her instructions. After the picnic lunch, and after they had cleaned up, they could choose their teams. She expected everyone would play and that the teams would be evenly matched. If they weren't, she would arrange them so they were.

She next appointed team captains, one of whom was Emma, the other Junior. That done, the children and adults spread out to eat, basking in the spring sunshine. Second Cousin LeRoy took his lunch with Miss Liptrap. He talked little, nodded frequently, and chewed a great deal.

Forty-five minutes later the picnic lunch was finished, with a cleanup completed to Miss Liptrap's satisfaction. She and Mr. Armstrong would now organize the game.

In order to accommodate the twenty-six children in the school, each team was to be made up of thirteen players. Nine would play at a time. After a full inning of play, four of the children who started the inning would be substituted so that those youngsters waiting could enter the game. After each inning, there would be another round of similar rotations. Miss Liptrap would be sure that everyone played the same amount. The game would last nine innings and no more, even if there were a tie at that point. There would be no base stealing. Mr. Second Cousin LeRoy would be the plate umpire and chief; Miss Liptrap would be the field umpire. She would defer to his expertise. Everyone understood.

Second Cousin LeRoy now called the team captains to him. He tossed a coin high into the air. How it fell, with Emma calling, would decide which team batted first. Junior's team won the toss and elected to go up first. Emma's team, with Emma pitching, took to the field. Emma was known to have a good arm.

And she did have a good arm that day. Although she was throwing against a team of many strong hitters, she allowed very little scoring with her hard and wicked fastball. But her own team hit no better, so by the start of the ninth and final inning, and by the time everyone was getting tired, the score stood six-all. It looked like they could end with the tie Miss Liptrap had predicted. Second Cousin LeRoy said the game had the kind of low score that happened in the major leagues. Miss Liptrap reminded him, and all, that there would be no extra innings. A tie was always a good way to end things, assuming that's what would happen.

The first batter of the top of the last inning, Junior's

team batting, struck out. The second batter up, however, somehow dribbled the ball far enough out and toward third base that there was a scratch hit. With a runner on first, one out, Junior took a time out to confer with his team. He was to bat next. It was late in the game and they needed to score.

After him came up the eighth-grade girl who was likely to hit; she had driven in two of their six runs; so if they got somebody in scoring position, on second base, then a hit from her would likely get them the game. What did they think? Should he go for the bunt?

The team agreed — he should bunt. He would probably be a sacrifice, but maybe he could lay the ball down the third base line too, like the batter before him, and even get on base. They broke up their conference with Junior intending to bunt.

Junior stepped to the plate. It was pretty clear that Emma knew what he was up to. She was grimacing like she was going to throw hard. Her eyes were narrowed and flashing between her half-closed lids.

Junior's counterstrategy was to try to make her believe he was going for an outfield hit. And, just to be sure she thought that, he was going to take the first pitch, as if he expected a bad pitch. He would give her the impression he would have swung away, had he thought she still had any stuff. Yes, he was taking all the way, even if the pitch were hard and down the middle.

It was — it was hard and straight down the middle. Junior watched it go by.

"Strike," bawled Second Cousin LeRoy.

Emma got the ball back from her catcher and studied it for a moment.

Then she looked at Junior. Her teeth were clenched and her hair hung over her eyes. This time she really stretched back for her throw.

As she released the furious ball, Junior moved over the plate, squaring to bunt. Unfortunately, Emma's next pitch was not quite as nice and down the middle as the first one had been. It was just as hard as, harder even, than her first — that part of it was excellent. But the rest of it was high, and way inside.

The ball struck Junior with a glancing blow to his forehead, as he turned away to avoid it. It then rolled off foul toward first. Junior shuddered for a split second, slowly released his bat, and sat down, right on home plate, feeling blackness closing in.

Second Cousin LeRoy stepped over the catcher and caught Junior under the arms, just before the sitting boy was about to collapse backward. After that, things got a bit unclear for Junior.

Junior became aware of being lifted and held upright from beneath his arms. He was thinking that he would just as soon try to walk off the field, and to catch his breath, but then someone grabbed him by the ankles. He found himself carried from both ends, sagging and hanging in the middle like wet spaghetti noodles, toward the wooden table with the big thermos bottles. By the time they got him there he was getting awake, and the thermos bottles were gone. He wondered where. He was about to tell them he was fine, even though his head hurt, but the words somehow didn't come out. All in all, he decided he wasn't quite ready to sit up — he needed another few seconds. He could hear them talking a mile a minute all around him. He heard Second Cousin LeRoy's voice, then Miss Liptrap's, then more chattering from the children. He heard Emma say she was sure he was all right.

He half opened his eyes. There was still darkness at the edges, although he could see ahead and above himself without difficulty. He noticed how blue the sky was, and how white the clouds were. Lord, but he loved the spring. He closed his eyes again, vaguely wondering what they were going to do with him.

He considered laughing, even though his head hurt. Sounds were diminished, and became fewer. No one was talking. He could hear the teacher — he assumed it was the teacher — rattling around in the box of kitchen utensils under the table. It was the teacher, definitely. He recognized the hiss of her breathing. He couldn't figure out what she was up to. He kept his eyes closed, still resting. He needed just another few seconds, then he would go back to the game.

About the time he no longer heard Miss Liptrap making a clatter in the kitchen box was when he decided it was time to get up and get started again. He opened his eyes. There was the teacher leaning over him, looking straight down at him. He began to sit up, to show her he was ready to play ball. As he began to push himself up, he saw what Miss Liptrap was doing. She was holding a huge butcher knife with both hands, one hand at the tip of the blade and the other on the handle. Junior was about to bolt when Miss Liptrap put a sharp elbow on his chest and firmly pushed him back down onto the table. A wave of terror swept over Junior, but he wasn't strong enough yet to raise himself against the teacher's insistent elbow.

A split second later he became aware of something cool on his forehead.

He realized that Miss Liptrap was rolling the side of the cool metal knife blade over the bump raised by the baseball. She wasn't pushing very hard. He let it go on for a bit, but decided that the slight pressure of the knife blade created as much discomfort as not. Still, it did soothe too. He let her roll the broad face of the blade back and forth over the bump again. All in all, he didn't like it, cool or not.

"Can I sit up?" he asked, the blade against his forehead.

"You may, yes. And Junior, it's *may* I, not *can* I." He saw her step back slightly, raising the knife.

Junior sat up. The teacher held the butcher knife with both hands. She kept her eyes on him.

"Do you feel sleepy?" she asked as she stared at

him.

"No. I'm thirsty. Can I go get a drink?" He was as dry as death.

"May. Use 'may' when asking permission. 'May I go and get a drink,' is what you intended to say, I believe." She was still watching him.

"May I go and get a drink?"

"No, you may not! Stay still for another minute. Tell me if you feel sleepy. Are you sleepy? Do you want to go to sleep?"

Junior watched the long knife moving in her hands. She seemed to be swaying from side to side. Her eyes did not leave him.

Without warning, Junior leapt off the table and ran full tilt for first base.

"Junior Armstrong! Come back here this instant!" rasped Miss Liptrap, pointing the knife at him.

Junior kept right on fleeing until he reached first base, where he turned and looked back at Miss Liptrap, his would-be assassin.

The teacher was about to demand again that he come back to her when Second Cousin LeRoy bellowed: "Hit batter. Automatically gets first. Play bawl!"

Emma looked at Junior. He was standing with one leg stretched back touching the base pad, the other off the base and leading toward second. He was rocking on the balls of his feet, ready to run at the crack of a bat. He was also keeping track of the teacher, out of the corner of one eye.

"Don't you think you should let some one run for you?" Emma called.

"You didn't throw it that hard," Junior answered.

"Play bawl," again roared Second Cousin LeRoy, as the kids began to take the field. Emma trotted up the mound. She began rubbing the ball with both hands, preparing for the next batter.

Meanwhile, Miss Liptrap realized she was still standing by the table, with the big knife in her hands.

Emma began pitching to the next batter. Actually, it was only a cake knife.

Turtle Soup

"The snapping turtle has a vicious temper and should be handled carefully. It strikes with amazing speed and its jaws are capable of tearing flesh severely. The strike often carries the forepart of the body off the ground. The safest way to carry a snapping turtle is to grasp it by the hind limbs while keeping its head down and the plastron toward you and well away from your legs. Do not carry large specimens by the tail: they can be severely injured by having their caudal vertebrae separated or the sacral region stretched. When handled, snappers emit a musk as potent as that of musk turtles. Snapping turtles normally are docile when submerged, but even then they can and sometimes do bite viciously.... The snapping turtle is delicious and is eaten throughout the range; excellent soup can be made from it ...."

— *C.H. Ernst and R.W. Barbour,* Turtles of the United States *(1972), University of Kentucky Press*

I.

The Token Creek Mill Pond was large enough to support an impressive range of wild life. Among the fishes there were plenty of blue gills, sun fish, crappies, small mouth, even walleyes to catch. Muskrats dug their burrows throughout the marshes above and below the pond, as well as in the banks of the pond itself. There were white-tailed deer, rabbits by the gross, chipmunks, wood mice, moles, voles, raccoons, 'possum, and skunk. In the early morning you might see a brown-red fox stopping for a drink before returning to its den somewhere up on Big Hill. There were several kinds of snakes, crayfish, three species of frogs, plus upwards of a hundred sun-loving mud turtles that, from May until September, basked along the muddy shoreline or on the partially submerged timbers at the foot of the old dam. Mallard ducks came every year to raise their peeping broods.

And, every few years, a snapping turtle turned up. Snappers were not tolerated, but even with standing orders for execution keeping them rare, you could worry one might be lurking in a submerged lair at the lower end of the pond. If you went down there, onto the old wooden dam, and sat very still, and peered long enough into the limpid water, you might even see a snapper's bulldog head slither from out of the sunken timbers. And if you lay there quietly, without moving a muscle, a fish would eventually edge up, attracted by the turtle's fascinating tongue, beckoning from within its darkened yaw. When the fish came near, very near, the warted snout would stab out so quickly that the fish was still jerking and twitching as it was swallowed. The same would surely happen to anyone's hand, at least the hand of anyone foolish enough to reach down into the water, among the crevices and the extensive wooden foundation. If you got a fish line snagged down there, you left well enough alone and cut it. You didn't go following it under water with your fingers, to try to retrieve the hook or lure, because a big old snapper just might be lurking down under there somewhere, ready to have a few of your fingers for lunch.

Second Cousin LeRoy claimed that, properly prepared, snapper made a darn good soup. Uncle August seconded this opinion, but added that when you were eating snapping turtle soup you had to forget it was made from something that not only looked like a snake, but was probably a good part snake too.

Second Cousin LeRoy figured once you got the shells off, the top and the bottom, you dressed out a snapper like anything else, of course making sure you got rid of that musk gland on the back end.

II.

In the spring after the bad winter, the Mill Pond hosted five pairs of mallards. After the time of dipping courtship rituals and jocund quacking, all five couples produced a brood of peeping ducklings. Folks stopped by to watch the families cruise the pond or walk the banks in dancing lines. Though there was plenty for the ducks to eat, in and around the water, several neighbors scattered corn along the banks anyway, to ensure the well being of parents and offspring. Emma and Junior went to the Mill Pond every day to check on the duck population. They counted twenty-eight babies; the mallards nesting at the upper end of the pond had four little ones, the other pairs — five or six each.

Uncle August loaned the kids his binoculars so they could watch the ducks from the bridge.

Suddenly, the counts started coming up short. One set went from six down to three within a week. Soon after, three other families each lost two. The kids sounded the alarm. Uncle August concluded something might be preying on the ducklings at night, because someone was almost always around watching during the day. It was suggested that fox from Big Hill were guilty, although the possibility that raccoons or skunk were involved wasn't dismissed either. Then, early one morning, when Second Cousin LeRoy was down by the pond, he witnessed the last duckling in a nervous line suddenly engulfed from below by a hideous mouth and head. As the duckling was dragged under, its frenzied mother and siblings paddled and flapped away from a whorl of broiling water that marked the descent of a good-sized snapping turtle.

"Soup," declared Second Cousin LeRoy.

Second Cousin LeRoy, along with his friend, Old Tillman, started fishing for the snapper that evening, using chicken necks on number-ten treble hooks with steel leaders. They used 120-pound test line, the heaviest Brother Bob carried in his store. After the baited lines were cast out into the pond, the shore ends were knotted around thick stakes driven into the bank. Second Cousin LeRoy and his sidekick set the lines at dusk, when the ducks were ready to call it a day, to avoid worry about any of them diving down for the chicken necks. Just before dawn the two men walked down to the pond to wind in the lines.

In a couple of days they had the snapper hooked on three different baits, with all the hooks swallowed. It took them a good three hours to drag the big turtle close enough to the bank to get a look at him. He was big all right. Old Tillman got so involved in the tugging and hauling that he toppled into the water, coming up face to face with the wild-eyed reptile. Fortunately, Second Cousin LeRoy was able to drag hard on the lines, keeping the turtle from striking, while frenetic Old Tillman mucked and thrashed himself to safety. By this time, word of the huge turtle had spread, so a minor throng began to assemble for the spectacle of landing.

When the two men, with the help of some bystanders, got the turtle close to shore, Second Cousin LeRoy was able to sink a gaff into one of its rear legs, giving some amount of control over the flailing animal. With the help of Old Tillman, Second Cousin LeRoy dragged the enraged turtle well onto the bank.

Still, it kept anyone from approaching closely by opening its beaked mouth and trying to strike. Uncle August took Emma and Junior down to see the snapper. It could have weighed 70 or 80 pounds, maybe more. Eventually the men pushed, slid, and pried the combative beast onto the Mill Pond yard where they cut the lines hooked down its gut. But with the lines cut they lost control of its front end, allowing the turtle to turn on Second Cousin LeRoy with blood in its eye. Second Cousin LeRoy dropped the gaff and backed off, returning advantage in the contest to the menacing turtle.

With the crowd circling, the turtle stood high on its arched legs, hissing and lunging. Old Tillman tried to keep it from lashing out by shoving it backward with a broken mall handle, which the reptile got hold of and started mincing in its powerful jaws. When it was obvious the snapper not only wouldn't release the wooden handle, and with no lines or the gaff for control, was successfully maneuvering back toward the Mill Pond, Old Tillman took up his ax and with impressive aplomb, cut off the turtle's head. Only then did the furious jaws release the well-splintered handle.

Old Tillman later took the severed head home to nail on his woodshed door. Meanwhile the decapitated cadaver went swerving drunkenly around the mill yard, while people and dogs leapt out of its way, its spouting neck weaving a trail of blood and regurgitated horror that was clearly partially digested duck parts.

Eventually, as the dripping thing slowed to a swaying hulk on four weakening legs, the men were able to run ropes around it. They hoisted the dying monster into the bed of Second Cousin LeRoy's wagon for the trip to his place, and the dressing out. Geeing his horses,

Second Cousin LeRoy swung the turtle-laden wagon out of the mill yard and toward Token Creek. The crowd followed as the wagon rolled slowly over the creaking wooden bridge. Old Tillman, still covered with black mud, put on his hat and sat up beside Second Cousin LeRoy. At the end of the bridge, Second Cousin LeRoy turned his team toward the village. Brother Bob walked immediately behind the trundling wagon, twanging a Jew's harp. The others followed in a gesturing, noisy cortege.

They suspended the turtle from a tree in Second Cousin LeRoy's front yard, using rope tied around the great animal's back legs. That way, the blood could drain out while they got ready to butcher it. Normally, butchering would be pretty straightforward, but some of them argued about how to go at it. If it were a deer, say, you would gut it, skin it, then cut it up, first by quarters. Then you laid out these quarters to be further divided from there. The problem at hand, with their turtle, was to get the upper and lower shells off before anything else could be done. Second Cousin LeRoy said he didn't see a problem at all; the shells were just an extra layer of tough skin, as far as he was concerned. Getting everyone to stand clear, he used a hatchet to hack a separation around the sides of the turtle, at the juncture of the keeled upper shell and the thinner under shell.

Then he lit into the carcass with a crowbar and two claw hammers. Indeed, he succeeded in lifting the shells cleanly off the body, which he gutted and skinned as he would have any other big game animal.

They hung it from a pole. Second Cousin LeRoy and Old Tillman, each with one end of the pole on a shoulder, carried it over to Brother Bob's store. It weighed in, on the meat scale, at 57 pounds. That was enough turtle to make soup for everybody within ten miles.

"Let's take him back so we can cut him up," said Second Cousin LeRoy.

"We could make soup for all of us, right now," cried little Junior, who had been so impressed throughout the whole adventure that he thought a village picnic was in order. The idea caught on.

Brother Bob gestured to the shed behind his store. He motioned for the group to follow him. There, in the back of the storehouse, on a chain connected to a rafter, hung a round, cast-iron cooking pot big enough to hold a missionary.

Brother Bob started pushing aside crates and cases to make a path to the great pot. When they had pulled it outside, they loaded it onto a tumbrel cart. The crowd wheeled it over to Second Cousin LeRoy's yard, following along behind Second Cousin LeRoy and Old Tillman bearing the turtle.

"Now then, what do we need for turtle soup besides turtle?" Second Cousin LeRoy asked.

"Vegetables," some one said. "Carrots, potatoes, onions, cabbage, turnips, parsley."

"You need to start with boiling water," said big Mrs. Stella Hoogewind.

"Chicken stock is good for flavor. I'm willing to contribute some," said Widow Olivia Oliverson, with a big smile for Second Cousin LeRoy, who grinned right back at her, saying he sure did appreciate her kind offer, to which she replied that she just loved cooking and sure did like to see a man who did too.

"We've got some real nice leeks we just dug up," said Mrs. Chelydress. "Is it all right with you, Linneus, if we donate a few?" she asked her husband.

"Fine, fine. We can go and get them right now so we can get cooking," he replied.

While the various folks were off fetching contributions to the community soup, Second Cousin LeRoy, Brother Bob, and Old Tillman built a tripod to hold the cooking pot. Axel and Charlotte Lawrence donated green logs for the job from a pile not yet cut up for fence posts. Axel brought them over in a wagon.

A lot of time was spent spiking and lashing the

logs together; they knew the pot would be pretty heavy
when things got cooking. A bucket brigade brought in
water from Second Cousin LeRoy's pump. Dry firewood was stacked and the cooking fire started. Meanwhile, Uncle August and Grandpa brought in two oak
tables, placed them end-to-end, and covered them with
newspaper.

Several chopping blocks appeared. The outdoor
kitchen was ready by the time the vegetables started
arriving.

"Here we are," said Big Mrs. Hoogewind, hand-
ing over a sack of potatoes. Mr. Chelydress arrived with
his basket of leeks. The carrots were donated by the
Yon Hamsums. Grandma sent over Emma, with Junior
helping, lugging a peck of fresh turnips and a big sack
of onions. Uncle August and Aunt Melodie contributed a half-dozen heads of new cabbage. Parsley came
from Mrs. Lawrence.

"You've got to have garlic, lots of garlic," declared
the now mud-free Old Tillman, as he set down a bag of
healthy looking bulbs, taken from storage.

The accumulating vegetables were stacked for pro-
cessing at one end of the work tables, while at the other
end Grandpa and Second Cousin LeRoy, with Uncle
August holding the knives and giving advice, under-
took the dissection of the great turtle carcass. None of
the men knew much about turtle anatomy, but proceeded nonetheless, guided by their experience with
other game, and with farm animals. Widow Olivia
Oliverson watched with encouraging approval as quarters were transformed into cuts, cuts into slices, and
slices into cubes, which she then rinsed and rubbed with
salt as Second Cousin LeRoy handed them to her. Second Cousin LeRoy observed that they worked well together.

It took over an hour for the water in the great pot
to reach a boil, giving the cooks time to prepare the
vegetables. When the water was boiling hard, the vegetables were dropped in and the fire reduced. Widow

Olivia Oliverson added her chicken stock. Meanwhile, the turtle meat stood ready. It was only noon.

The company agreed to work in shifts, keeping the fire going strong and checking the soup. The turtle meat would be added to the vegetable base about two o'clock. Five, maybe six hours of cooking after that would be enough. By evening the soup would be ready. Some of the group would come back around seven to put more tables out onto Second Cousin LeRoy's front yard, for space to feed the dozen plus participants in the upcoming supper. Ice from the store's icehouse was to be brought over for two tubs of drinks on Second Cousin LeRoy's front porch. Ice cream makers, filled and ready for cranking, were brought in. Extra salt was brought from the store.

At eight that evening, with the sun setting into a red sky, Brother Bob played a fanfare on his harmonica, calling the group to the table, and as a signal that Uncle August was ready for his pre-meal speech. With the group in place, except for Second Cousin LeRoy who was tending the bubbling soup, Uncle August began.

First off, Uncle August announced that Grandma Armstrong, Big Mrs. Hoogewind, and Widow Oliverson had all tasted the soup. Dire predictions and fears to the contrary, the ladies had found it about as close to perfection as anybody could probably hope, so this gathered company was definitely in for a treat. But before the community cookout got under way, there were some people to recognize and to thank for their contribution to the evening's conviviality.

There was, of course, Brother Bob, who had supplied the grand cooking pot (*there was long applause*).

And, there were all the good folks who contributed the vegetables, not to mention Widow Oliverson, whose chicken stock certainly added a dimension of flavor to the soup that everyone was about to appreciate in just a few minutes (*more applause*).

Next were the cooks, which included just about everybody here as far as he could tell (*laughter*). They also must thank Axel Lawrence, who had sacrificed some good future fence posts for the tripod *(applause)*; and we can't forget Stella Hoogewind for her ample... advice and fine potatoes *(laughter and applause)*. And now, they all needed to honor their host and hunter, Second Cousin LeRoy Armstrong, who would hopefully say a few words so they could get down to the soup *(applause as Second Cousin LeRoy hurried over from the steaming cauldron)*.

"I thank you, August, and everyone. I'm not sure if I'm the host here or a guest, what with all the help we've had. To tell the truth, we're all hosts and all guests here tonight, since we all somehow or other had a hand in making our soup. You know, I've been thinking about this turtle we're about to eat. From the size of him, he must have been living down there in our pond for a long while. So while we've been going about our business up here, keeping things going as best we could, he's been down there in the pond with leeches hanging off him, waiting for a fish, or a duck, or maybe even somebody's arm to come along. What I mean to say is, it was good we caught him and got rid of him. He was a bad one. I'm pretty sure my friend here, Old Tillman, agrees. After all, Mr. Tillman did elect to pass some time with the turtle — right down in the water with him, having a face-to-face talk *(laughter)*. I think the turtle did most of the talking though; he dominated the conversation, I'd say *(more laughter)*. Well, our Mill Pond's safer now. I can't say I didn't have a good time of it, getting that old snapper. I did. He made this one heck of a day. Now, I think we should get on with our doings. Soup's on! *(long applause, followed by eating)*.

III.

As the company pursued its happy banquet, pausing from time to time to dance to Brother Bob's harmonica, and, as the wonderful aroma of tasty soup floated out into the gentle night, in a bog east of Token

Creek there was stirring.

A young turtle, hatched out that spring among the muck and ooze, began a journey. The turtle was a bad-tempered little snapper that had outgrown its niche in the bog; it had to move on; the supply of water bugs, waterlogged worms, and strayed minnows was no longer sufficient for its increasing appetite.

Sinking its front claws into a mass of roots at the edge of its lair, it hauled itself out of the water and onto a clump of marsh grass. The turtle stretched its head up into the warm darkness, alternately listening and sniffing. Detecting no evidence of predators, it struck out, floundering away from the deeper portion of the bog toward higher ground, from where it might get wind of larger quarters and wider water. It had to clamber and struggle to leave the area of low water and intertwined roots, moving through webs of algae, across damp hillocks of coarse grasses, and finally thrashing into an expanse of cattails. The cattails were followed by a difficult tangle of marsh cranberry. Eventually it labored out of the cranberry. It rested for a time, without retreating into its shell, listening and smelling.

Striking out again, it reached firmer ground, with shorter grasses and small flowers making the going easier. It kept on until it came to a gentle slope covered with only scattered weeds and nettles; it climbed this embankment, at the top of which was the road. The earth was dry there, dusty and lacking odor.

The turtle looked about for several minutes, swaying and waiting, yet unable to choose a direction. It moved its head from side to side, sniffing for information.

After a few minutes, it turned west. It held to the edge of the road, shuffling tentatively along, still sampling the air, still rocking its head from side to side, nostrils flaring all the while, in search of an improving scent.

As it crawled on, the night breeze began to stir. The moving air stopped, started, stopped, then stirred again. After a while, the breeze became definite, beginning to flow steadily along the clearings, through the woods and brush, across the lush fields, and down the quiet gravel road where the fierce little turtle plodded onward. The air blew only mildly at first, yet soon increased, to become constant and plentiful across the animal's sharp, maleficent face.

Quite suddenly the snapper began to stride faster, for in the rich night gases and wafts it had sensed open water somewhere on ahead. It kept to the sandy shoulder of the deserted road, away from impeding stones, scuttling forward with increasing energy as its instincts confirmed and reconfirmed that it had chosen well: there was sweet water not far away.

The moon was in its zenith by the time the revelers in Second Cousin LeRoy's yard had begun to scratch and talk of heading home. As they stood and stretched, and gathered plates and glasses, to pack bags, to wake sleeping children who had long ago curled up in quiet clusters to peer at the many stars, thick vapors sliding across the Mill Pond flowed thickly and seductively over the tireless snapper's nostrils. The excited animal rushed on with great determination. Moments passed.

Then it saw before it the great body of placid water. It paused for a satisfied few seconds, taking in long draughts of the rich air rising off the shimmering pond. Then, in a frenetic dash of anticipation, it scurried across the wooden bridge connecting the road to the Mill Pond's yard. From the mill yard, it turned down the grassy banks. The silver sweet pond lay before it.

The snapper stopped one last time. It scanned, with smoldering yellow eyes, the innocent, moonlit expanse. The animal now slithered easily over the last few feet of dewed grass, touching, finally, the warm mud at the pond's edge. Quietly and stealthily, the reptile slipped through the surface of the silken water.

Submerged, it glided without hesitation downward, toward the dark regions beneath the Mill Pond dam.

The Big Dipper

Follow the drinking gourd,
For the old man is waiting,
For to carry you to freedom
If you follow the drinking gourd.

On Thursday, July 14, 1921, Cousin Dillard Armstrong of Merrimac, Wisconsin, fell through the floor of his corncrib. His weight, which was hardly excessive, snapped out a yard-long by yard-wide section of the sturdy two-by-twelve floorboards. Both Dillard's legs went straight down, down farther than they should have, for he found himself dangling over open space under the corncrib instead of landing on the solid ground he had always known to be no more than a few inches underneath. He nearly panicked, thinking he was about to drop into some void — perhaps a vast, undiscovered cavern or grotto once eroded by the great river, or an unknown cave whose roof had suddenly begun to crumble after years of supporting the old farm and its buildings.

Dillard hung there for a long moment, taking stock of the situation, letting his heart slow down, waiting for the pit of his stomach to stop churning.

Dillard's arms were spread over the intact flooring on either side of him. He began to realize he wouldn't fall farther — he was firmly supported. He could tell that the boards under his arms were solid, with no give to them. He saw he might be able to get himself out. He would do that cautiously.

He gathered himself. He started slowly, first lifting both legs upwards, gradually bending and raising his knees until they nearly touched his chest. He held himself that way, in that position, for a few seconds; the floor he held onto still seemed good — no sounds of giving or cracking. Deliberately and cautiously, with care, he twisted himself sideways at the waist, to bring his left leg up and between the joists. Maintaining an even motion, he inched the leg over the floor beside him, stretched it out, and planted it on the hard portions beyond the break. He waited a few more seconds, then extended and freed his right leg in the same way, with the same unbroken movements. He stopped again to listen.

Dillard still heard nothing. He then arched himself upward at the middle, to raise himself over the hole, finally able to roll to safety like a skater rolling away from broken ice. He lay there for a moment, on his stomach, catching his breath, feeling slowly more secure, and curious, for he could detect old air rising from the dark opening beside him: musty, stale air. He paused once more, minding his senses.

Warily and gradually, he moved his head toward the strange opening, and inhaled. What he smelled was not the wet, seeping rank of a cave — it was drier, cooler air — more like that of a root cellar, or a tunnel.

He kept himself alert for a moment, then peered at the edges of the square hole where he had broken through the floor. Broken wasn't quite correct. The ends of the boards at the side of the hole were not splintered or jagged. Three adjacent lengths of the planking that ran across the joists were gone, as if they had been cut out. It may have been that the floor had once been patched in that area; there were short sections of planking elsewhere around where repairs appeared to have been made. But the ends of the planks that formed the opening were smooth to the touch, polished almost, a better joint than he would have expected for rough flooring. He wondered if they dated from when the floor had been laid. Looking at the top edges of the partially exposed joists, he saw that the lost section of floor hadn't even been nailed in place — it had been fitted into the opening, very carefully fitted like a section of a cabinet or some other piece of furniture, or better yet, like a trap door. Funny he hadn't noticed it before, for all these years, considering all the times he'd been in the corncrib.

Gingerly, he reached into the hole and ran his fingers along the sides of the joists under the opening. The joists facing the opening were smooth too, not at all rough. There was also no question they were solid.

Groping farther, he found hard earth beyond them. The gap that had taken him seemed to be just under this one section.

Still, he was not yet ready to stand on floor he remained unsure of. He rolled to the wall of the corncrib where he raised himself on his hands and knees.

He looked for nail heads in the floorboards where they would have been fastened to the underlying joists. He detected dim lines of nails repeating every three feet. Although the old, square heads were not easily seen, they were there. He aimed his feet for the nearest line and stood. The floor did not creak or flex.

Stepping from one nail line to another, Dillard strode out of the corncrib, back into the warm sunshine. He went to get some help, and a lantern.

His wife, Wren, was in the house. He hurried to

tell her about the collapsed floor. He would ask her to stand by while he investigated. It would be unsafe to do it alone, not knowing what he was dealing with.

"Wren, I just fell through the floor of the corncrib. There's a cave or something under it!" Dillard exclaimed as he burst into the kitchen where she was kneading bread dough.

Wren stopped. She was startled and immediately worried. Her husband was a steady man, not given to outbursts. If he was excited, he meant business.

"My land, Dillard, what did you say?" was all she could muster. His words had registered, but didn't make sense. His manner raised her concern.

He slowed down and explained what had happened to him while he had been cleaning the corncrib. They needed to find out what was going on. There could be danger. They might be over a limestone cavern that was ready to cave in, like those around Blue Mounds or Mount Horeb.

Wren placed the bread dough into buttered pans. She covered them with a damp towel, then wiped her hands on her apron. She firmly took Dillard's arm.

They rushed out, to the machine shed, where they gathered up two kerosene lanterns. Dillard asked Wren to hold onto them while he pulled down an eight-foot ladder stored on the machine shed rafters.

Wren wondered if they shouldn't drive to the post office to telephone the county sheriff. They decided they should first try to handle the situation themselves. It could be that this cave, or whatever it was, was no more than a covered-over basement from a former building. The farm had been in operation for over ninety years, so the corncrib could have been built over a foundation that hadn't been completely filled in. Wren said she hoped it was that simple.

She didn't like the idea of living on the top of a cave that might swallow them at any time.

Dillard carried the ladder to the corncrib, but he

wasn't ready to go back in yet. He went around to the barn and located a pair of two-by-sixes stacked near the calf pens. He carried the boards out to the corncrib where he slid them in, one at a time, perpendicular across the flooring, making a bridge over the distance he would have to walk, or creep, until he reached the opening. Wren lighted a lantern and handed it to Dillard. He was ready to enter.

"You know, this crib's only, maybe, thirty feet from the barn. It could have been built over an abandoned cellar, or an old part of the barn," Dillard said to Wren. This was quite possible. He was thinking more clearly now, having subdued his scare from the partial fall through the floor. Such thinking reassured him.

When he entered the corncrib however, with the lantern in one hand and crawling awkwardly on his knees and the other over the two-by-sixes, he felt a twinge of fear growing in his chest. When he got close to the open floor, he went down on his stomach. With the lantern held up, he slid himself forward until his head was over the opening.

Again he smelled the stagnant air he had detected before. He confirmed that the edges of the boards where he had gone through had once been cleanly dressed — no question about it. He lowered the lantern into the hole.

He could see a dirt floor perhaps six feet down, on which he saw the section of lost floorboard, broken in the middle. There were some chunks of rubble around the boards, no doubt pulled down when the boards fell into the vault that was now outlined by the lantern light. The space below him was some four feet wide, a great deal less than the ten-foot width of the corncrib. The walls of the chamber were fieldstone. Mortar held the stones in place. It sure looked like an old basement, except that he could see what appeared to be a stone ceiling further on. Dillard pulled up the lantern and backed out of the corncrib. Wren was waiting.

"There's some kind of crypt down there. Let's get the ladder in. I want to go down. I'm pretty sure it's safe. The floor's solid and the space underneath isn't very deep or very wide. The crib's sitting on firm ground except in the place where I went through."

Wren nodded and helped pick up the ladder.

With Wren helping to steer, Dillard maneuvered the ladder into the corncrib. It took some effort to turn it down into the hole, but they eventually felt it touch the dirt floor of the vault. This time Dillard and Wren both walked into the corncrib. Dillard swung himself onto the rungs, grinned at his wife, then disappeared into the fusty chamber with his lantern.

What Dillard found was not only puzzling, but exciting. The space was a good eight feet long, half the length of the corncrib, by hardly more than four feet wide at the dirt floor. The chamber had an arched stone ceiling, made from well-joined stones. The opening in the ceiling, under the flooring in the corncrib where Dillard had first fallen, and now had purposely descended, was clearly intended to be an entrance, or an exit. The stone room was only slightly damp, probably from ground water behind the stone walls, but he saw no seepage.

Indeed, the dirt on which he stood was dry enough in spots to be powdery. The end of the chamber, the end away from the barn, was a dead end; a wall made of the same joined stone as the walls and ceiling. In the direction of the barn there seemed to be no end. Dillard headed that way.

The passage narrowed to two-thirds the height of the room, and reduced to perhaps three feet in width. It led off under the back of the corncrib, straight at the barn. Dillard followed the passage, a feeling of elation growing in him.

Surprisingly, the passage came to an abrupt end at the barn's foundation.

Dillard studied the stones where the passage

stopped, moving the lantern's light slowly across them. After a minute, he figured out that the stones there formed an arch, the same height and shape as the tunnel. At one time the passageway must have opened into the lower level of the barn. It had been closed off.

Dillard returned to the room under the corncrib. He put down the lantern and picked up the two pieces of broken floor that had fallen down. Both were roughly broken in the middle, one around a knot. The middle had weakened and broken when he had stood on it. Oddly enough, the boards had been fastened together on their undersides, at each end, by a short piece of oak two-by-four.

They had once formed a cover, or a door. He called up to Wren.

"Come on down. It's safe. I fell through an old trap door."

Wren easily managed the opening, bringing down the second lantern. They inspected the strange room and tunnel together. Wren wondered if they hadn't perhaps found an abandoned storage space. She did agree with Dillard; it wasn't likely to be the remains of an old basement, considering the room and passageway had a stone roof. What could it have been used for? Feed grain or storage maybe? It must have been that the barn and the corncrib were at one time connected.

They climbed out and went to the barn to check the foundation, inside where the tunnel would have met it. That end of the barn was now used for calf pens. Dillard climbed into one of the pens and began inspecting the foundation wall. He found the faint outline of the arched doorway that he had detected from the underground side.

"Here it is. You can see that there was an entrance here once. It's been sealed off. Look, the mortar is just a little different than in the rest of the foundation."

Wren entered the pen and had a look. She agreed.

"It was some kind of underground storage room," she decided. "Maybe to get corn to the barn without going outside in the winter."

Dillard wasn't' sure. In any event, it was possible that this vault, or whatever it should be called, was part of a building that was part of the first barn. But what confounded him was the trap door, if it was a trap door, in the corncrib. He was inclined to get an opinion from some one who knew the history of the area, or who knew about how they built these old barns — maybe one of the old-timers would know.

"Let's see. This barn was built about nineteen hundred, after the first one burned down. Dad said it was put up right over the same foundation as the old one."

"How old is the corncrib?" Wren asked.

"Goodness knows. It's probably the original with a new roof. Dad said it escaped the fire. He was always patching it, that's for sure."

"Then it might have been built before the Civil War," Wren suggested.

"Just like the house," Dillard added.

* * *

And that was how the Merrimac, Wisconsin slave tunnel was discovered.

Within six weeks of Dillard and Wren's descent into the stone walled vault, it had been inspected by nearly three dozen neighbors, by the County Commissioner and two of his staff, three engineers from the State Department of Bridges and Highways, the County Sheriff, an architect from Milwaukee, four historians from the Wisconsin Historical Society in Madison, and two more from the University plus several of their students. The underground room and passageway were measured, described, photographed, inspected, admired, sketched, and certified safe. The vague opening in the barn wall was chiseled open by a state archeologist and a small crew, following which the lieutenant governor, trailed by an entourage of staff and a couple of newspaper reporters, plus some politicians, came by to declare the tunnel a state historical site. This official dedication resulted in an article about the discovery in the *Wisconsin State Journal,* prompting minor weekend streams of curiosity seekers, Civil War enthusiasts, amateur historians, professional historians, and folks just out for a drive. By the end of the summer, there had also appeared a representative from the Chicago office of the National Association for the Advancement of Colored People, who was writing an historical account of the Underground Railroad in the Midwest, all eight grades of Merrimac grammar school, and a high school history class all the way from the East High School in Madison. There were a lot of others.

Dillard never did get to use his corncrib that fall of 1921, nor in future years for that matter. By virtue of its status as part of an historical site, Dillard was asked to keep the old building empty so that the entire layout could be seen and appreciated. Dillard was obliged to store his 1921 corn crop at a neighbor's.

The next year he built a replacement crib on the other side of the barn. He did not complain; the State Historical Society offered to foot the bill, in exchange for his agreement to accept visitors, by appointment, to the old slave tunnel.

II

On Friday, June 4, 1948, August and Melodie Armstrong of Token Creek, Wisconsin, received an invitation in their mailbox. It was dated the previous Monday, and asked them to visit Cousins Dillard and Wren Armstrong, still living on their farm outside of Merrimac. In particular, the note asked that August and Melodie bring along young Emma and Junior Armstrong. It was time the two children had a tour of the slave tunnel.

Cousins Dillard and Wren also hoped that Grandpa and Grandma could come too — they hadn't seen them in a good while. After consultation among the invited parties, the invitation was answered in the affirmative.

On a sunny Sunday, two weeks later, they set out, with Uncle August driving. They drove up the Portage Road, Uncle August, Aunt Melodie, and Grandpa in the front seat; Grandma was in the back, along with Emma and Junior. They would spend the night at Dillard and Wren's, so this was a real outing.

In the car, Grandpa explained to Emma and Junior who Cousin Dillard was. He was one of Grandpa's first cousins. Grandpa's father, George Armstrong, and Dillard's father, Aiken Armstrong, were brothers. George and Aiken were the sons of Great Grandfather Levi Armstrong, the first of the Armstrong family to live in Wisconsin.

"Grandpa, that makes Levi your grandpa," Junior laughed.

"And my grandfather too," said Uncle August.

"And, our great-great-grandfather," Emma said to Junior.

Grandpa went on with the history. It began with Levi Armstrong. Old Levi had been an abolitionist before the Civil War. In fact, he had married a lady named Susan Tallman, the half-sister of a famous Wisconsin abolitionist named William Tallman. The story was that it was Levi who in fact had persuaded this William Tallman to join in the movement that had helped runaway slaves fleeing north to Canada. Tallman ended up getting so involved in the movement that he made his house a station on what was called the Underground Railroad.

Underground didn't mean "under the ground," but secret routes that were taken to get out of the South. There were no trains involved, but the places along the way where the runaway slaves hid were called stations. Anyway, Mr. Tallman's house later became a state historical landmark.

But, until Dillard fell through the floor of his corn-crib, closing on thirty years ago now, no one had known about the slave tunnel on the Armstrong homestead, which had been Levi's, then Levi's son, Aiken's, before Dillard had taken it on. That's why the discovery of the tunnel had been such a big event, because it looked pretty sure that great-great-grandfather Levi had been working along with the Tallmans, hiding fugitive slaves moving along the railroad. Levi was a part of history.

"What does a slave tunnel look like?" Emma wanted to know.

"It's as much like a room as a tunnel," answered Aunt Melodie. "Except it's usually under the ground. But it can be a tunnel so you can go in one end and escape from the other if people like slave-hunters are after you."

"It goes from one building to another, so if they hid people in the barn and somebody came looking, the people could get to another building, or away," added Grandma.

When the travelers arrived at Cousin Dillard's farm, the first thing every one wanted to do was see the slave tunnel. The tour started in the great barn.

Dillard explained that he had removed the calf pens so the entrance to the tunnel was accessible. He had lanterns ready to be lighted, hanging by the arched stone door.

"The entrance was most probably hidden behind something when it was in use," Dillard explained. "Maybe a cart, or some sort of big shelf that could have been moved fast."

They started in. Dillard led the way, with Emma and Junior close behind him. The long, narrow passage was lit only by Cousin Dillard's lantern, and the lantern that Uncle August carried, at the end of the procession. Junior and Emma kept close to each other as they followed Cousin Dillard. They listened to him

tell the history of the tunnel, how it was built, how fleeing slaves might have had to hide there until it was safe
to travel on to the next station on the Railroad, using
the Big Dipper to point the way. Junior and Emma said
they didn't understand what Cousin Dillard meant by
that — that the Big Dipper pointed the way. When
they got under the corncrib, in a larger space, Cousin
Dillard stopped and told them how the Big Dipper can
be used to find the North Star, which is always in the
North, over Canada. That's where the slaves had to
get to, to be safe, because slavery wasn't allowed there.

"Emma and Junior, do you know there was another name for the Big Dipper, back then?" asked Uncle
August.

Neither of them knew what it could have been.

"It was called the Drinking Gourd. That's because
it's shaped like the dippers people used then, which
they made out of gourds. The Big Dipper and the Drinking Gourd are the same thing," Uncle August explained.

"There's even a song about it," said Second Cousin
Dillard.

And, right there in the dim lantern light, standing
in the stone-walled sanctuary, under the old corncrib,
Cousin Dillard started singing the song, in his soft, kind
voice. He sang slowly and carefully, so that the kids
could hear each word. He sang *Follow the Drinking
Gourd* and the refrain was wonderful:

> *Follow the drinking gourd,*
> *For the old man is waiting,*
> *For to carry you to freedom,*
> *If you follow the drinking gourd.*

Then Cousin Dillard told them about the song,
what the words meant. He told how, before the ter-
rible Civil War, and even while it was going on, slaves
trying to escape to freedom knew they could use the
Big Dipper, the Drinking Gourd, to point their way

north, and along the Underground Railroad. He told about people who were part of the Railroad, the conductors, the stationmasters, the Quakers in Ohio, and all the other abolitionists in the different states along the way, from way down in the South all the way to the North. And he told the kids that their great-great-grandfather was sure to have been a stationmaster, maybe even a guide that they called a conductor. He might even have been the old man in the song.

"We can go outside, when it gets dark, and have a look at the Drinking Gourd. I'll show you how it points to the North Star," he offered.

With that, the party climbed up the ladder and back into the sun.

They had a late supper. Even so, there was too much light when they had finished to see the stars. The days were long now. Grandpa, Uncle August, and Cousin Dillard went out to look at Dillard's Holsteins, which he was soon going to be selling. Grandma, Aunt Melodie, and Cousin Wren went out to the flower garden. Wren wanted them to pick out some plants for cuttings, that they could take back the next day. Emma and Junior went back to the slave tunnel. They were no longer apprehensive. They entered through the corncrib.

They studied the walls in the lantern light, and talked about how long it must have taken to build the ceiling. They wondered who did it. They touched the sepulchral chill of the stone walls. They crept along the narrow passage to the old barn, where they stood in the arched doorway for a moment. They returned, quietly, to the underground room. Junior climbed up the ladder so he could inspect the trap door. He noticed that the edges were worn smooth, perhaps from people rubbing against them as they entered or left. He told Emma and she climbed up too, and felt the wood. People must have gone in and out a lot.

Had the wood been smoothed down from all the

recent visitors rubbing past it, or had it been worn this way a long time ago, when the tunnel was being used?

They wondered if the opening into the corncrib might have been for ventilation — the tunnel was pretty closed in, or would have been with the barn entrance closed. They would ask Cousin Dillard what he thought.

Junior was sitting on the earthen floor, looking around the bleak chamber. Emma was holding the lantern, lost for words. Junior sat for a while, then put his arms around his knees. He was shivering.

"People had to live in here," he whispered.

"Until it was safe to leave for the next station, up the line," Emma responded. "Maybe they came out at night." Her voice was hushed.

"It makes me feel sad, Em."

It did Emma too.

III

Stars were shining and twinkling in the deep field of sky when the family climbed the pasture hill behind the darkened farm. At the top, they gathered close together, looking up into the night. They saw the great universe about them. They could feel its distance and its depth as they stood in the darkness.

They saw the many layers of stars, some that seemed so close, many more so far off. Uncle August and Cousin Dillard pointed to constellations. They found Cygnus, the swan, out toward the East. Hercules was nearly straight overhead, but it was hard to figure out exactly where his leg was, and which points of light made his sword, there were so many stars around.

The Drinking Gourd was easy. It was clear.

Cousin Dillard talked again about the Drinking Gourd, admiring it, showing how it was used to locate the North Star. He knew the names of the stars in it, and some in other parts of the sky.

While Cousin Dillard and the others were whispering, Emma heard a sound from Junior. She moved closer to him and listened. Her brother had begun to weep. He edged away, so he wouldn't be noticed like that, crying almost silently while he stood there, following the stars, feeling tiny and lost, listening to Cousin Dillard tell of searching for freedom, of the past, of the Underground Railroad, of old Levi Armstrong, of the world then...

Emma noticed Junior's tears, shining on his face, but she looked away, to steel herself. No one else seemed to see his tears, flowing ever so quietly, sparkling in the glowing starlight. She wanted to move close to him, to touch him, to let him know she understood, but she was afraid she too would start to weep. And so he stood apart, alone.

Emma saw Junior wipe his tears away, with the back of his arm. But they came again. He moved still farther from the group, enough away so they might not see his feelings, his confusion. Emma watched his silhouette. His head was turned up toward the Big Dipper. She could see him tracing the constellation's outline, through blurred eyes like her own, following the line from Drinking Gourd toward the North Star. She stood watching, working against her own tears.

The group had become silent. They were all looking upward. Cousin Dillard stirred after a moment. He moved off, to be by Junior. He stood close beside him, searching above. He laid a hand on the boy's shoulder.

"It's all right. I cry myself when I look up there," the old man said.

Bird Dog

Ale, man, ale's the stuff to drink
For fellows whom it hurts to think ...
— *A.E. Housman*

There was a time, after they shipped him home from overseas, when Second Cousin LeRoy let things slide, everything slide — letting himself get too fat, shaving maybe once a week at best, and not keeping himself or his place any too tidy. He swore more than was necessary. If he started talking, you were in for a long session, because once he got going it was hard to get a word in edgewise, particularly when he'd had a few, and he was taking a few fairly often.

He wore bib overalls, never less than a size too small because the fit of his clothing lagged behind his expanding girth. In the summer he spent most of his time fishing at the Mill Pond, pulling in crappies and sunfish by day, or at night going after bullheads. He tended to smell like the fish he had just cleaned.

The family began to worry about Second Cousin LeRoy's not working, but after a while he took a job at the packing plant, where he was put in charge of cleaning up the slaughter floors after a run. It was stinking,

gory work. "It ain't the worst job," was his description
of it, a point that could be argued. Once in a while, he
didn't show up for work, like slightly before trout season (Second Cousin LeRoy believed in getting an early
start in such matters), or on the first day of deer season.
Such transgressions were overlooked by the bosses, because the fact was that Second Cousin LeRoy did his
work well, browbeating and berating the men under
him to be certain every last bit of mess was cleaned up
after a run of animals. His absences were infrequent
enough, as far as the plant supervisors and other big
shots were concerned, to excuse a little hookey. It was
difficult to find men who could abide by such bloody
work for long, let alone do it well, and even with enthusiasm.

With his steady job and pay, Second Cousin LeRoy
could afford regular, after-work stops at the Burke Road
Bar and Grill, for some end-of-the-day cheer.

Being a sport, he felt obliged, as compensation for
his ranting and scolding during the day, to order up a
round or two when any of his men came in for a drink.
It didn't take these birds long to realize there were easy
pickings if they followed Second Cousin LeRoy to the
tavern after the shift. So Second Cousin LeRoy and his
crew came to be considered the tavern regulars. They
usually played cards when they got settled in. Sometimes Second Cousin LeRoy won, pounding his cards
onto the table as he took tricks; sometimes he lost, still
pounding cards onto the table. The plant shift ended
in mid-afternoon, so Second Cousin LeRoy could, if he
chose, and he often did, get comfortably potted after
work and still make it home to feed himself before he
turned in.

When fall came, Second Cousin LeRoy switched
from fishing to hunting. He hunted pheasant, quail,
geese, rabbits, squirrel, pigeon, muskrat, raccoon, deer,
anything that had meat on it. He claimed to have eaten
porcupine and even woodchuck, more than once. He

sometimes talked about how some fall he would go hunt elk, way out West, in Wyoming or maybe Montana. He hunted everything with a 12-gauge, changing shot according to the kind of game he was after. He had a freezer full of wild meat and you could always get a cut of venison at his house, even in the middle of the summer. Of course, when it was handed over, you got with it a package of outlandish talk about how he had come by it, like shooting the deer from the hip because he hadn't had enough time to get his gun to his shoulder, or maybe how the deer had tried to sneak around behind him, but he being substantially smarter than the deer, got it anyway because he had known what it was up to.

Most people wouldn't hunt with Second Cousin LeRoy. He talked incessantly when he was with a bunch of other hunters, and he was always calling to them if he couldn't see them: all his noise scared off game. The upshot was that he pretty much hunted alone, which turned out to pay dividends — absence of talking meant game didn't always sense hunters were out, so if he were downwind from his intended, he could get in close for a shot. There was also the unforeseen factor that weight played in his good fortunes. Being heavy, he had to move relatively slowly, meaning he walked quietly. Stealth by default really got him in close for a shot. He almost never came back empty-handed from a foray. One November he got a deer after he had been in the woods for not even an hour. After he had dressed it out and dragged it to the road, he tied it over the front fender of his car, then drove over to the Burke Road Bar and Grill to show it off. After he had sat in the tavern long enough to get a pretty good snoot full, some of the boys decided to have some fun.

While Second Cousin LeRoy was inside, telling for the umpteenth time about how he had sneaked right up and practically sat on the poor deer, they took it off his car and hung it in the garage behind the tavern.

When Second Cousin LeRoy finally came rolling out of the bar, he was far too overflowing with love of life to notice the deer was gone. Off he drove, weaving home without giving a self-satisfied thought to the buck he was supposed to have draped over the left fender of his Chevy. When he got home, he managed to get himself into the house and flopped on his bed for the next twelve hours.

The next morning, Second Cousin LeRoy recalled that he had gotten himself a nice buck the day before. He went right outside to get it, but of course couldn't find hide nor hair of the thing, although he knew it should have been tied onto his car. After he looked around and realized that his deer was definitely missing, no question about it, he scurried over to Brother

Bob's store, madder than ten pigs, intending to telephone the sheriff.

"Somebody's stole my buck," hollered Second Cousin LeRoy as he burst into the store. He then started accusing everybody he'd ever heard of or seen of stealing his deer.

A couple of the men who had sneaked the buck off his car the day before were at that moment in the store, telling about their joke. When Second Cousin LeRoy paused for breath in his tirade of the missing deer, they all had a good laugh. Second Cousin LeRoy told them they were a bunch of thieves and deer robbers. Lips pursed, he stormed out, to fetch and to butcher what was rightly his.

One kind of hunting where Second Cousin LeRoy wasn't too successful was pheasant hunting. When he went out he usually didn't get skunked, but he might shoot only one, or if really lucky, two birds. To his neverending chagrin, when he'd arrive at Brother Bob's store to survey the Saturday hunt, he would find nearly everyone had taken maybe three or four birds, and a couple of hunters would even have their limit of five.

Second Cousin knew none of them was a better hunter than he was, and they sure weren't better shots either. After thinking about it, he realized they got more birds because they used a dog. A dog flushed up pheasants toward you, so you were offered a nice approaching shot. If you hunted without a dog, most of the time a bird wouldn't flush; it would just run in the other direction, from one corn row to another, or from one cover to another; you hardly ever even saw it, let alone got a chance for a shot. But, if a bird was made to fly up in front of you because your dog was charging him, you had bird on the table that night for dinner, not to mention a few in the freezer for the long winter. Second Cousin LeRoy decided to locate himself a dog. He started asking around.

He wasn't going to settle for just any mutt. He

looked at a few local dogs, but wasn't able to locate the dog that he imagined was out there somewhere. He had been looking for a while, and had reached the point of almost deciding on an expensive retriever from a kennel over in Dodge County, when his supervisor at the packing plant told him about a tavern keeper over near Prairie du Chien who was known to sometimes have a good hunting dog for sale, one that the man had trained himself. Second Cousin LeRoy found out where the tavern keeper lived and located his tavern. Unfortunately, it was a Sunday when he arrived at the town, so the tavern was closed. Luckily, the man lived behind his establishment, so after some negotiation Second Cousin bought a two-year-old, good-natured and certainly alert, brown and white Border collie named Sergeant. The dog was in fact exceptionally smart and turned out to be a first-class bird dog.

Second Cousin brought home his dog in a late September, two weeks before that year's pheasant season. Right away, Second Cousin LeRoy took it out into the cornfield between his place and the Creek. Within half an hour, the dog flushed about thirty birds (Second Cousin LeRoy's estimate). Second Cousin LeRoy got so excited when he saw pheasants flapping in all directions that he doubled-timed it back to the house for his shotgun. He needed to verify this dream, and back he and his dog went to the field.

The dog was a true canine genius. It seemed to know exactly what Cousin LeRoy wanted it to do. It would zigzag through the cornfield, point, backtrack, or even charge without having to be told. If Second Cousin LeRoy even whispered, "Sit, Boy," the dog sat. If he told it to run, the dog ran. He decided to test the dog to the limit. Second Cousin LeRoy told the dog to sit. It did, and didn't seem to move a muscle when Second Cousin LeRoy toddled off and away from it, down the edge of the cornfield.

Second Cousin LeRoy walked a good quarter mile

from the dog. It was watching him but gave no sign of moving. Second Cousin waited for a few more minutes. Finally he called, "Okay, Sergeant. Sic 'em."

Sure enough, the dog trotted into the field where Second Cousin LeRoy heard it dashing back and forth across rows. Within a minute, it had flushed a fat, ringnecked pheasant that flew downwind, right toward LeRoy's 12-gauge.

The dog didn't even bark when Second Cousin fired.

"Okay, fetch" he ordered. The dog brought over the dead bird, laying it ever so gently at Second Cousin LeRoy's feet. Second Cousin LeRoy thought he had arrived, the dog was so good.

"Good boy, good boy," he kept telling it. He sat right down in the field and hugged the dog. The dog licked his grinning face and he laughed out loud.

Second Cousin LeRoy then tucked his illegal bird under his coat and headed back home, with Sergeant marching behind.

Second Cousin LeRoy dressed and feathered his pre-season bird on his back porch, away from the road, to avoid prying eyes. That done, he and the dog spent most of the remains of the day goofing around in the yard. The dog would romp and yap, and chase Second Cousin LeRoy if he tried running; it would stop the second it was told to sit, or stay. If Second Cousin LeRoy ordered it to stay, and then he threw a stick, the dog wouldn't budge until it got the order to fetch.

It could roll over, sit up, beg, bark, prance, or shake hands, and even play dead, on command. Second Cousin LeRoy knew there was going to be so much pheasant eating that fall that he and his dog were both going to stark squawking and flapping by the time they were finished. What a dog.

He thought about letting it sleep in the house. It would, come winter. Maybe even in his bedroom, when he got it straightened up. For now, he made up a bed of old blankets and a pillow on the enclosed part of the back porch, off the kitchen. The room would stay comfortable if the door from the kitchen were wedged open. He put out bowls of water and people food. "Good boy," he told the dog. He petted and praised it constantly.

On the following Monday and Tuesday, Second Cousin LeRoy came directly home from work.

"Got to get my dog ready for pheasant season," he told his drinking buddies. His men went to the tavern anyway, but there was substantially less carrying on without LeRoy around to set them up. Meanwhile, Second Cousin LeRoy arrived home earlier in the afternoon than he had for a long time. As he drove into the yard, he cranked down he car window and called, "Here, Sergeant!"

The dog pushed open the porch door and came bounding out to him, ready for fetching and romping. What a hunting team they were going to be, said Second Cousin LeRoy to the dog, petting it happily.

On Wednesday, Second Cousin LeRoy came home right away again. He wanted to do some advance work with the dog. It was a warmer day than usual, so after about an hour of practice, Second Cousin LeRoy had got up a sweat, plus the dog's tongue was hanging out and it was panting. Second Cousin LeRoy held up his hand.

"Enough for now," he told the dog. He went into the house where he located a cold bottle of beer, and a bowl filled with fresh water for the dog. He returned to the front porch with beer under his arm and holding the bowl.

"Good boy," he told Sergeant, and placed the bowl down. The dog started lapping away. Second Cousin LeRoy stopped to scratch his back, bear-like, against a porch post. After that exercise, he sat down at the top of the porch steps to uncap his beer. The dog walked over to sit right next to him. At the hiss of the bottle opening, the dog tightened up. It sniffed toward the beer, then started growling right in Second Cousin LeRoy's face.

"Hey, friend, want some beer?" teased Second Cousin LeRoy, holding the open bottle under the dog's nose. The dog shuddered, snarled angrily, then began barking like crazy, crouching down on its front legs and up on its hind legs. Second Cousin LeRoy pulled the bottle away but the dog lunged for it so quickly that it caught it between its jaws, and yanked it out of Second Cousin LeRoy's hand. The dog then proceeded to shake the bottle back and forth, like it was trying to break the neck of a flopping bird. The beer went flying all over the porch and Second Cousin LeRoy.

"Hey, hey! What's the matter with you?" screeched Second Cousin LeRoy.

With that, the dog dropped the empty bottle and turned toward his bewildered master, snarling loudly and showing its fine, long teeth and speckled gums.

Then it seemed to move forward. Second Cousin LeRoy wasted no more time in getting into the house and slamming closed the door. The dog stood outside the door, barking and glaring at him. Second Cousin LeRoy was baffled. He went to the bedroom and changed his beer-soaked overalls. "Too bad it was the last bottle," he grumbled.

After he had changed, Second Cousin LeRoy peered out the window to assess the situation. The dog had now settled down and was resting on the porch. The empty beer bottle lay out in the yard. Second Cousin LeRoy took a broom for protection and went outside, ready to scoot back into the house if the dog started up again.

It didn't. The dog started wagging its tail and jumping up happily, as if it were pleased its master was back outside.

"Come over," Second Cousin LeRoy ordered guardedly. It rushed toward him and begged for a cracker, which Second Cousin LeRoy gave it.

"Let's go for a walk," said Second Cousin LeRoy. The dog dashed down the driveway.

They trotted up the road, the dog sniffing here and there, and running ahead, but always returning to his side if Second Cousin LeRoy called. He was mystified by the dog's crazy behavior a few minutes ago, and why it went after the bottle of beer. But Second Cousin LeRoy had no answer, and he soon postponed further worry when he started looking at the fields beside the road, calculating how many pheasants were probably in them at that very moment.

They moved cheerfully along, soaking up the warming sunshine and the tang of autumn. The dog raced down to the Creek to plunge in after a stick that Second Cousin LeRoy threw. The dog brought the stick up to Second Cousin LeRoy, who patted the dog's wet head and fed it another cracker. A few minutes after they had crossed the bridge, they heard the moaning whistle of the far-off afternoon train bearing down on the Windsor station. They turned back for supper.

The next afternoon, after work, Second Cousin LeRoy stopped by the Burke Road Bar and Grill with his men, to have a couple of quick ones. But he was in a hurry to get home and tend to his dog, so he told his cronies to deal him out of the card game. He told them about how good the dog was, and how promising for the pheasant season, but for the life of him he couldn't figure out why the animal had spooked when he had opened a beer.

"Maybe it don't like the smell," somebody said.

Second Cousin LeRoy drank up. He bought two bottles of beer to take out. He left without buying a round.

When he drove into his driveway, the dog came cavorting out to meet the car, tail wagging and very excited. Second Cousin LeRoy stopped the car, opened the door, steadied himself, and lifted himself out. He belched good and loud as he did, pleased with himself and ready to entertain the dog.

"Hey, boy!" called Second Cousin LeRoy as the dog ran to him.

Just about the time he spoke, the dog slid to a dead stop on the gravel. It leveled its eyes on Second Cousin LeRoy, sniffed once, sniffed again, then began snarling at him as if he were some trespasser. Second Cousin LeRoy backed toward his car when he saw the dog's sudden change, groping for the door handle. The dog started circling, glaring at Second Cousin LeRoy, its head turned sideways. Its lips were curled with rage. With his hand behind him, and not taking his eyes from the advancing dog, Second Cousin LeRoy found the handle to the car door. He pulled it open and thrashed back into the driver's seat, slamming himself in.

The dog dashed at the car and stood on its hind legs, its front paws on the driver's side window, barking. It fixed its gaze on Second Cousin LeRoy and bared its long teeth, snarling tremendously. Frustrated by the rolled-up window, it clamored onto the car's hood and barked at LeRoy through the windshield, pawing and scratching until it tore off one of the wiper blades.

Second Cousin LeRoy wasn't sure what to do. He seemed trapped; he made a move toward the passenger side of the front seat but the dog caught on and jumped off the hood, ready for LeRoy to come out that way. Finally, Second Cousin LeRoy cranked down the window a crack and firmly ordered the dog to sit. It snarled at him. He repeated the order, getting angry himself.

The dog hesitated, but sat.

"Don't you budge," said Second Cousin LeRoy. The dog watched him with furious eyes but did not move.

Second Cousin LeRoy waited for a minute, then opened the door on the driver's side and slid guardedly out. The dog continued to stare at him, malice glowering in his eyes, but it did not budge.

"Stay," ordered Second Cousin LeRoy. It did and Second Cousin LeRoy hurried to the house. Once in, he locked the door behind him.

He ate a troubled dinner. Here he had, hands down, the best bird dog he had ever heard of and bang, out of the blue, the animal would all of a sudden go berserk for no apparent reason. It was a big enough dog, and especially a smart enough one, to be afraid of. If it decided to attack, he would have his hands full. What if the dog all of a sudden went nuts like this when they were out hunting?

What would he have to do?

A troubled nap followed the troubled dinner. Second Cousin LeRoy tossed and worried, waking in starts. Was it his own smell? Was it the smell of beer? What?

When LeRoy got up, he washed his face and went to the kitchen. He poured himself a cup of coffee and sat down at the table. He sipped his coffee and pondered the dog, which was now whining and whimpering out on the front porch, wanting to come in. Second Cousin LeRoy went to the door and looked though the window at the top. The dog wagged its tail when it saw him, and whined some more. Second Cousin LeRoy said, "Hey Sarge." The dog put its paws against the door, looking forlorn. LeRoy decided to take a chance. He opened the door.

The dog came in as friendly as anything, licking Second Cousin LeRoy's hand and banging its flailing tail against everything. LeRoy offered it a piece of summer sausage from the icebox. It carefully took the meat from his hand, ate it, and then started licking Second Cousin LeRoy's hand. He gave it clean water in its bowl, gave it a good portion of bologna, sat down at the kitchen table and began to read a stray book he found there. Tomorrow he'd ask his supervisor at the plant if he had any ideas.

The supervisor said that usually border collies were

pretty good-natured, but they were so smart that they needed to be kept busy, so maybe it was just looking for excitement, or needed more to do. Maybe when LeRoy was gone at work the dog got worried and angry. The supervisor also pointed out that Border collies had a very keen sense of smell. Did LeRoy think the dog might smell some of the slaughter floor on him? Did Second Cousin LeRoy make sure he was always good and cleaned up before he left the packing plant?

"Most usually am," said Second Cousin LeRoy. He had lately taken to washing up good, and putting on fresh clothes, before he left for the day.

Well then, said the supervisor, he just didn't know either.

Second Cousin LeRoy went directly home again that afternoon. The dog was exuberant when LeRoy arrived and got out of the car — there was no growling or bad behavior. It was just happy to see him again. After supper they ambled up the road, enjoying the quiet. When they got back home, Second Cousin LeRoy sat down on the front porch with the dog beside him, but it had begun to cloud over and the wind was rising, so LeRoy decided it was time to go inside and light a fire. He stood and stretched. The dog jumped off the porch and began chasing the last of the leaves that were floating down in the wind. Second Cousin LeRoy was thinking of the opening of pheasant season, on the up-coming weekend. It occurred to him that he should go over his shotgun and check his shell supply.

"Hey, mister dog. Let's go in," called Second Cousin LeRoy. They went inside.

LeRoy took out his Remington and laid it on news-papers he had spread out on the kitchen table. He sprinkled gun oil on a cloth and began to clean the gun. The dog sat on a chair, watching the goings-on. A couple of drops of oil were needed under the pump slide, then in the internal mechanism. He cycled the gun a few times to distribute the oil. Nice and smooth, he noted. Next he screwed together a rod and cleaned the barrel. He put the choke back on and made sure it was set right. He would use number 6 shot. He found the shells in a box in the pantry and put them in his hunting coat, which he hung in the back porch room where the dog lived.

"You can keep and eye on that," Second Cousin LeRoy told the alert animal.

Second Cousin LeRoy went over to the refrigerator and pulled out a beer.

He was about to pop the cap when, out of the corner of his eye, he saw the dog looking at him with its nose raised. Second Cousin LeRoy put the bottle down on the table, without opening it. He took the oily gun cloth he had been using and covered the bottle with it. Then he went to the sink and washed his hands. That done, he called the dog.

"Come 'ere boy," he said gently. The dog went to him, wagging its tail. It began to enthusiastically lick his hand, and Second Cousin LeRoy began to think.

"Dog. Go out on your porch and sit," ordered Second Cousin LeRoy. The dog obeyed. LeRoy walked behind him and closed the screen door between the kitchen and the enclosed porch. The dog turned and sat down near the door, watching through the screen, head sideways as if it were wondering what was about to happen.

"Good boy," said Second Cousin LeRoy and the dog wagged its tail.

LeRoy went to the kitchen table and removed the gun cloth covering the unopened bottle. He took his knife from his pocket, flipped out the opener blade, and pried off the cap. Without taking a drink, he waited to see if the dog would react. He didn't have to wait long — within no more than ten seconds the dog began growling, then it started barking. Second Cousin LeRoy quickly recovered the bottle with the oily gun cloth. He went to the sink and washed his hands, dried them, and walked to the screen door. He opened it for the dog, who came rushing in, nose in the air and growling. The dog walked around the kitchen, nose up and eyeing Second Cousin LeRoy. It continued to growl deep in its throat, searching for a scent.

"Sit now!" ordered Second Cousin LeRoy. The dog stopped, beginning to sit but looking ready to jump. It kept looking around, but sat. It studied Second Cousin LeRoy, with its head cocked to the side, growling intermittently. Slowly it cheered up, starting to wag its tail when Second Cousin LeRoy said "Good boy."

"Rest," said Second Cousin LeRoy. The dog lay down. It continued to halfheartedly sniff the air and to search around the kitchen with its eyes, but now with an honest-to-goodness hangdog look, as if it had realized it had made a mistake. After a couple of minutes, with Second Cousin LeRoy saying nothing and standing very still, it stretched out with its chin on the floor, and moaned.

"Sergeant, stay here," Second Cousin LeRoy whispered to the dog.

LeRoy picked up the beer bottle, with the gun cloth still over it, and walked outside. He left the house door open. He walked to his car, opened the driver's side door, and got in. He leaned over and opened the passenger window a third of the way down. He placed the bottle and rags carefully on the passenger seat, and then got out of the car, but behind the open car door, so he could quickly get back in.

He reached in the car and tapped the horn. The dog came prancing out of the house and toward LeRoy, its tail wagging. It ran up to LeRoy and licked his hand. LeRoy bent down to pet it and it licked his face.

"Okay, back home," ordered Second Cousin LeRoy.

As the collie trotted back toward the house, Second Cousin LeRoy, still behind the open car door, reached for the beer. He drank it down in one long draw, announcing completion of the feat with one of

his famous belches. He placed the emptied bottle back
on the seat. Still well behind the car door, he called the
dog.

It left the porch in its usual energetic romp, but
three-quarters of the way to the car it slowed down
and began to sniff the air. Second Cousin LeRoy could
see its nostrils flare and pulse. The dog stopped and
looked at Second Cousin LeRoy, sniffed again, and then
started growling. It began to stalk toward him.

"Hot dog," yelled Second Cousin LeRoy and
plunged into the car, locking himself in. The dog began
running around the car, looking for an entrance. It
leaped on the hood, barking in a near frenzy at Second
Cousin LeRoy. LeRoy reached across the seat, picked
up the empty beer bottle, and threw it backhand out
the partially opened passenger window.

The dog went after it, barking wildly. When the
dog reached the skidding bottle, Second Cousin LeRoy
quickly opened and skedaddled out the car door, making for the house. The dog heard, and realized it had
been tricked. It gave up attacking the bottle and turned
for the chase. With narrowed eyes and ears drawn back,
it sprang after the fleeing Second Cousin LeRoy who
was now almost up the front porch steps. As dog and
man ran, the dog rapidly closed the distance between
them. As LeRoy reached the house, the dog got its teeth
into his overall leg. It yanked back but Second Cousin
LeRoy's momentum tore him loose and he bounced
through the door and inside, slamming the door behind him.

Panting, Second Cousin LeRoy peered through the
keyhole. The dog was on the porch, raging and barking at the closed door, a patch of denim Oshkosh B'Gosh
hanging from a lower front tooth.

"Son-of-a-gun temperance society dog!" called
Second Cousin LeRoy as the animal scolded and carried on outside.

"I've got to brush my teeth first," sputtered LeRoy,

heading for the sink.

He had never been overly responsible with a tooth-brush, but today he brushed as if he were about to meet three dentists. He next shaved without even stropping his razor. A bath followed. He pulled off every stitch of clothing, throwing it into a pile in a corner. Down to his ample birthday suit, he scampered to the wood stove, grabbed the hot kettle, and emptied the steaming wa-ter into his tub. He added cold water, poured in soap, testing the mixture with his toe, then plunged in. He thrashed and splashed, scrubbed, rubbed, washed, and re-washed. He washed his face, his arms, his back, his stomach, his hair, his neck, and his stomach again. He washed his hair a second time, paused for a moment to catch his breath, then began another round of scrub-bing. He rubbed himself cleaner than clean, newer than new, fresher than fresh.

Puffing from his effort, but satisfied that his fren-zied lathering had done the job, he scrambled out of the large tub and bounded into his bedroom where he dried himself with two towels, using a third for his hair. He put on fresh clothes from the bottom up. He even took out a new pair of socks. He brushed his hair and splashed on lotion.

His ablutions were done.

Twenty minutes later he was looking out of a win-dow for his dog. It was resting on the front porch, watching the blowing leaves in the yard. Second Cousin LeRoy strode out onto the porch and called, "Here, boy! Here Sergeant!"

The dog jumped up, studied him for a second, sniffed, then sprinted happily to him, tail wagging. He bent down and it licked his face.

"Good boy," said LeRoy, and handed it a cracker.

LeRoy and the dog went into the house, where LeRoy told the dog to stay.

He then went back outside and located the empty beer bottle, which he wrapped again in the oily rag and dropped, with great care, into the trash barrel at the side of his house.

The next morning Second Cousin LeRoy and the dog drove back out to Prairie du Chien to find the tavern owner. Second Cousin LeRoy left the dog in the car while he went into the tavern to talk to the man, and have a bottle of orange pop. The man scratched his head when he heard the strange story. All his dogs were pretty smart — they came from a good line, and were ever so good-natured. And yes, they could smell something a mile away.

"But this sure is a new one on me," the man said. "I can't explain it, but I guess it's possible he don't like the smell."

Second Cousin LeRoy thanked him and went back to the car. He got in and gave the dog a rub under the chin, and drove home.

The following Saturday, Second Cousin LeRoy and Sergeant were out early. By ten o'clock they had their limit of five pheasants. They stopped at home for the dog's reward of extra crackers and a dish full of dog food that Second Cousin LeRoy had bought. When the dog was finished, Second Cousin LeRoy tucked a pheasant feather under its collar. Then, side by side, the two of them walked over to Brother Bob's store with their birds.

The other hunters were coming in by now. Everybody was pretty impressed. It turned out that Second Cousin LeRoy was the only one who came in with the limit that morning. The dog was looked at, petted, and praised.

After a while some of the men said they were going up to the Burke Road Bar and Grill for a few beers. They invited Second Cousin LeRoy along. He hesitated. He looked at the dog. Well, no. He'd pass, thanks. Just now he had all these pheasants to dress out.

Treasure Hunt

La primavera all'apparir brillante...

They closed down the Token Creek Mill one spring day, many, many years ago now. The mill hadn't been busy enough, they said. It was losing money, not carrying its weight. So they stopped the water wheel, let the old miller go, shut the doors, dismantled the machinery (which was sold to an outfit in North Dakota), and got ready to clear out. During the removal, the owners decided it wasn't necessary to cart out all the small stuff right away, like milling tools, or all sorts of pulleys and chains, and, some later whispered, the company safe. The workers who came up had orders from Chicago to remove all the heavy equipment, but anything the people out west hadn't bought was to be stored until another crew could be sent to get it. The problem for the company people was leaving behind anything useful just sitting around inside the old building.

Once the place was empty, even with the windows and doors boarded up, somebody or other was liable to get in and carry off the valuables. The men in the mov-

ing gang decided that the best thing to do was to bury
what they weren't taking with them. They wrapped
everything in burlap — in greased burlap if it were metal,
so it wouldn't rust — carried it all out somewhere, dug
a good-sized pit, lowered it down, and covered it up.
The men marked the spot with an iron stake. Then the
crew loaded the big wagons, tied down, tightened up,
hitched up, and early on a promising spring morning
rumbled away to wider fields and richer waters.

And that's how things stayed for a long while. The
gray mill stood empty and still, the steady Creek flowed
by day and night, the Mill Pond sparkled and flour-
ished, and the land around the mill lay fallow. As best
they could, the folks of Token Creek maintained the
plank bridge across the old wooden dam, and they kept
the old dam itself in pretty good shape. On and off,
farmers pastured sheep in the sloping field above the
mill, keeping the field from getting overgrown.

But for some reason or other, nobody from the mill
company ever came back to check the building, nor to
dig up all that lay hidden. That's why there was a real
hoard out there somewhere, all wrapped up and shining, ready to be found. A buried treasure.

Uncle August figured the buried treasure story was
pretty much, and no more than, a story — one that had
been concocted, expanded, supplemented, and embel-
lished over time — an original fiction, blown way out
of proportion through the years by people daydreaming and wishing for something better. The yarn had
grown considerably since Uncle August had first heard
it; the part about the company safe had appeared only
about twenty or so years ago. Early on, the cache was
said to have consisted of no more than a few tools, some
grain shovels maybe, a few lengths of chain, some rope,
and whatnot. As the years eased by, the treasure's value
compounded. During the long winters, when things
were slow because you couldn't work outside, you could
go down to Brother Bob's store and hear all about the

Token Creek treasure from folks sitting around playing checkers, or euchre, or just talking about one thing and another. The treasure was marked with an iron stake, they said. You just needed to find that stake and start digging, assuming the iron wasn't rusted down to the ground by now.

Old Tillman, Grandpa's grizzled hired man, was convinced that there sure was a lot of valuables out there somewhere. And even if the safe was empty, its steel and locks were bound to be worth something. And maybe it wasn't empty, because the mill had been closed down in one big rush of a hurry, as he recollected. The bosses weren't even around when the place was boarded up. The men who came up just loaded all their heavy machinery, including those wide leather belts, even the water wheel, into the six-team wagons, and pulled out.

Old Tillman figured the crew must have buried the treasure at night, because nobody had seen any of them go outside the mill yard during the daytime. In fact, the only time anyone from the gang went off site was when a couple of them came up here to the old store for provisions. Tillman remembered the wagons rolling past at the crack of dawn that spring morning, a long time ago, just after he had come to Token Creek. Why the owners never came back to get their things was beyond him. Anyway, it now belonged to whoever found it, and she was out there somewhere, that treasure, not necessarily close to the mill, either. It was more than likely out in the open hillside, up above the mill, or somewhere in the woods that had grown up east of the mill site after the land wasn't used; it could be even higher up, on Big Hill even, in all the woods up there. Just because nobody had been able to find it meant nothing. It could well be that some fool had pulled up the stake without knowing what he was doing.

Junior heard the treasure tale for the first time one

Saturday night at the store, when Uncle August had taken him along to watch a round of checkers.

Uncle August was playing with Brother Bob, and the two were a good match for each other. Junior was more or less following the game, but was also listening in on Old Tillman and Second Cousin LeRoy, who were sitting by the wood stove exchanging cock and bull. When Old Tillman brought up the treasure story, Junior got very interested, because Old Tillman was making it all sound very convincing. Tillman himself had gone out maybe a hundred times looking for the iron stake, but nothing ever came of his efforts. Not to be outdone, Second Cousin LeRoy, who knew the country well because he was always out in it, fishing and hunting, claimed to have gone out maybe twice that, but he'd never had any luck either. Junior was surprised to hear Second Cousin LeRoy claim Uncle August had gone out looking with him a few times. Junior later asked Uncle August about these excursions, when they were walking the cold walk home at the end of the evening.

"Well, spring days seem to draw me away. That's when most go looking."

Junior asked Uncle August if he would take him, and Emma, out hunting for the buried treasure. Uncle August said he would, as soon as it got warm enough.

When Junior got home, he ran upstairs to tell his sister about the buried treasure. By the time he reached the point of Uncle August promising to take them out looking for it, Emma was pretty excited too. Just imagine, she said, fabulous loot right out there near the abandoned mill.

"Old Tillman said there was a safe that might weigh 500 pounds," Junior reported.

"Did he say if there was money in it?" she asked.

"Not for sure, but he said that you had to find an iron stake. Why would they use an iron stake, Em?"

"It lasts longer than wood." Emma had it all figured out.

"I wonder why those people from Chicago never came back to get their treasure."

"Maybe they died," Emma said in a whisper.

Emma and Junior decided they'd try to get a date firm for the upcoming treasure hunt. They scurried downstairs to talk things over with Uncle August and Aunt Melodie. Uncle August expected they'd be able to go out by the middle of April, when the country was clear of snow and mud.

The next day at church, Junior told Grandpa about the spring treasure hunt. Grandpa said it sounded like fun. He'd gone out a few times too, although not in the last few years. If Junior and Emma didn't mind, he'd go along on their trip too, as soon as it got warm enough, of course, and when the fields were dry. Maybe just before spring plowing.

The sermon that Sunday was about King Solomon and his riches. Emma and Junior glanced knowingly at each other as the minister described the fabulous wealth of the fabled king. They were looking forward to April.

The rest of the winter dragged on, as cold as anyone could remember. If there wasn't more snow than in the past twenty years, there wasn't any less either. When the thaw finally did arrive, it was only grudgingly followed by the smallest makings of spring, with at best, two days between chilly rainstorms interspersed with snow flurries. The weather didn't let up enough for dry fields until nearly May. By then, the interminable waiting had carried Junior and Emma from disappointment, through impatience, and well into frustration. They began to argue for starting the treasure hunt, rain and bad weather or not.

Finally, it looked like the first Sunday in May was going to be possible — there had been no rain for over a week and the temperatures were going up.

Grandpa was definitely going along. They would

leave right after church. Junior said he didn't understand why they should have to go to church at all on such a special day. Aunt Melodie said they did, so that was that. Uncle August somewhat calmed the waters by declaring his hope that the minister would be merciful enough to keep his sermon to a reasonable length.

They set out just after ten, from their rendezvous at the store steps. They headed west, walking along the gravel road toward the Mill Pond. Late the night before, the wind had shifted around to the southwest, behind a dry warm front rolling up from the southern plains. The morning was bright and pleasantly mild. The explorers walked beneath endless herds of low, flat-bottomed cumulus, trailing the weather front and casting rapidly moving shadows across the land. Emma and Junior were in the lead; Grandpa and Uncle August walked together a few yards back. The plan was to go as far as the Mill Pond, then cross the wooden bridge over the dam, and on up to the big field behind the mill area. They had decided, in their winter discussions, that the old mill men could well have buried the treasure somewhere in this higher ground, now pasture land for whoever wanted to use it. The big field was spotted with rocks, so besides looking for the iron stake, they would keep their eyes peeled for unusual rock piles, in case the treasure was marked with something like an Indian sign.

On the walk down the road, the kids were struck by the number of birds they heard and saw. Robins were everywhere, scolding and chirping in the budding trees. Near the Mill Pond, the party paused to watch a pair of wrens inspecting a stand of cattails. Grandpa pointed out a red-tailed hawk perched on the very top of a maple, off in the cemetery next to the schoolhouse. Emma spotted a yellow and black bird watching them from a bush. Uncle August said it was a goldfinch that arrived just about this time of year. Intermingled with the agreeable cacophony of robins and wrens were the strident callings of the red-winged black birds that were setting up territories along the marshy edge of their route. There was one about every hundred feet, perched on a fence post behind the ditch, or hanging on a waving reed, making a great show of ruffling its red shoulders, and berating its neighbors.

"There's a sound of spring I never get tired of," Grandpa said.

Farther down from the road, in the bogs, wide leaves of skunk cabbage appeared among the thick patches of pale orange and delicate green marsh marigolds. When the breeze lifted up a particularly strong odor of the skunk cabbage, Emma and Junior held their noses and giggled.

Emma asked to pick some marsh marigolds. Grandpa and Uncle August decided they saw a dry-looking spot to cross the ditch, but there was unseen water under the soft hummocks of grass; Emma got her feet wet, but did get some flowers. She was grateful Aunt Melodie had packed a change of socks for her. She sat on the side of the road and dried her feet while Grandpa wiped out her boots. They laughed and called her the first casualty.

Soon after, the road forked, one branch heading northwest toward the mill, the other turning southwest toward the distant Blue Hills. The group took the road toward the Mill Pond and Big Hill. When they reached the sparkling Mill Pond, the frogs were carrying on so much that their throaty croaking nearly drowned out the songs of the birds. The moment Emma and Junior stepped onto the wooden bridge that would take them to the mill yard, the frogs shut down and they all could hear the birds again, including the pigeons and sparrows on the mill roof. Bobolinks were singing in the field above them.

They moved on, taking in this jamboree of spring, anticipation growing, until they arrived at the edge of the high rocky pasture. The new grass of the pasture was still low; if there was even a part of an iron stake showing somewhere in the expanse, they should be able to see it.

There were others in the field. They made out three figures at the far western side. The figures were walking beside the fence line there, moving up the slope toward Big Hill. Grandpa took out his binoculars to have a look. It was Second Cousin LeRoy and Old Tillman, followed by Brother Bob. Each of the distant travelers carried a shovel on his shoulder.

Grandpa was not surprised. He passed around his binoculars; they watched the three men climb higher, up into the far slope of the old pasture and into the woods at the bottom of Big Hill.

"It looks like they're headed for the west section of the hill," Uncle August decided.

"Maybe we'll run into them later on," Grandpa added.

The part of the field Junior and Emma wanted to cover was pretty big. The strategy that sounded best was to spread out in a long rank, each of them walking about ten feet apart. That way, they could sweep across a good part of the area, scanning the ground in front and beside themselves. Given the size of the pasture, they estimated a couple of dozen crossings would be needed, maybe more. Emma and Junior were to take the two middle posts; Grandpa and Uncle August would take the ends. They began at the eastern boundary.

They walked with their faces to the wind, into the fragrant spring wind. They took their time. At the west fence line, where they had seen the other party, they turned back. The soft-blowing wind now brushed them from behind, gently ruffling their hair, while the sun warmed their backs.

It was afternoon by the time they gave up the search. No one had seen the iron stake, nor any other unusual markings. They gathered in the upper end of the field after their last sweep.

"I think we should eat," Junior proposed.

They decided to picnic right there at the top of the field, where they could enjoy a long view of the valley below them, with its crossroads village, its fields, with the scattered farms and tiny roads running off and away. They could see some of the Blue Hills off to the west. While they were spreading out, they saw Second Cousin LeRoy and his two companions come out of the woods a few hundred feet above them. Emma and Junior stood and waved; Grandpa waved a sandwich and Uncle August gestured toward the lunch baskets. The three men headed toward the picnickers.

"Just in time for lunch," Grandpa called as they came nearer.

"Great day to be out," whooped Second Cousin LeRoy, spreading his arms.

When Second Cousin LeRoy and his comrades reached the group, they put down their shovels and sat down for a chat. They said they were heading back to Token Creek to have their own lunch. Uncle August and Grandpa convinced them there was more than enough food and drink to go around, so they stayed.

As they all ate, they talked about spring planting, and the prospects for the summer. Grandpa told Old Tillman it looked like they could start the plowing to-morrow. Tillman said he had checked over the plows; he'd get them out when they got back. Grandpa had the harnesses oiled and ready; and of course the horses were champing at their bits.

The talk turned to the buried treasure. Emma and Junior wondered why Second Cousin LeRoy and his friends had gone way up to the high part of Big Hill. Old Tillman explained that they had gone up that high because nobody remembered ever looking there before. Second Cousin LeRoy said that was right, but they'd come up dry as usual. Still, there was a lot more ground up there.

Emma explained her group's having swept across the big pasture, walking abreast, looking for clues. They'd seen nothing either. Junior said yes to that, but mentioned that Emma had stopped a few times to pick some purple violets and those little golden buttercups. She had put some in her hair; the rest were for Aunt Melodie and Grandma.

They agreed that the treasure sure was an elusive thing. People had been hunting it for years, with the same results. You wondered how those old mill men could have hidden it so well. Second Cousin LeRoy's opinion was that those geezers didn't want anybody, maybe not even themselves, to have an easy time locating it. Uncle August wondered if there really was a treasure after all. Old Tillman said he very much thought so; besides, a lot of people would have been fooled if there weren't.

Second Cousin LeRoy thought that there probably was a rich treasure around them. It was just hard to see where — they lived in a big place. Besides, Second Cousin LeRoy said, Old Tillman should know. He was around when the mill got closed down. He was a witness, so to speak.

Brother Bob shrugged his shoulders, suggesting he certainly didn't know.

What did the kids think? Second Cousin LeRoy asked.

Both Junior and Emma said they sure hoped there was a treasure — they liked hunting for it. Grandpa said that, either way, it didn't hurt to keep looking for it. That was the fun of it, after all, the looking and the hoping. He'd been searching, on and off like the rest of them, for a long time. He always enjoyed going out on one of these rambles. Everyone did.

Second Cousin LeRoy said it was good that the kids had been introduced to the treasure, and that they would start coming out, to keep the rolling stone rolling, in a manner of speaking. There was a lot more ground to cover. There were places nobody'd even considered yet. Where would they go next?

Brother Bob wanted to tell them something, in response to that question. He held up his little writing tablet that he always had with him. They waited while he paused for a moment, then carefully wrote:

"Even higher."

Wasn't that the truth? The whole summit of the hill needed to be explored and searched. They smiled at the thought.

The kids were lying on their backs, full of food. They were studying the sky, watching the churning clouds that were forming in the west.

"There's one that looks like a pig," Emma said, pointing.

"Where?" Junior asked.

Emma pointed again.

"I see it," said Grandpa

"It's changing. It's getting thinner now."

"I think it looks like a dog," Junior said.

"The wind must be strong up there. The clouds keep changing."

"Now it's a cow," Junior decided.

"I still see the pig," Emma giggled.

They laughed and laughed, all of them. Then they settled down and were quiet for a while, resting and looking up.

Second Cousin LeRoy and Junior both fell asleep, but not for long — Second Cousin LeRoy woke himself and Junior with his snoring. They laughed again, especially Second Cousin LeRoy.

It was time to get back. They got up and stretched. They gathered up their paraphernalia, and took a last look down the valley. They started for home, down the hill toward the Mill Pond and the village, walking in a line.

As the troop filed across the Mill Pond bridge, the frogs felt their steps, and ended their chanting. They could hear the robins still, calling and calling again, and the red-winged blackbirds along the road. The hawk had left the tree above the cemetery.

"When can we go hunting the treasure again?" Junior asked.

"After spring planting, once things settle down," Uncle August answered. "There will be more days."

"Today's been fine, even if we didn't come across anything," Grandpa concluded.

"May is the best month," said Second Cousin LeRoy.

"Have we decided where we'll go next trip?" Grandpa wondered.

"Even higher," answered Junior and Emma, in one voice.

Horse Sense

Grandpa William Armstrong was a very good farmer — better than a very good farmer, a superior farmer. There was no question about it. He was a man who could raise pretty much anything that would grow in Southern Wisconsin: field crops, garden vegetables, fruits, and flowers, even asparagus. Grandpa had a knack for choosing seed corn that produced tall, dark fields with bumper crops, year after year. People said he had the gift, that he was endowed with a true green thumb. He had the ability to look over a piece of land and then tell you how many acres it was. He understood crop rotation and he plowed deep.

Grandpa had started contour planting before almost anyone had even heard of it. He was held in high regard for his ability to predict weather by just looking at the sky, checking the wind, and reading his barometer. He knew the names of clouds.

He could fix most farm machines, even hay balers and threshers; he could build a stone wall without using mortar, he could figure out the best spot to drill a well, and he had helped plan or build at least half the barns within twenty miles of Token Creek. Besides plants, land, and everything that went with them, his knowledge of farm stock was not questioned. He understood animals, he kept them clean and healthy, he made sure they were watered in the hot summer, kept warm in the cold winter, and at all times well-fed. Grandpa spoke kindly to them and about them. He was familiar with their habits, their strengths, weaknesses, quirks, tics, and needs, be they milk cows or pigs. He knew about beef cattle, sheep, goats, dogs, cats, geese, ducks, rabbits, and to the best of his abilities, horses.

Grandpa had been around horses since he was a boy, meaning he had, as he so wryly put it, learned over the fullness of time to tolerate the darn things.

This was not a boast. Grandpa was not a boastful man. He just did not hold horses in high esteem. He said you never knew when one might decide to sneak up behind you, ears back, to try for a nip at your backside. A horse looked out for itself; a horse would push a poor dumb cow completely out of the way to get at hay it thought was sweeter, or what appeared to be the bigger stand of grass, or the deeper end of the water trough. Horses were like cats in his book: self-centered and self-serving. He said their beauty was over-rated and their intelligence much exaggerated. It was his contention that pigs were so much smarter than horses that, come the day there were animal intelligence tests, pigs would come out on top of horses. With a lot less effort and aggravation, let alone a fraction of the time needed for training horses to just start and stop, you could teach a pig to roll over, or walk backwards, or turn in circles, even fetch sticks. Pigs could even dig up fishing worms. Dill the spotted pig was a case in point; not only could the pig do all those things, he could even count. No horse had ever learned to count.

Still, you needed horses for a lot of the heavy jobs around a farm, like plowing, or pulling wagons and other such unwieldy things, from one place to another. Horses were among the irksome but necessary aspects of farming.

That's why Grandpa kept and used horses — because they were necessary. Nor did his feelings about them keep him from taking good care of them. He worked them thoughtfully and pampered them as he did the rest of his animals.

But, he didn't love them.

The fall that Junior was seven, one of the farms over by Cottage Grove went up for sale, after the only son of the place was killed. The boy had fallen from the silo. His parents were so devastated by the death that they decided to get away entirely, to move down to Illinois, near the wife's folks, where they could start over. When the accident happened, Grandpa and Grandma were there visiting, having stopped over with some gladiolus bulbs. Grandpa drove the boy as fast as he could to the doctor's, but there was no saving the poor little guy because his neck was broken. Anyway, late in the winter, the farm was sold to a neighbor, who bought it for his daughter and new son-in-law.

The couple selling the farm wanted to give Grandpa and Grandma something by way of thanks for support during the tragedy, so they up and gave a horse. It was a bedraggled strawberry-roan mare named Truth. Truth had been withheld from the sale of the farm's livestock specifically for Grandpa and Grandma. Grandpa thought she, the horse named Truth, looked all set and ready for the glue factory, with her distended belly and sway back. He even discreetly inquired if she was by chance with colt. He was assured she couldn't have been — there were no male horses on the farm.

There was also a question of whether Truth could see very well, since she seemed uninterested in what was going on around her. Then again, she pretty much ignored you when you told her to "get up" or "walk."

She was out of touch, depressed and dejected, you might say. You had to tell her two or three times to start moving, or stop, depending on her state of motion.

Grandpa and Grandma didn't need another horse, particularly one that looked like it was on its last legs, but they couldn't very well refuse the gift, considering the circumstances. So, on a drizzling March Saturday, with the temperature none too warm, the dejected looking quarter horse mare, tethered to the back of Grandpa's wagon, moped down the Windsor Road, with Grandpa having to walk beside it for encouragement and moral support. Grandma was obliged to drive the team.

When the morose parade dragged through Token Creek, the participants' backs to the rain-spitting wind, Second Cousin LeRoy came outside his house to shout encouragement. Brother Bob waved Grandma and Grandpa into the store for coffee, but they wanted to keep going. Eventually the drenched troop arrived at the farm.

Everyone was shivering. Even the horses were cold, especially Truth, who was in a state of trembling and shaking when they got her into the barn. While the hired man took care of the Percherons, Grandpa dried and rubbed the quivering mare, wondering all the while what he would do with the poor thing. He decided the best thing was to keep her for garden plowing and light work for a while, if she lived past spring. Just to be sure Truth kept going, he started giving her extra rations of oats, and told the hired man to keep an eye on her. He would get the vet to look at her too.

The very same weekend that Truth arrived, life got even more complicated, because Grandpa's young sister Mabel up and announced that she had become engaged to a young man named Carl, from Wyoming. Carl had just been hired as the principal at the Windsor High School, not far up the road from Token Creek. She had met him while they were both students at the teachers' college at the University. Carl hadn't returned to Wyoming when he got his degree. He decided he liked Wisconsin and took a teaching job down in Milwaukee, teaching history and science at one of the big high schools there. He and Mabel had kept in touch. In fact, they had seen each other quite a lot over the past couple of years. When Carl came up to hear History Department lectures, or work at the University library, he was always invited to stay over at Grandpa and Grandma's spare room, as Mabel's guest. Grandpa and Grandma liked him, and they hoped for a marriage. Carl was straightforward and well spoken, with a gentle wit. He and Grandpa appreciated each other. He also knew a lot about animals.

Mabel and Carl had decided to get married in the late summer, just before they went back to teaching, or in Carl's case, running a high school. They had located a small farm up the Burke Road, which they were going to buy. They could take possession right after threshing was done. They wouldn't farm the land themselves, since they'd both be busy teaching. They would rent out the fields.

Grandpa and Grandma were so pleased with the news from Mabel that they suggested she invite Carl up for the next weekend, for a little celebration.

Mabel got out the buggy and drove right down to Brother Bob's to telephone Carl long-distance. He told her that he was delighted with the invitation, and would be there.

On the Friday following the arrival of the gift horse, Carl arrived by train at the Windsor station. Mabel and Grandpa met him with the buggy and team. On the drive back to the farm, Grandpa told Carl about the sad old horse with the big belly that had been given to them. He would try to keep it going, he said, but the poor thing might not make it, although it seemed to be holding its own since it got to the farm. That evening, after chores, Carl asked to have a look at her.

Grandpa took him to Truth's stall.

"I took a look at her teeth when I got her," Grandpa said. "Her teeth aren't bad. And her temperature seems normal, but she sure is swollen up." Grandpa touched the horse's belly and it groaned.

Carl nodded, looking at the horse.

"We've been brushing her down a lot too, so she looks a lot better than when she came. She's always hungry," Grandpa continued. He ruffled the new supply of hay that the horse was busily eating.

Carl was studying the horse carefully. He climbed into the stall and kept her from taking another mouthful of hay. The horse pushed at him a little, wanting to get at the hay. Carl pushed her back and opened her mouth.

Grandpa was right — the animal's teeth were in good shape, very good shape. The molars were high. He checked her eyes and found they appeared satisfactory too. Grandpa had shod her since she arrived. Her feet looked fine. He ran his hands over the horse's belly. The horse didn't move, but groaned.

"She's not an old horse," Carl said.

"She's younger than I first thought," Grandpa agreed.

When Carl was done looking her over and had climbed out of the stall, the horse resumed eating, but watching the two men.

"Well, what do you think?" Grandpa asked.

"I think your horse is carrying a foal," Carl answered. "She's low on spunk because there's a pretty good size colt in there. She's big enough for two, almost."

"Oh, I don't think so," Grandpa said with conviction. "Why, there weren't any male horses on poor Olaf's place at all. He assured me that she wasn't bred. I think she wasn't looked after too well, after the boy died. They were pretty distraught, which is understandable. She's looking better because we're feeding her so much. As for this big belly, it's more than likely she'd been given bad oats up at the other farm. If she's going to get better, I expect she'll start to shrink pretty soon."

Carl studied the animal for a while longer. He reached into the stall and pushed on the horse's belly. It groaned again, and lowered its head. Carl looked back at Grandpa. He raised his eyebrows and nodded.

"Seems like a colt in there," Carl said.

"The vet said he'd be able to come by next week. He'll know," Grandpa said, a little put out.

At supper, Grandma asked Carl if he'd had a look at the gift horse. He said he had. What did he think? she asked. He said he thought it was going to foal. Grandma, sensing something in the wind, asked her husband if that was right. Grandpa shrugged.

"Could be, but I doubt it," he said.

Mabel came to her future husband's defense:

"I'm sure Carl's right, Brother. People from Wyoming grow up around horses. They've got horse sense," she declared.

Carl kept quiet, but he looked amused; he was pleased that Mabel took his part without question.

"We'll see," said Grandpa, and dug into his dinner. He was not overly talkative for the rest of the evening.

On Sunday, they had a big dinner at noon, so Carl could catch the afternoon train back to Milwaukee on a full stomach. Uncle August, Aunt Melodie, Emma, and Junior had been invited to make it a party. The kids were greatly taken with the newcomer. Aunt Mabel brought up the possibility of a baby horse arriving one of these days, which caused great excitement for the two children. Grandpa said they'd wait and see about that.

Late that afternoon, after Carl had left and while Grandpa and Grandma were saying goodbye to the youngsters, both of them asked if it was true that there really was going to be a new colt on the farm, and what

Grandpa thought about naming it. Grandpa said he didn't know if there was going to be a colt or not, but the vet was coming in a couple of days, so they'd be sure then. Uncle August said that from what he knew of Carl, even though he had only talked to him a few times, the man could well be right.

"We'll see," said Grandpa.

In the middle of that night, Grandpa was awakened by horses whinnying in the barn. At the same time, Basil the dog started barking, and Dill the pig took up the call from his pig house, with squealing and grunting. Grandpa took down his 12-gauge and went out to the barn with a lantern to see what was the matter. He and the dog found Truth in the process of giving birth to the second of a pair of partly colored colts.

Grandpa was astounded. He didn't know where to turn first and before he could even think about helping, the two little creatures were out, and up on wobbly legs, beginning to nurse. The mother glowered at Grandpa, as if daring him to enter her stall.

The colts had unusual markings — nice patches of white on their faces, with dappled spots on their bellies and quarters, sort of like the Indian horses in paintings. Before he returned to the house, Grandpa hooked an extra pail of water on a stanchion, for the new mother. He also poured a generous scoop of oats into her feeder, and pitched some new straw into the stall. He made sure she had enough hay, then hurried to reassure Grandma.

"Must have been one of those Gypsy horses from last year that sired her," he told her.

When Uncle August stopped by the next afternoon, he looked over the mother and offspring with approval. All three seemed quite healthy. He asked Grandpa if he thought he wasn't getting a bit rusty when it came to judging the condition of horses.

"Well, she looked more sick than pregnant when she got here, didn't she?" Grandpa asked stiffly.

'Today's the first time I've seen her," answered Uncle August. Uncle August was enjoying this conversation.

Grandpa didn't respond, so Uncle August kept it up.

"You probably got confused because she was carrying two colts, not just one," he said. "They must have been quite a load. No wonder you thought she was low-slung. They've got real nice markings. Just think, two colts. Still, I always thought you knew your horses. At least, that's what people would say, I suppose. But then, people will talk."

"I never claimed for certain that she wasn't going to have a colt."

"Or colts," said Uncle August.

"I just said that Olaf told me she wasn't. I took him at his word," Grandpa explained.

And here began Grandpa's tribulations.

When Carl arrived for the next weekend's visit, the entire family met him at the train station. The kids couldn't tell him fast enough about the twin colts. He had a look at them as soon as the group reached the farm. Carl thought they were very handsome, indeed, and very healthy. They had fine markings, and the way they walked, they might eventually be good buggy horses. He hadn't failed to notice, either, that the mother gave an improving impression, now that she was relieved of her burden. She was coming along well. He thought she'd turn out to be a good horse, this Truth.

"You know, that's what the vet said too," contributed Mabel, smiling at her brother.

Emma told Carl that they had waited for him to help name the babies, since he was the only one who had known about them coming. Gosh, even Grandpa hadn't known.

Grandpa remained silent.

Carl said he considered their request an honor. He suggested that they make a list of names they liked, then vote on the ones that seemed best. Later in the evening they settled on "Stars" and "Stripes," because the white face of one of the colts looked like two stars, and the white on the other's face was like two interrupted stripes. They were beautiful horses, no question about that.

The story of the unpredicted colts quickly spread. Down at Brother Bob's store, on a Saturday no more than two weeks after the foals arrived, Grandpa took a lot of ribbing.

"Hey Will. Were you just horsing around when you said that horse Truth was sick?" some one asked.

When Grandpa complained to Grandma about all the teasing, she said she thought the man who gave him the horse was the one who had made a mistake. Olaf had said quite definitely that Truth was not bred, so Grandpa should not feel like he had goofed, too much.

This was Grandpa's defense on his next trip to the store: he had believed what he had been told — a reasonable mistake. This defense didn't get him very far.

"Now Will, you just can't hang your harness on that," chuckled Second Cousin LeRoy. This brought a good laugh from the crowd.

Grandpa was just too popular and good-natured a man to let off the hook too easily. A fair number of neighbors stopped by his farm over the next few days to inspect the handsome colts. Of course, they also came by to rib Grandpa some more about his boner. Early in the summer, a newspaper reporter who covered Dane County got wind of the story:

Token Creek. Saturday, June 14. Most people who know William Armstrong wouldn't question his farming. He raises some of the best corn in Dane County, for one thing. And half the community around knows that Will and Kate regularly take a lot of flower prizes at the fair every year. Their gladiolus are second to none. There are those who say Will knows horses too, most of the time. Well, just this past April the first one of those times when he wasn't totally up on his horses happened to our friend Will.

At the store out at Token Creek, they say that Will came by a horse that he declared was next in line for the glue factory.

According to a reliable source, Will had more than once insisted that the horse had a swollen belly because it was sick and worn out, and it was so tired of living. So even though Will cared for it with great kindness, it just stood around like it knew its end was near.

The trouble was the horse wasn't the least bit sick — it was just carrying two very large foals. The other trouble was that Will argued with a couple of experts about whether the horse was going to foal, Will claiming it was not.

One of these experts was his new brother-in-law-to-be, who happens to be a horse authority from Wyoming. You can imagine farmer Willliam's surprise when the supposedly broken-down mare gave birth to a set of frisky twins that a lot of people say are Pintos (a breed from the Southwestern United States).

We hear that Will is going to start a subscription to a horse magazine, so he can read up on the subject of swollen horses, just in case another gift horse comes to him.

That evening Grandpa drafted a letter to the newspaper, stating he wished to cancel his subscription. Aunt Melodie talked him out of it.

"Don't be sour grapes, Will. You have to admit that Truth the horse fooled you," she said.

"And foaled you too," added the merciless Uncle August.

In the end, Grandpa put the letter in his desk to think about it. In time, the teasing died down and Grandpa began to laugh about the incident. Once in a while, he would run into someone who might offer a feeble joke about his misreading the horse, something along the lines of looking a gift horse in the belly, or similar such nonsense. He began to take it in stride, for this horse affair was turning out for the best, because by late summer, not only were the twins bounding joyfully around his pastures, but the mother had definitely become quite perky herself. Indeed, she was so much so that one morning when Grandpa hitched her to a mower, she yanked it around for three hours without a break, allowing him to cut almost four acres before noon that day.

Grandpa decided that, after all was said and done, he was better off for the old gift horse, and he was going to keep her. And, she wasn't really old after all, and she was getting to be pretty good-natured; and to boot, he had the two good-looking colts that folks told him were probably worth something. Still, he knew he couldn't keep all three of them — the mother and her two offspring. Five horses, counting his team, were beyond the farm's resources. Come winter, the colts would have to go. He gave the whole affair some careful thought.

Emma, Junior, and Grandpa were leaning on the pasture fence one evening, squinting into the setting sun and watching the mother horse and her two colts nuzzling each other. All of a sudden, as Emma saw Grandpa smiling and chuckling to himself, she realized he was up to something.

"Grandpa, what are you and Grandma going to give Aunt Mabel and Uncle Carl for a wedding present?" she asked. She caught Junior's eye.

"Do you know, Em?" Junior asked. He recognized that his sister was on to something.

"Maybe," she answered. She was looking at Grandpa.

"Well, if you two can keep a secret, I might tell you," he said. Actually, he was just itching to tell them.

Emma quickly nodded.

"We can, we promise," Junior whispered.

"Grandma's going to give them one of her big quilts,

and a set of dishes. I'm fixing up their barn some, on the inside."

"They won't have any animals for their fixed-up barn, will they?" Junior asked. He too began to see which way the wind was blowing.

"Maybe they're going to get some," Emma said, smiling at Grandpa.

"I guess we'll see," Grandpa responded. He looked slyly toward the horses.

"Grandpa, are you going to give them the two baby horses?" Emma asked, clapping her hands. Junior began jumping up and down with excitement.

"Well, yes, that's right," Grandpa told her. "But remember, it's a secret. We especially want Carl to be surprised. Remember you two, it's a big secret, just between us."

Emma and Junior asked Grandpa how he and Grandma had decided about the colts as their wedding present.

"Well, I got to thinking how Carl knew, the minute he saw Truth there, that those nice little colts were coming along. Then, when they arrived, it was pretty clear he really liked them. So I said to Grandma that it seemed a shame to sell the little guys, considering how Carl would be happy to have them. I said we should give them to Mabel and Carl as a wedding present. Grandma heartily agreed with the idea. You know what she even said?" he asked.

"What, Grandpa?" both children asked.

"Well, she gave me a fine compliment. She said my idea showed real horse sense."

Fish Story

... once, on this earth, once, on this familiar spot of ground, walked other men and women, as actual as we are today, thinking their own thoughts, swayed by their own passions, but now all gone, one generation vanishing after another, gone as utterly as we ourselves shall shortly be gone like ghosts at cockcrow.
— *G. M. Trevelyan,* An Autobiography and Other Essays

Dramatis Personae:

- *Knutson Yon Hamsum, Wisconsin Game Warden*
- *Alice Chalmers Yon Hamsum, Knut's wife*
- *Brother Bob Armstrong, storekeeper of Token Creek*
- *Second Cousin LeRoy Armstrong, a local sportsman and character*
- *Olivia Oliverson Armstrong (Aunt Ollie), Second Cousin LeRoy's Wife*
- *Junior Armstrong, the son to Second Cousin LeRoy's second cousin*
- *Emma Armstrong, Junior's sister and older by two years*
- *Grandpa William Armstrong*

- *Grandma Kate Armstrong, Grandpa's wife*
- *Uncle August Armstrong, half brother to William; guardian to Junior and Emma Armstrong*
- *Aunt Melodie Armstrong, August's wife*
- *Mabel Armstrong Swann, Grandpa's younger sister*
- *Uncle Carl Swann, Mabel's husband*
- *State Wildlife Department employees (Trillin and Abe Eyfniphcz)*
- *Chorus*
- *Governor, politicians, functionaries (in pantomime)*

Prologue

Enter Chorus

My friends, come with me! Come away! Let us travel together. Let us, during these fleeting, sweet moments we have here together, make a journey of our hearts and minds. Let us wander away, in our imaginations, back to another time, turning, turning our thoughts and dispositions, with gentleness, to an era now far passed and of memory fading. Let us take ourselves away, to that kindly span when our dear relations and loyal friends, now gone, were themselves young, and newly embarked upon life's journey, as many among us now are.

Let us go there, to them, on this stage, in this play, in our imaginations.

Let us find them, ourselves seeking them, with warm hearts and countenances smiling, in those sweet past days, even briefly, so we may see the lives they lived, visit their quiet hours and their hours of great business, in those fair times that can be no more. Ah, those wonderful, long-ago years, that bounteous and promising time.

Let us, together then, imagine that we are there,

watching, hearing, feeling, so we may witness a most true, yet strange story, of great fish and of fabled fisherfolk. You agree? You will go? You are prepared? Then we shall go, and here are soon arrived.

The stage is slowly lighted to reveal a large, marbled hall, akin to the interior of a temple. There are many doors, office doors, adjoining the space; gesturing and conferring figures leave and enter the offices; groups of men come together and disperse.

Our venerable chronicle of angling, quite soon to unfold in its entirety before us, takes its origins here. As you see, these are not the bucolic environs and bounds of the village of Token Creek, although the narrative will play out and find its end there, in that most wonderful of corners on this fertile earth. No, no, the beginning is here. The genesis of our tale arises from among and along the smoothly hewn marble halls of enlightened government, in that noblest of great structures, in that repository and vibrant symbol of our democracy hereabouts, within our splendid Wisconsin State Capitol, as you now see it revealed.

To the high walls of this magnificent edifice, to enter amid the echoing ferment and conniving din of politics unrelenting, the then-director of the Wisconsin Wildlife Department came each year, year after year. He came to this place, with his perennial requests for money, to fund a trout stream restocking program. Each year he badgered the governor, asking his monetary blessing for this much-needed affair, and each year he saw his request flow into the great shuffle of budgetary paperwork. And, sadly, with the arrival of each early summer, when the perspicacious governor's budget descended from the normal rounds of scrutiny, trade-offs, and bickering examination, there remained not even a single verbal iota, nor numeric mention, relating to the replenishment of game fishes. And large was the

Wildlife director's perennial and woeful chagrin! That there was clear need for reestablishing the nearly defunct trout fishery was undeniable. Local catches had long been incrementally diminishing; each passing spring brought a poorer return. The dearth in the trout catch was, we must admit, the result of years of over-fishing, almost exclusively out-of-season, by the many, very many, discreditable poachers dwelling upon our richly-soiled countryside.

Several locals, among them Second Cousin LeRoy Armstrong and Brother Bob Armstrong of Token Creek, appear stage left. They are all carrying fish poles — many are also carrying recently caught fish, which they jocularly show to each other, each admiring the others' catch. They lurk about, obviously enjoying themselves. They gesture derisively toward the politicians and functionaries.

The astute governor, whom you see on the dais to the right, was more than aware of the habits of the sly and nefarious country populace. After all, he was from among them. He knew their ways. Thus, when asked why he ignored the incessant entreaties from the bewildered and chagrined Wildlife director, he declared that if the local denizens were so darn piggish as to over-fish, then it was there darn hard luck if trout were hard to come by. He was not, no sir, going to start raising fish for them. Let them eat summer sausage.

A group of lawmakers assembles. The distinguished members greet and congratulate each other, with ceremony and deep bow. They then sit. One among them soon rises and holds forth. He waves his arms as he mimes a great speech. When he is finished, and has put some of his colleagues to sleep, there is sudden animation in part of the crowd — nearly half of them rises and applauds feverishly.
The remaining members sit, arms folded and scowling.

Thus it was that the waning days of the once-renowned trout fishery were not to be ignored, nor so cavalierly, as the governor would have it, put on the back burner. Late of a budding spring morn, redolent with the touting of daffodils and the scent of cherry blossoms, there arose from among the legislatures, housed high in the towering Capitol, an illustrious member of the minority party. This member gave forth, in a ringing and stentorian voice, an impassioned — not to mention accusatory — fish speech.

In an oration worthy of archival immortality, he wove and spun the sad tale of the state's feeble reputation among those who would pursue trout fishes.

He raved, he cried, he spoke in a shaking and sorrowing voice, filled even with suggestions of true emotion, telling that while these fair lands were bountifully graced with miles, yea miles upon miles, of happily rushing streams, the taking of trout had become a sport feebly akin to nonexistent. You would have thought, he told them, that our glistening waterways would be brimming and churning with these oversized, succulent fishes that would leap, mouths agape, toward even the inkling of an artificial fly. Alas for the harsh reality! Oh woe the unhappy fact! Rainbow trout in Wisconsin had gone the way of the great auk.

In truth, dear friends, the faded glory of our Wisconsin's trout fishing was a mortifying embarrassment. As far as this honorable member was concerned, oh yes, the present fishless humiliation was the fault of none other than an irresponsible governor, supported by a mob of myopic lawmakers of the same egregious, hidebound ilk, that is, members of his party. Oh shame, oh shame.

A portion of the body of lawmakers arises, applauding and gesturing toward the speaker. Soon after, a second group arises, responding in quite an opposite fashion. Chaos reigns.

The offended politicians of the sanctimonious majority party (the governor's) responded with vehement celerity to this demagogic ranting. How could anyone, they demanded, claim that our favored land was anything less than a sportsman's paradise? One might ask here, even had they known, these majority folks, in their heart of hearts that trout fishing was not the premier sport in their neck of the woods, or plains, whichever. What are politicians for, if not to disagree with each other and then make a deal? In any event, this cogent query of the minority party was clearly a means to cast aspersions on the majority. It was a minority, potboiling ploy to divert attention from larger issues, such as buttermilk prices, or the unspecified problems of cheese factory owners.

A newspaper lands on the stage. The Chorus retrieves it, reads it for a moment, then smiles. He resumes his speech:

Next upon the scene, as you have seen, plops the ever-carping and perpetually self-satisfied newspaper, the notoriously outspoken *Capital Times*. Plunging itself headlong into the piscatorial fray, the pesky gazette not only reprinted the honorable member's recriminatory fish speech, as well as the opposition's incoherently flailing response, it added some privileged information it had ferreted out somewhere or other. It asked if the reading citizens were aware that sales of out-of-state fishing licenses had sounded a new bottom this year? Going further, the editors and scribes produced secret statistics showing that our burbling waterways were not only markedly deficient in rainbow trout, but that our gurgling brooks and purling freshets represented some of the paltriest and laughable stream fishing in the entire, far-flung, and proud region know as the Upper Midwest!

"Consider," sputtered the tempestuous tabloid, "that trout fishing supplies aren't even carried anymore by many, many of our sporting goods stores. Admittedly, casting for walleye, or cork fishing for crappies and sunfish still keep our beloved sportsmen occupied, and fish pans cracking. We grant that many of our fishing emporiums do well in the cork, hook, and line departments, yet ask yourself this: how many high-booted gentlemen and ladies are to be seen nobly wading into the rushing froths of our innumerable sparkling rapids, snapping fly rods and lugging creels, nets, and whatnot? Not a lot, that's for darn sure. How shall our esteemed governor respond? Is this not a most obvious deficiency for which he, who is assigned to lead, is most surely the responsible culprit?"

The great body of lawmakers assembles. Some members gesture disparagingly at each other. There is pushing and shoving. Others beat their chests. Some do cartwheels. One stands off to the side and holds his nose.

When the aforementioned diatribe appeared, the minority party was handed an unanticipated, yet certainly welcome, gift with which to further harass the beleaguered governor. The newspaper's hyperbolic bombast was copied and circulated among legislatures and of course, among the teeming, ever-fickle public. The article was a clear indictment, a declaration of war. The cry went up — would our honorable governor care to explain his complete and absolute lack of interest in enhancing the reputation and revenues of our milk and honey land? Did not the sad sales of out-of-state fishing licenses make painfully obvious, to anyone who could bait a hook, that the governor was not, was now not, and would never be, the fisherman's friend? Step forward and explain, governor, they thundered.

The governor soon realized that he had little chance of gaining the upper hand in the expanding piscine brawl. To head off the possibility of fish becoming an issue in the year-after-next election, he publicly declared, on radio and in print (indeed, in the redoubtable *Capital Times*), that the chief of his Wildlife Department was to study and consider the need for a fish restocking program.

Further, it was declared that consultations with the astute and neighboring state of Minnesota had been undertaken. Minnesotans had a fish program. We should learn from them. It was expected that recommendations for the establishment of fish revitalization and renewal, in Wisconsin, would be forthcoming, within 30 days and no more!

The breakneck Wildlife Department study was immediately begun. It was soon to demonstrate that the affable Minnesotans had been, for years, completely, moreover entirely, successful in keeping trout fishing a percolating affair. They had done so by means of a far-flung, comprehensive, and regular restocking infrastructure. The fiscal aspects of their labors were most gratifying — because there were so many fish to catch as a result of stream restocking, fisherman from all sorts of unusual places, from East, South, and West, came to blue-watered Minnesota to fish. There was a positive cash flow into the program. There were fish galore.

The governor steps forward from the milling crowd on stage. He raises his arms for quiet, and gets it.

The embattled governor quickly came around. In keeping with the obligatory ostentation of his high office, he announced, in a speech delivered from atop the glistening steps of the state Capitol building, that: "As for a fish restocking program, by golly, we can't afford not to have one."

Thus it was that the governor of the state of Wisconsin became the sportsman's friend. He introduced a trout replenishment bill into the legislature well before the summer recess. Bipartisan support was rampant, frenetic, and tumultuous. The fish bill raced through the boisterous chambers. Members clamored to be sponsors. All took credit for its advent. Within the week of his speech on the Capitol steps, the bill landed on the governor's desk. He signed it with full alacrity and expansive pride, using fourteen different fountain pens, surrounded as he did so by dozens of posing politicians.

Things began to move after the law was signed. The following year, as spring was showing itself as a possibility, an entire state-organized and sponsored fish restocking system had been put in place. From fish farms in all parts of our great country, the state bureaucracy had arranged for the purchase of multitudes of coddled rainbow trout, destined for planting in our many unsullied streams. These colorful fish were all delivered to the state in late winter. They were placed in scores of great ponds and holding pens, constructed at key locations in the counties, prior to eventual dissemination.

One of the many new trout ponds was erected close by the fair village of Token Creek, in Dane County. Token Creek, as we know, was home to Second Cousin LeRoy Armstrong, among others.

And now, finally, to the sweet environs of thriving Token Creek. It is early on a blustery March day. The fish-restocking program is about to begin.

Act I
(in prose form, read by the Chorus)
Scene One: *At the Trout Pond*

Knutson Yon Hamsum, sturdy and veteran Wisconsin game warden stood, arms akimbo, at the edge of a neat and spacious concrete trout-holding pond, newly built at Token Creek. The trout pond lay a few dozens of yards downstream from the Windsor Road Bridge, on the Mill Pond side. It was only recently that the ice covering the Mill Pond had broken up. Warden

Yon Hamsum was watching, with great satisfaction, the elongated trout enclosure and the present activity around it.

Hard by stood an impressive Wildlife Department tank truck, from which were pouring, down a wide chute and into the ample fish basin, large, flopping, and certainly healthy rainbow trout. As the squirming load spewed forth, the mass of fish skidded and slid so rapidly down that Knut was unable to detect individual specimens. He saw only a blur of fins and tails, highlighted by flashes of red from the speckled sides of the passing hoard. Knut had expected to be able to count the fish, or at least estimate the accuracy of the load, but enumeration was impossible, given the speed of their flow into the trout pen.

Well, anyway, he thought, there were probably even more than the five hundred listed on the shipping form. The department always got some extra in case a few were banged up during transport.

Knut looked up into the sharp, blue sky, blowing with biting northern air. His craggy face was flushed with cold. He removed a glove and drew down his fur ear flaps onto his ears, then quickly replaced the glove. He should be grateful there was no snow, he considered, or even sleet, for this auspicious unloading. March was roaring along like a perverse lion. It had been fifteen degrees when he had left home this morning. Right now, the wind made it feel below zero.

Knut intended to remain at the fishpond for the rest of the day, guarding it, marking and establishing his ominous, official presence. At the outset of the state's new program he needed to warn the local reprobates, right up from the start, against fishing before season, and especially in this brimming new trout pond. Seeing Knut hanging around would be their warning. And, he would stay around unrelentingly, from dawn until dark. Of course, Knut wasn't about to perform such rigorous duty by just gawking and stomping his feet to keep away the cold — not at all. Once the trout were in the pond and he had fed them, he would pass his day's vigil, and many of those to come, in his warm, chugging, little orange-red patrol truck, with its efficient heater heartily blasting. At noon, he'd take his lunch on over to the Token Creek store, where he would eat by the warm stove he knew Brother Bob kept going. He'd buy a bottle of Doctor Pepper to go with his sandwich, then have a cup of scalding coffee.

Such visits to the country store would emphasize to the loafers gathered close around the warm stove that anybody who was caught down by the trout pond would be in a mess of trouble. By golly, people around here had to realize that there was a serious effort going on, trying to get this new stream-restocking program to work.

Yes sir. You bet. Knut planned to come to the trout pond every day, if he could. He would arrive before light sometimes. Although it was unlikely, maybe his noonday visits to the store would allow him to get a bead on any violators prowling around. After a week or two, he might consider letting up on this schedule to tend to his other duties. You could be darn sure, though, that he'd visit the pond whenever he was nearby. If somebody were skulking around, he'd find him. He'd never pop in at the same hour, either. He intended to give them no gift of predictability. The lurking fish robbers were probably watching the unloading at this very moment, some with binoculars he'd bet, scheming for ways to withdraw a few easy trout before the late April distribution to the area streams.

The two Wildlife Department men, Trillin and Abe Eyfniphcz, who were working the tank truck, waved to Knut to signal the unloading was done. Knut waved back to them, and called his thanks. The two subwardens folded the fish chute onto the side of the idling truck, tied the device down, and then quickly climbed into their big vehicle. They were happy to be out of the wind. They were off in a roar, heading back to the State garage for hot coffee and a lot of standing around talking, Knut was sure.

Knut in turn trotted to his diminutive patrol truck. He started the noisy engine but didn't stay in the cab. He went to the back to fetch a bag of fish food.

"One fifty-pound bag daily per 1000 adult fish," the instructions read. Easy enough — half today, half tomorrow, and so on down the line. He dragged the fish food bag out of the truck and threw it over his shoulder. He wondered what fish food for trout consisted of. Lots of protein, he was sure, plus a good measure of dead bugs too. He lugged the bag to the edge of the pond where he put it down and opened the drawstring. He began scooping the food into the fishpond with his hands, scattering it as best he could. The moment the pellets hit the water the fish were at the surface, gobbling and thrashing about, mouths everywhere. These fish sure weren't shy like regular trout, Knut observed. He wondered how long they would last in the streams, once they were loose. They were too fearless of people as far as he was concerned. They'd be easy to catch.

When Knut had finished the feeding, he returned to the truck with the half bag of fish food. He slid the bag into the covered bed, closed the tailgate, and then clambered into the warm cab where the heater had been running full-tilt.

He pulled off his gloves, his cap, and coat. He scratched his head. It was now very quiet around and about, he observed. Nobody was even driving by on the road. He took his thermos from the seat beside him. He poured himself a portion of coffee. He savored its warmth. He had started early that day. Now he would take some time to relax, yet keep a sharp and watchful eye out.

Scene Two: *At the Store*

Three hours later, at a few minutes past twelve

noon, Warden Knutson Yon Hamsum parked his rattling, misfiring truck in front of the Token Creek store. He hurried up the steps of the white building, carrying his lunch pail.

Drawing open the heavy door, he stepped from the biting chill of the cloudless March day into the comfort and calm of the dimly lit grocery store and hardware emporium. Knut lifted off his cap as he entered, stuffing it into a coat pocket.

He stopped there and set his lunch pail on the floor, so he could carefully open and remove his coat, thus making his silver warden's badge plainly visible on the front of his Wildlife Department shirt. No harm in striking a little fear and respect into the hearts of the restive suspects, he told himself. Knut picked up the lunch pail and continued on in.

Brother Bob Armstrong was watching Knut's entrance. Brother Bob was standing behind the counter that ran the length of the grocery portion of his store. Brother Bob Armstrong was unable to speak, because of the war. Still, he got along pretty well by all accounts — his store was definitely prospering. It was clean and well stocked. Knut was certain beyond any reasonable doubt that this Mister Brother Bob Armstrong was one of those he needed to keep track of when it came to trout fishing at the wrong time and place. Knut strode to the counter.

Brother Bob waved a large hello.

"Hello, Robert. I'll take a bottle of Doctor Pepper, if you please." Knut laid down a dime and a nickel.

"I'll take some of your coffee after my sandwich, if

you've got some going."

Brother Bob nodded his agreement to both orders. He gestured toward the cooler as he took Knut's money. Knut went to the cooler, pulled out the bottle he wanted and headed for the radiating wood stove at the back of the store. He was looking forward to a quiet lunch by the glowing heat.

"Afternoon, Knut," sang a cheerful voice from the obscurity in the rear of the store.

Knut squinted into the cozy dimness. He saw who it was that had greeted him, although the voice was one he should not have been surprised to hear. Yes, it was the booming tenor of Mr. LeRoy Armstrong, known to many as Second Cousin LeRoy, since it appeared he was related more or less in that way to the throngs of Armstrongs, in and around Token Creek. Mr. Second Cousin LeRoy held the position of first place on Warden Knut Yon Hamsum's list of known-but-never-apprehended pre-season fishermen, out-of-season hunters, and off-season trappers.

Many were the times, over Knut's long years of honorable tenure, that he had stalked this Second Cousin LeRoy Armstrong along the banks of some shining stream or sparkling pond, during pleasant spring days, well before to be sure, the official game seasons. Numerous were the hours that Knut had lain in ambush in some golden woods or breeze-blown field, on crisp fall days, far in advance of the regulation pheasant shooting. And too, many were the cold days that the old warden had huddled, stock-still and waiting, in the hushed snows of winter, long prior to the allotted time for deer hunting, hoping to entrap this Mr. Armstrong. All his efforts had been without success, unfortunately.

During all these busy years and decades of attempting to catch in the act the elusive Second Cousin LeRoy, Knut had found not even one of the rascal's rabbit snares, nor a single trap, they being so cleverly hidden and often moved among the weeds and grasses of the woods and clearings around and about Token Creek. No, it must be admitted — Knut had never even come close to nabbing this crafty poacher, who knew the countryside better than anyone else.

Apprehending this wily desperado was a challenge yet to have been met. It could be, Knut had lately come to fear, that such a moment might have to be passed on to those who followed.

"LeRoy," acknowledged Warden Knut, nodding toward the extensive figure lounging in front of the hot stove. Knut located a chair and pulled it close to the heat. He draped his coat over the back of the chair. He sighed, sat down, and opened his lunch pail, in which he found an oversized meatloaf sandwich.

Apparently Second Cousin LeRoy was the only other person in the store besides Brother Bob.

"Getting in some big fish, I notice," commented Second Cousin LeRoy, a note of glee lurking on the surface of his rich voice. Knut had just taken a bite of his sandwich. How did LeRoy know they were big?

"Season opens May first," mumbled Knut, chewing and looking hard at Second Cousin LeRoy. He swallowed after some more chewing. "Not before," he added.

"Already got my license," Second Cousin LeRoy informed him, the teeth of his broad grin visible in the lowered light.

Knut took a second deliberate bite of the enlarged sandwich. He chewed slowly, savoring his wife's famous meatloaf.

"Glad to hear it," Knut eventually said.

"No sirree, I have never missed buying my licenses for a good while now," declared Second Cousin LeRoy, waving cheerfully as he said this to Brother Bob, who had strolled over to listen. "I always get my licenses, now that we need them. I buy 'em right here from my dear relative and close friend, Brother Robert himself.

You know, Brother Bob's a well-known fisherman in his own right."

"A well-known, out-of-season fisherman, in his own right," Knut said as he chewed. The sentence came out in such an indistinguishable mumble, that Brother Bob and Second Cousin LeRoy had no idea what was said. Finally, Knut swallowed and could speak more clearly: "I'll be around here regular, until the fish are planted out," he threatened, a split second before taking another tear at his sandwich. He chewed for a long time. Second Cousin LeRoy scratched his nose. Brother Bob sat down on a chair on the other side of Warden Knutson. "Pretty much every day," Knut added, for reinforcement.

The group fell silent. Except for the crackling of the stove, and Knut's chewing, there were few other sounds to be heard.

Act II

Scene One: Second Cousin LeRoy's April soliloquy, with Brother Bob as witness. It is two weeks later. The two men are sifting on the wooden steps of the store, peering in the direction of the State trout pond. The weather has become unusually warm, and they are in shirtsleeves.

"Well Robert, it looks from here like Old Knut has let up on spending his every waking hour down at the trout pond. He's been down there watching for us just as much as checking the fish though, you can be sure of that. But, you know, I haven't seen him for upwards of four hours now. Maybe he's finally tending to all his other work that he's been neglecting but still getting paid for. You'd think, by the way he hangs around those fish, that he was worried some poor hungry soul might make off with one or two and upset the whole fish program. Doesn't he hover around them just like a mother hen? And you know what? He'll be back here today again two or three times before dark, sooner or later, you can bet your life. And tomorrow, he's going to pop in, for certain, even before the sun comes up; he'll park that truck of his behind the mill and lie in wait, like a fox trying to catch a rabbit. He's sure wanting to leap out and snatch hold of some poor citizen who might be just innocently walking by. Well, he ain't going to catch none of us rabbits."

Here, Second Cousin LeRoy laughed out loud; Brother Bob began to giggle the strange expression of mirth that his damaged throat permitted.

"Still, you've got to give the old fox credit. He's kept us cooped up here ever since the day those fat, over-fed, nice tasty trout were put in that overcrowded, fancy storage bin of his, right under our noses, and here we sit helpless. You know, little Junior went down there the other day, while Knut was feeding those penned-in fish of his. Knut started eyeing the boy, and acting suspicious of even him, so Junior felt he had to explain himself, so quick did he pick up on Knut's attitude. Just like that, the boy up and told Knut he maybe wants to be a game warden when he grows up, and started asking Knut all sorts of foolish questions.

"Of course, all the time Old Knut was lecturing about what a noble and rewarding profession wardening was, Junior was surveying the fish. Ha! The boy tells me that the fish are as big as carp and as tame as kittens. Knut told Junior that the Wildlife Department's going to start, very soon, planting those fish all over the county. Junior says the fish come right to the surface if you throw anything into the water, even a stone. They could be dipped out, with a net. They're not afraid of people at all. You wouldn't need even a hook and bait. You got any nets in your store, Bob?"

Brother Bob nodded in the enthusiastic affirmative, before breaking into his distinctive giggle again.

"But, how're we going to get down there, to sample

a few of Knut's trout that we, as taxpayers and license buyers, paid for anyway? Outside his job, I like that old fox, but I sure don't want him swooping down without even saying hello. Doesn't he ever take a day off? Doesn't the man rest?"

Brother Bob shook his head slowly and morosely, meaning probably not. They sat quietly for another few moments, faces to the warmth of the early spring sun, listening to the sounds of the countryside. Quite suddenly, Brother Bob sat up very straight, and tapped the daydreaming Second Cousin LeRoy on the shoulder. LeRoy looked at him. Something was up in Brother Bob's brain.

Brother Bob held up his hands in a gesture that indicated he had something to communicate. Second Cousin LeRoy became alert and interested. Did Robert have an idea? The man's demeanor suggested a creative mind that had been hard at work and now had come up with something.

Slowly, with deliberate movements, Brother Bob held the palms of his hands together, his fingers together and extended. He then separated the palms of his hands and held them above his head.

"What?" asked Second Cousin LeRoy, not understanding the gesture.

Brother Bob maintained his hands as they were, but lowered his head, as if bowing.

"Bowing?" asked Second Cousin LeRoy. "Mountain?"

Brother Bob shook his head, indicating no, then repeated the gestures, this time with his mouth moving.

"Praying?" asked Second Cousin LeRoy.

Brother Bob indicated yes, with strong nods of his head. He gestured that Second Cousin LeRoy should keep going — he was on the right track.

"Let's see... praying... worshipping?"

Brother Bob gestured that Second Cousin LeRoy

should keep going. He held up his hands again, palms open, extended fingers again touching at the tips.

"Lets see now... praying, church... steeple?"

Brother Bob clapped his hands in approval. Then he put his hands together, put his fingers between each other, and reversed his hands so that his intertwined fingers were facing upwards, as in the children's rhyme, "Here is the church, here is the steeple, open the doors and see all the people."

"Church, steeple... people. Robert, you aren't thinking of going to church?" asked Second Cousin LeRoy with puzzled surprise.

Brother Bob shook his head. He would try to convey another message. He pointed toward the trout pond, and made gestures of pulling a fish up with a fish pole.

"Okay, you're not going to church. Let's see. The fish are going to church?" He was laughing as he asked this foolish question.

Brother Bob pounded his forehead in frustration. He walked down to the bottom of the steps and faced the still-seated Second Cousin LeRoy. Brother Bob drew himself up very tall, stuck out his chest, and strode back and forth in front of the bewildered Second Cousin LeRoy. Brother Bob kept tapping his chest over his shirt pocket. He then stopped and drew the outline of a star in the air.

"Hey, I get it. You're Knutson, our game warden."

Brother Bob danced a short dance of emphatic approbation, then repeated the entire sequence of gestures, from the praying gesture, the steeple, and the people, ending with his charade of Warden Yon Hamsum.

Slowly, slowly, Second Cousin LeRoy raised himself and spoke.

"Do you mean to suggest, Robert, that we might try to visit the trout pond when Old Knut is off to church?" he asked in a hushed voice, looking about to ensure they were alone.

Brother Bob nodded craftily, with obvious pleasure — he had conveyed his message. He then held up a finger, to mean that Second Cousin LeRoy was almost, but not completely, there.

However, before Second Cousin LeRoy could ask more questions, Brother Bob abruptly scurried up the steps and into the store. He returned with a pencil and a small pad of paper. He wrote out a sentence for Second Cousin LeRoy, then handed him the pad. Second Cousin LeRoy read aloud: "If he does come by on Sunday, he might not stay long. Even if he comes by to check, he'll want to go to church with his wife."

Second Cousin LeRoy held the pad for a moment, then looked affectionately at Brother Bob. He smiled warmly at him. Brother Bob too smiled, and spread his arms in a gesture meaning, "There you have it."

Second Cousin LeRoy placed a large hand on Brother Bob's shoulder. "Now, Robert, I understand. At first I couldn't keep up with you. I finally caught on. You say that Knut might not hang around here for long, if he comes on Sunday. Why yes, that makes sense. In fact, it makes darn good sense. It's a true brainstorm. And me, it takes me a while to grasp the speed of your thoughts. Foxy Old Mr. Knut has probably missed church for three Sundays in a row now, what with his haunting us from dawn to dark. But he's got to go to church this week, or people will begin to talk. After all, he's a deacon or something like that, a real pillar of the church ... or at least, a rafter. Let's say he's a pew, a pew of the church. Haw.

"Yes, yes. He will for sure be off to church. And, when he is there, when he is off there, then the daybreak will truly be ours. The dawn by the fishpond will be our time, ours for the fishing. Robert, you are a man of wonder. You see things that others do not. Of course, of course, now even I understand. But I understood only long, long after you did."

Brother Bob here laughed his unusual laugh, as Second Cousin LeRoy clapped him warmly on the back. Second Cousin LeRoy had more to say, and held up a hand, asking for further attention.

"Before dawn Robert, before the crack of dawn, we will meet. Let it be here at your store, before the sun is even thinking about rising, before it gets light, so when the day arrives, we will be on the spot and able to see what we are doing. We will be ready at first light. Let us, however, use bait and line. When I think about it, I don't want to just scoop up the poor things. That's not fishing.

"No, that is not fishing. I am a fisherman, you are a fisherman. We, Robert, we are fisherrnen. Let us not forget who we are. We will catch fish only as true fishermen do. We will bait our lines."

As Second Cousin LeRoy took a second to catch his breath, before launching on a few dozens of more words, Brother Bob lay a warning hand on his sturdy arm. Second Cousin LeRoy calmed himself. He stood still as a post.

Brother Bob cupped a hand behind his ear, indicating that Second Cousin LeRoy should listen for something. Second Cousin LeRoy too placed a cupped hand behind an ear.

Then he also heard what Brother Bob had detected: out on the road, to the west and still at a great distance, could be distinguished, if one were very quiet, the occasional yet approaching report of a backfiring vehicle.

"Knut is coming," whispered Second Cousin LeRoy.

Brother Bob nodded, rolling his eyes. The two men sat back down on the store steps to wait.

Time passed. Ten minutes later, Mr. Knutson Yon Hamsum clattered past the store in his undersized, orange-red truck. From their perch high on the store's steps, Second Cousin LeRoy and Brother Bob Armstrong waved to the warden, smiling cheerfully. Knut returned their waves and grinned, then drove to the fishpond for his vigil.

"You know, I've seen that bird so many times, he's getting to be a regular Dijon view, just like I remember the French people used to say," concluded Second Cousin LeRoy.

Scene Two: Very early, before dawn, on the following Sunday.

Enter Chorus, and later, figures. Music: W.A. Mozart, Piano concerto Number 21, in C major (K467), 2nd movement

Now sleep the rustic folk of Token Creek, taking deserved respite from their long labors of the previous day, taking pause from the efforts that filled their gainful hours. And, as the good people doze and dream, gathering their strengths anew for the toils of labors yet to come, overhead flows the great, dark vessel of the hushed universe, where strata of winking stars and sparkling galaxies sing of expanses that pass the understanding of those who would stand beneath in mystic awe. Around and about, the gray country meadows and shaded woods rest deeply still, as do the houses wherein lie the sleeping citizens. Only from time to time, and but at long intervals, is the full hush of the clear spring night broken, by the call of a staring owl, or the bark of a lightfoot fox. Thus, above the quiet earth, and in solemn majesty, the great moonless night turns softly on, holding sway over the placid land and its worthy creatures.

But lo! There steals forth upon the high-arching, black-curtained vault, the first russet glow of another returning day, a rising glimmer of rebirth, away there beyond the low hills and silent fields to the east. At first, the shimmering is yet no more than an imperceptible alteration among the flickering and glimmerings of the encircling starlight. Yet, the radiance climbs surely, in unrushed splendor, up and into the deep, great firmament. Now, with the light it brings to the land below, one can see here and there the form of a tree, a bush perhaps, a patch of grass by the roadside.

And, as the ruddy light grows and defines the forms of the peaceable landscape, there comes too, comes with it, a song in the rich air of the fading darkness. It is a faint wind, a breeze, born lately as a boon companion to the incipient dawn. This zephyr that stirs with the morning light carries in its arms something new and wonderful, bringing with it wafting hints of renewal, of green sprouts and purple violets, of warmth and sunshine, of nests and song. It brings with it a story, a tale, as it flows, a cheerful message brought from its happy trek from the south, a story that whispers of northward migrations, of snowdrops beneath trees, of daffodils. It brings along cheer, for all, saying in its fragrance that it is time to put aside the long months of cold and waiting. Oh yes, the awakening air carries along a fine melody with a sweet refrain — a song that announces the gentle spring that is a'coming in, moving up to meet us, is now but just around the corner, arriving to awaken the long-dormant fields, to warm the rime-chilled woodlots, to tickle the brooks and streams to laughing and chattering, as they begin their flow and chant of the burgeoning season.

And hark! Are those footfalls we hear upon the crisp gravel of the tiny road? Does the streaming light of a million stars, and the blush of the expanding dawn, reveal shadows that move forth, here beneath the dome of early morning? Yes, there are two forms, two forms abroad, seeming to have materialized at the very moment when an anxious rooster of a nearby farm called four times then stopped his cheering. What are these forms? Who are these phantoms of the dawn? Are they men or beasts? If men, who might they be, up and out at such an early hour, and for what purpose? Let

us look carefully. Let us watch and wait, for they now
arrive close by.

Here they are, two men. Yes, there can be no doubt,
there are two men walking along. They are drowsy
perhaps, from the shortness of their rest, yet they appear purposeful in their intent to travel forth. Each man
is carrying something upon his shoulder. What are the
objects? It is difficult to determine, in the faintness of
the pre-dawn, for the men are yet little more than faint
silhouettes, as they pass quietly by. Perhaps the things
they carry will be seen as the light grows.

Yes, they can be identified — the objects are long
poles, fishing poles. And one of the shadows, the nar-
rower, seems to be holding a cloth beneath an arm. A
gunny sack? What for? Let us follow stealthily, to learn
their errand.

The tranquil waters of the new fishpond lay not
far off the little road, along which the yet unknown
figures make their way. A small track leaves the road, a
few feet beyond the stone bridge. This track, whose
center shows the beginnings of new, spring grass, par-
allels the cheery flow of the Token Creek. The shadows
turn off the road and onto the track, gliding over it noiselessly, moving inexorably toward the fish enclosure at
it's end. Suddenly, they halt, for they are now above
the waters wherein the pulsing crowds of gluttonous,
yawing fish wait for the full flood of dawn, when food
from above might well, as it always has, rain down upon
them in plethoric abundance.

The two dark figures speak no words, communi-
cating it seems by the sure understanding of each other's
imperceptible gestures; there is confident, long-practiced
knowledge here, for they seem to know what to do,
and where to step without even a glance about. It is
certain each possesses deep understanding of every foot
of the munificent land, of each fence and field, of every
barn and woods, of the very position and placement
even, of each path and byway.

At the edge of the somber fishpond they stand for a moment, the men holding themselves still and alert, attuned to the rustlings and twitterings arising from the land that is awakening with the advancing dawn. Can we identify these men yet, as the light of the morning begins to filter through the trees? One of the immobile figures is quite large. The other is as tall as the first, but far less circular. Who are they?

But hark now again, for one of them has whispered. With that whisper the voice can be known, and too the man who utters it. It is a voice we have heard before, for even in near inaudibility we recognize the cheerful tones of Mr. Second Cousin LeRoy Armstrong, prominent resident of the village of Token Creek. The figure with him must be, of course, his constant companion in high adventure, Mr. Brother Bob Armstrong, affable keeper of the Token Creek Grocery Store and Hardware Emporium.

The stealthy silhouettes remain stark still for passing minutes, moving so little they seem to be a part of the waning night from which they have come forth. Yet, if we observe carefully, we see their heads turning ever so slowly from right to left, and back again, scanning the little world about them. They make small signs to each other, with their arms and hands, as they look and listen. They are surveying, verifying, ensuring that they are alone, that only they stand hard by the copious schools beneath their steady feet. Then, one of the figures nods, and the other nods in response.

The long fish poles are brought down from the shoulders and stood upright. The stouter end of each device is placed upon the edge of the concrete enclosure. The figures next perform an operation upon a length of line arising from the slimmer end of each pole. They are baiting hooks. A moment later, each man quietly lowers a baited line into the tranquil liquid of the new fishpond.

Third Movement, Mozart's Piano Concerto Number 21.

Quite suddenly, the stealthy figures, heretofore working in unrushed calm, adapt a furious activity. The surface of the fishpond, but a moment ago shining and smooth, without even a ripple, explodes into a turmoil of thrashing fish as the lowered baits touch the water. The water roars with movement. Two fish are instantly hooked — bending poles are raised to bring the squirming prey into the waiting hands of the shadowy fishermen. In an instant, the fish are unhooked, thrust into the wide gunny sack, the hooks rebaited, and the lines once again dropped into the churning mobs below. Again, within seconds, a pair of flailing fish are raised from the frothing chaos of gills and fin, popped into the sack, hooks once more replenished, and the process begun anew, fish after wiggling fish.

End music

But soft! The madding pace of joyful gathering has not blunted the fishermen's keen ears.   Even as they energetically hold forth, drawing to themselves the cornucopia of windfall fish, they listen unrelentingly for signs of discovery of what the swarming sanctimonious would surely name a most questionable early morning occupation.

Even as they proceed apace in their bounteous harvest of future suppers, they maintain their keen-honed senses at full alert, hearing all that transpires in the stirring land around and about them. Suddenly, the busy Second Cousin LeRoy halts his descending pole in mid-cast. With the pole resting still in his hands, he closes his eyes in concentration, and trains a practiced ear out toward the darkened, western horizon. Brother Bob, noticing and taking frank warning from his companion's markedly altered stance, makes the same pause, even holding his breath to quicken and enhance his aural faculties. Thus standing, each harkens for a moment. Then, each looks to the other with a nod of knowing and comprehension, for both have extracted, from out of the background shushes and whirrings, those nearly inaudible, yet strident, detonations that could only be emanating from the tailpipe of a familiar, orange-red official truck.

"Knut," whispers the vocal member of the pair. The other gestures his accord. Knut comes.

With hardly a noise, and carefully, without seeming to rush, yet with a practiced celerity in which no move is wasted nor in vain, each figure gathers his pole to himself, and sheds from its hook the bait that had been about to be employed in the capture of yet one more among those many gaping trout. Each tosses the bait into the water below. Then, together, they steal off into the dense and surrounding understory of fallen logs and bushes, within the encircling woods. One figure is carrying a bulging sack.

A safe distance away, and hidden from view behind a mass of dense scrub, the two peer back into the dimly lit environs. At ease, they wait there for the sure arrival of a well-known state employee of long and zealous term. As they attend his coming, and as each passing moment provides an increase in the volume of the claps and knocks of Warden Knutson's colorful conveyance, the two lounging men smile to each other. They breathe deeply of the fresh, morning air, and hear the songs of the waking birds. As they rest and listen, they feel the joy of the day welling up within themselves.

Soon, Warden Knutson will guide his croaking truck down the little track that the two shadows so recently followed. The warden will stop his vehicle, get out, and after feeding the fish in his charge, will remain for but a few more minutes. As the sun's glow appears above the eastern horizon, he will take his leave, assured that indeed, his charges are safe and sound, not yet affected by a little touch of LeRoy in the dawn, nor brushed by the noiseless passing of our Brother Bob. Knutson will drive off, to his Sunday's worship, after whose ceremonies and celebrations, he will take a well-deserved day of rest. As he enjoys his respite, he will remain confident that he has carried out his weighty obligations. He will say to himself that he has stead-fastly protected the plans and property of the brave state which holds him in its most praiseworthy regard.

Upon the warden's departure, Mr. Second Cousin LeRoy and Mr. Brother Robert Armstrong will, in turn, leave their cover. They will smile at their good fortune and at the new day, and amble cheerfully to the home of the former.

There they will take a cup of rich coffee, prepared for them by Olivia Oliverson Armstrong, loving and devoted wife to Mr. Second Cousin LeRoy Armstrong. Mrs. Armstrong will, along with her dear husband and his silent kinsman, pass a sunny morning of fish clean-ing and packaging, intending for deep freezer storage the bounty so wondrously provided.

Act III
Enter Chorus. It speaks.

Now arrives the full bloom of May, month of warm-ing sun and a thousand flowers. Everywhere can be heard now the chant of birds, everywhere can be seen the new green of leaves; around and about comes the scent of blossoms, the buzzing of bees.

Today, this first day of May, is of particular and noted importance for some. Not only does the day mark the beginning of that most welcome of all months, it is moreover, the day which heralds the onset of this year's officially sanctioned trout-fishing season.

Second Cousin LeRoy and Brother Bob Armstrong have been early out and along the banks of the rushing creek called Token Creek. They have gone out with poles and lines in hand, with creels on their shoulders, and with pleasure radiating from their pleasant faces. Had we observers been as early to field as this fine pair, who were up with the rising sun, we would have learned early of their activities. But, we were not then awake, so we must join the sporting comrades after they have already returned from their rewarding outing, as they sit and clean fish.

Scene One: Fish cleaning, outside at Second Cousin LeRoy and his wife Olivia's house. The house stands across the road from the Token Creek store. Second Cousin LeRoy and Brother Bob are sitting at a wooden table on the porch.

Second Cousin LeRoy: *(sipping coffee, while holding up a wiggling fish in his opposite hand).* "Robert, Robert. What will people say of us? Only five fish between us, and after three hours of fishing? Still, it's better than last year. What was it? We caught maybe four for the whole season. How about the year before last? Was it five? All things considered, I think maybe Knut's fish program is working after all. These are big ones too. Look at this one."

Brother Bob: *(he turns to nod his cheerful agreement, while removing a large, squirming rainbow trout from a pail on the table; he inspects the fish by looking it in the eye and showing sympathy by extending his lower lip).*

Second Cousin LeRoy: "Well, if Mr. Knut comes by today, we can show him our legal fish. He'll be gratified, seeing we waited until the season opened." *(He winks at Brother Bob.)*

Brother Bob: *(He begins to clean a fish with a knife; he pauses to giggle at Second Cousin LeRoy's comment and wink).*

Second Cousin LeRoy: "You know, we should try to get out tomorrow early. I'm going to try to get out after work next week. You know, if we were lucky, we

could get enough for a fish fry. We could invite some of the folks in, like Will and Kate, and August and the gang. I'm sure Mabel and Carl could eat a few fish. What do you think?"

Brother Bob: (*He nods his agreement, and licks his lips*).

Second Cousin LeRoy: (*beheading a fish*) "Let's see ... Will and Kate, August, Melodie, the two kids; Ollie will be here of course; there'd be Carl and Mabel, you, me. How many is that? Eleven, correct? Suppose everybody eats two fish, some'll eat more. We need at least two dozen. We got a ways to go."

Brother Bob: (*He giggles again, then makes motions for a pencil and paper.*)

Second Cousin LeRoy: "I'll get them. (*He stands and goes to the kitchen door, which he opens with his elbow since he is still holding a fish; he speaks to his wife, who is inside.*) "Hey Ollie, Hon. Can we get our Brother Bob a paper and pencil? He wants to write something for us."

Olivia Oliverson Armstrong: (*from inside the house*) "I'll bring them out. Do you two want more coffee?"

Second Cousin LeRoy: "Sounds good."

Aunt Olivia: "I'll be out in a minute."

Second Cousin LeRoy: "Robert, you've got another brainstorm on the way. I can feel it in my bones."

Brother Bob: (*He stands, rinses his hands in a pail; then dries them with a towel.*)

Aunt Olivia: (*pushing open the screen door with her backside, carrying a pad of paper and a pencil in one hand, a coffee pot in the other; she is a tall woman, of cheerful disposition.*) "LeRoy, we're going to have to buy ourselves another freezer at the rate you two bring in fish."

Second Cousin LeRoy: (*holding out his cup while Ollie pours coffee for him; she then turns to Brother Bob and refills his cup.*) "We thought we'd do even better than we did — only five between us."

Aunt Olivia: "You've got a good four dozen in the freezer already, what with your early trip to the fishpond."

Second Cousin LeRoy: (*grinning at his wife, then gesturing toward Brother Bob.*) "What's our Brother Robert here writing? I can't take it — my hands are all wet. Can you take a look if you don't mind?"

Aunt Olivia: "I'd like to know myself. (*she takes the pad of paper from Brother Bob, who has been writing rapidly; she reads aloud.*) "We could invite Knut and Alice. Invite them to what? What are you two cooking up now?"

Second Cousin LeRoy: "By golly, a fish fry. We've got plenty to share, with those in the freezer."

Aunt Olivia: (*giving him a kiss on the cheek, and laughing.*) "LeRoy, LeRoy. You are incorrigible. You just want to tease poor Knut. And he's such a nice man. We'll just have to raid our stock."

Second Cousin LeRoy: "Ollie, Ollie. I see already that you approve of a party."

Scene Two: The following weekend, in the afternoon, on Second Cousin LeRoy's and Aunt Olivia's porch. A large table is set for a meal.

Second Cousin LeRoy: "Ollie, here come Will and Kate." (*He greets Grandpa William and Grandma Kate*

Armstrong). "Hello there, you two."

Aunt Olivia: "Hello, hello. I hope you're hungry."

Grandpa William Armstrong: "Melodie, it's good to see you. LeRoy, I hear you've got some fish to fry."

Second Cousin LeRoy: *(shaking hands with Grandpa while Aunt Olivia hugs Grandma, who has just placed a chocolate cake on the table.)* "We have three frying pans all ready to go. Is that one of your famous cakes, Grandma Kate? Maybe I'll just skip the fish and settle for about half this cake."

Grandma Kate Armstrong: *(She gives Second Cousin LeRoy a peck on the cheek.)* "LeRoy Armstrong, you'll never change. And Olivia, such a beautiful table."

Uncle August Armstrong: *(entering cheerfully with his wife, Melodie; the two children, Emma and Junior, run ahead to Second Cousin LeRoy and hug him; Aunt Melodie is carrying a large bowl.)* "Here come the potatoes."

Emma: "Second Cousin LeRoy, we've got a new song for you."

Junior: "Aunt Melodie taught it to us."

Second Cousin LeRoy: "Well then, let's hear it."

Aunt Melodie: "Maybe we should save it until we eat, and keep it a secret for a while. Then it will be a surprise for everybody."

Junior: "Aunt Ollie, can Emma and I go in the house and practice some more?"

Aunt Olivia: "Of course you can. Go upstairs. Then we won't be able to hear you." *(The children go into the house.)*

Second Cousin LeRoy: "First no cake, now no music."

Aunt Olivia: "Brother Bob will be along in a minute. He said he would close early. I expect Knut and Alice will be here pretty soon. I told them around six."

Grandpa: "LeRoy, aren't you something, inviting Old Knut? He's been after you for twenty years and here you are, about to feed him illegal fish."

Second Cousin LeRoy: "Well, he's been after you too, but he never knew it. You're just too foxy for the old buzzard. We've enjoyed a few of your early fish, as I recall."

Uncle August: "There's no denying it, Will. Come clean."

Grandpa: *(laughing)* "Is that another one of your puns?"

Uncle Carl and Aunt Mabel arrive. Aunt Mabel is carrying a one covered bowl.

Junior: *(from an upstairs window)* "Here's Uncle Carl and Aunt Mabel."

Uncle Carl: "Hello, everyone."

Grandpa: "Hello. I hope you two are hungry."

Aunt Mabel: "Carl's been talking about eating trout all week. He didn't even want lunch today so he'd have plenty of room."

Uncle Carl: "There's nothing better than fresh trout."

Uncle August: "I think you mean thawed, at least today."

Uncle Carl: "I'm not sure I could tell the difference, or should try to."

Second Cousin LeRoy: "We're waiting for Knutson."

Uncle August: "And Brother Robert."

Emma and Junior rush from the house, going to Uncle Carl. He hugs them both at the same time. They whisper in his ear, probably telling him about the song that they have ready to sing to Second Cousin LeRoy. The group laughs and chatters, enjoying the get-together. A moment later, an approaching commotion is heard. It is the clatter and occasional backfiring of a vehicle. The group stops to listen as the noise becomes gradually louder.

Second Cousin LeRoy: "Knut is coming."
Grandpa: *(holding a hand to an ear)* "Speak of the devil."
Uncle August: "Which one?"

Uncle August has said that because Brother Bob has just walked in, waving hello with one hand while the other is held behind an ear.

Brother Bob: *(He points toward the sound, with a smile on his face.)*
Junior: "Second Cousin LeRoy's got three dozen fish all thawed and ready to fry."
Brother Bob: *(He gestures in amazement, and thanksgiving.)*
Second Cousin LeRoy: *(clearing his throat to get their attention)* "Our guest of honor is about to arrive. It's our good luck that we always know when he's closing in."
Grandpa: *(to Emma and Junior, a finger touching his lips)* "Let's not get too much into whether the fish are fresh or thawed."
Uncle Carl: *(winks at the children)* "Fresh or thawed, they're just as good."

Knutson Yon Hamsum and his wife Alice drive onto the scene, in an orange-red truck that makes an incredible racket.

Second Cousin LeRoy: *(He goes to meet Warden Knut and his wife; he opens the truck door for Alice.)* "Alice, welcome." *(He then rushes around the front of the truck to shake hands with Warden Knutson; Aunt Olivia, Aunt Melodie, and Grandma go to Alice Chalmers, welcoming her warmly; Alice hands a huge covered dish to Uncle August; Grandpa and August shake hands with Knut; the kids hold back a little.)* "Welcome Knut, welcome. I hope you brought your appetite."

Warden Knutson Yon Hamsum: "LeRoy, I'm happy to see you. Thank you for inviting us. August, Will, how do you do? And who might these fine children be?"

Uncle August: "This is Emma Armstrong, and this is Junior. Rile and Leah's children."

Emma and Junior: *(They step forward and shake hands with Knutson and with Alice.)* "How do you do?"

Alice Chalmers: "William, it is so good to see you again. And August, my goodness." *(She shakes hands enthusiastically with both men, then turns to the children.)* "Hello there. I've heard many, many good things about you two from your teacher. Did you know that your uncle and I were schoolmates?"

Emma: "Yes, ma'am. Uncle August told us you were the best speller in the school."

Junior: "Now Emma is."

Uncle August: "Well, I'll have you know that Alice Chalmers won the State Spelling Bee two years in a row, when she was in the sixth and seventh grades."

Grandma: "Alice never talks about her accomplishments. We have to do it for her."

Alice Chalmers: "I always boast about one thing though, catching Knutson."

Second Cousin LeRoy: "That's a fish story I'd like to hear. Did you catch him in or out of season?"

Warden Knutson: "I'm the big one that didn't get away."

Aunt Melodie: "The story I heard was that you were hoping she would catch you."

Grandpa: "Knut bit, hook, line, and sinker, as I recall."

Second Cousin LeRoy: "We're ready to start frying whenever everybody's wants to eat."

Aunt Olivia: "LeRoy and I are going to do the cooking, and that's that. We don't need any help, so please sit down and enjoy yourselves. Especially you, Grandma Kate — start with some of the side dishes."

Second Cousin LeRoy and Aunt Olivia go into the house to start frying fish. The rest of the group takes seats at the table. They pass around dishes, and chat. A few minutes later, Olivia announces the arrival of the first platter of fish. Second Cousin LeRoy follows her, holding high in the air, like a waiter, a platter stacked with fish. He and Olivia distribute the fish, then they too sit down. Everyone begins.

Second Cousin LeRoy: "We'll start another batch when everybody's ready for seconds. Eat these while they're hot."

Aunt Melodie: "Here's macaroni and cheese, and potato salad. Look at the green beans from Mabel and Carl. The macaroni and cheese is from Alice."

Uncle August: "Just look at the size of these fish. One of them is practically a meal."

Grandpa: "I guess that means you'll have two more."

Brother Bob: *(He finds this comment terribly funny.)*

Grandpa: *(to Brother Bob)* "Don't let that keep you from seconds, either."

Warden Knutson: "By golly, LeRoy. This is just about as good a fish as I've ever tasted."

Aunt Olivia: "Here's more potato salad for you, LeRoy. I know you'll want some more of Alice's macaroni, too." *(She scoops out a huge portion of potato salad for her husband. Alice Chalmers passes him the bowl of macaroni and cheese.)*

Second Cousin LeRoy: "Thank you, thank you."

Grandpa: "As strange as it may seem, our second cousin here isn't a big eater of fish."

Warden Knutson: "LeRoy, you're always out fishing. I find that hard to believe."

Second Cousin LeRoy: "They're all right. I always eat one, and none is wasted. Ollie loves them."

Warden Knutson: "What I mean is, I'd have

thought you ate them all the time."

Second Cousin LeRoy: "I'm more partial to venison, I guess; and pheasant of course. I like rabbit a lot."

Warden Knutson: *(in disbelief)* "So fish aren't your favorite food, LeRoy?"

Second Cousin LeRoy: *(shrugging his shoulders)* "Not particularly."

Aunt Olivia: "Just watch how much of Alice's macaroni and cheese he eats."

Warden Knutson: "So why do you love fishing so much? I'd have thought, considering the amount of time you're out after fish, sometimes when I'd rather you weren't, that fish were your main diet."

Everyone is now listening to the conversation between Second Cousin LeRoy and Warden Knutson Yon Hamsum.

Second Cousin LeRoy: "Well, the fishing part is pretty good. I share with the neighbors. Of course, Brother Bob is a big eater of fish. And, as I said, Ollie eats what I bring home. She loves her fish."

Grandma: "And her fisherman." *(Olivia smiles and touches Grandma's arm when Grandma says this.)*

Warden Knutson: "My, my. Will wonders never cease? So, what's the never-ending attraction?"

Second Cousin LeRoy: *(pausing before he answers)* "Maybe it's when... they take the line, and start pulling back. I like that, the feel. It's hard to explain."

Warden Knutson: *(nodding slowly)* "I can understand that."

The company remains quiet for a time. Gradually, the passing of dishes and eating resume. Soon they are talking and gesturing happily.

Brother Bob: *(He stands and raises a glass to offer a toast. They all raise their glasses. Brother Bob looks at Grandpa and nods).*

Grandpa: (*rising to speak*) "I think Brother Bob wants me to make a toast to the fishing season. To the fishing season, which has been a darn good one so far."

Second Cousin LeRoy: "And I believe we need to add our thanks to Knut Yon Hamsum, and all the good people in the State Wildlife Department. This new fish program has sure brought bounty to our table today."

All: (*except Brother Bob*) "Hear, hear."

Warden Knutson: "Thank you, LeRoy."

Aunt Olivia: "Is everybody ready for a second round?"

Aunt Melodie: "Ollie, you and LeRoy just sit now. August and I will do the honors this time."

Second Cousin LeRoy: "Well, I don't mind. I'll just stay here and eat Alice's macaroni and cheese and talk to Knut. I want to know about this fish restocking."

Aunt Olivia: "Be careful of that big frying pan — it's heavy."

Warden Knutson: "By the looks of things, LeRoy, you and Brother Bob had a good week of fishing. Will, you and August must have thrown in a few. There's sure a mess of fish here to eat."

Grandpa: "We managed to get out some."

Warden Knutson: "I mean, you all certainly had the best luck I've heard of."

Second Cousin LeRoy: "We know the good spots. Plus a week of good weather helps."

Aunt Olivia: (*coming to her husband's rescue*) "Knutson, we're still waiting to hear about the fish restocking. It's been wonderful — look at the size of these fish."

Warden Knutson: Hmm. (*There is skepticism in his voice.*)

Aunt Melodie: (*She enters with a platter of freshly fried fish.*) "Here we are."

Emma: "Can we sing our song now?"

Second Cousin LeRoy: "Time for a song, every-

body. Here's Emma and Junior to sing for us."
 Emma and Junior:
 "Fishy, fishy, in the brook,
 LeRoy caught them on a hook,
 Ollie fried them in a pan,
 We'll all eat them as fast as we can."

All applaud; the children are asked to sing the song again; soon, they all join in.
 Enter Chorus. The party continues in the background. It speaks.

Well, not too many people wondered, or wonder when they hear this story, whether or not Warden Knutson knew that he was eating illegal fish. Knut was an intelligent man, and he was experienced. He'd know full well that it was unlikely that Second Cousin LeRoy and Brother Bob, even with help from August and Bob, could have caught three dozen trout during the first week of the season. That would have been a record for the books. Besides, they all worked during the day, and Brother Bob kept his store open late most days. And, finally, there was a daily limit. You see what I mean?

The party continues in pantomime. Eventually, they finish their meal, and the singing. They are ready to call it a day. They begin cleaning up. The Chorus remains on stage, watching from the side.

 Uncle August: "Ollie and LeRoy, this was just fine."
 Aunt Mabel: "What a wonderful idea to have this party. It's so nice when we get together. The fish were delicious."
 Aunt Melodie: "Alice, your dish was perfect."
 Second Cousin LeRoy: "I'll vouch for that."
 Warden Knutson: "Well, we better be on our way.

This was the best fish fry I can remember. But it's an early day tomorrow."

Aunt Olivia: "I never knew how complicated fish restocking could be. Thank you for telling us all the ins and outs."

Warden Knutson: "I liked the singing. Thank you, Emma and Junior."

Junior: "You're welcome, sir."

Second Cousin LeRoy: "Knut, it was a pleasure to see you, out of uniform."

Warden Knutson: "Well, it's nice to be off duty and forget about who's doing what, or who did what. And to eat such good fish in such good company."

Grandpa: "We hope to see you more often. We'll keep a lookout for you."

Second Cousin LeRoy: "It was our pleasure to have you and Alice. We should always keep in touch with old friends."

Uncle Carl: "Knut, it was good to see you again."

The men shake hands with Knutson Yon Hamsum. The women kiss Alice Chalmers goodbye.

Second Cousin LeRoy: "I'm glad you enjoyed the fish. I'll bet they were the ones you planted."

Warden Knutson: "Goodbye, goodbye, good friends." (*Exit, driving a small truck*).

The remaining characters disperse, gradually departing from the stage, until it is empty except for the Chorus. The lights begin to fade. The Chorus surveys the scene, looks at the audience and smiles; it then leaves the stage, waving as it walks into the darkness.

Speaking of Pigs

For many years, Grandpa William kept a small spotted pig called Dill. Grandpa had raised this pig from a grinning runt piglet, given to him by a farmer friend to settle some minor debt. The farmer's name was Dell, so at first Grandpa and Grandma referred to the animal as "Dell's Pig," but the name quickly evolved to Dill, which was easier to say. Dill was exceptionally intelligent; some considered him downright gifted — a wonder pig. Before his first birthday he had learned some impressive tricks: to roll over, to grunt to three, and to play dead. If you held an ear of corn above his head, he sat upright like a squirrel, front legs bent at the wrists, squealing and wheedling until you dropped the snack. He almost always caught it on the way down.

Whenever Junior visited the farm, the boy made a beeline for the pigpen to help the pig expand his repertory. By the spring that Dill celebrated his second birthday, Junior had succeeded in teaching the animal, among other antics, to walk straight backwards while looking over his shoulder, rolling one leg around and behind the other like an ice skater. Grandpa said he should have called the pig Sage rather than Dill, it being so clever. Grandpa liked puns.

While the pig tolerated squirrels, he disliked cats. He kept clear from his pigpen any of the half-dozen or so felines that lived off the farm. A cat that dared come sneaking and slinking around the pig house, hunting for mice, ran a great risk. The pig once got his teeth into the end of a fleeing tom who had made the mistake of trying to squeeze through rather than scramble over the pigpen fence.

In triumph the pig bit the end of the cat's tail clean off, but immediately spit the thing out in disgust. For half an hour afterward, the pig stood around spitting and hawking, holding his tongue out and grimacing. Finally he rinsed his mouth in the water trough and settled down. Uncle August declared that the way Dill felt about cats, he surely had some dog in him. He wouldn't have been surprised if one day Dill started wagging his tail, or barking.

Dill expected to be treated with civility. He would enter into an ostentatious sulk should you forget to call out a cheerful hello when you met him. From his perspective it would seem farm chores could be postponed, certainly for a moment, in favor of a chat. If, on a busy day, you hurried by his quarters with only the wave of a hand, then came back later to make amends, the snubbed animal would turn his head away and to the side, looking everywhere but at you. Then he would walk stiffly to the far side of his pigpen where he gave the deliberate impression of being occupied with some important matter, a worm on the ground perhaps, or a knot in a fence post.

Appeasement in the form of some savory treat, on the order of a new potato or an apple, was necessary to mollify his injured ego. He had another quirk: he withdrew to a dark corner of his pighouse, grunting mournfully, whenever a chicken was killed for Sunday dinner. Uncle August declared that such laments for a dying chicken justified the widespread contention that pigs were among the more sensitive and feeling of animals.

"Whoever heard of a pig who contemplated death?" Grandma asked. "Such foolishness."

Grandma's opinions notwithstanding, the spotted pig was surely one of the smartest animals on the farm, although hardly the equal of Basil, the auburn and white Border collie, whom the pig held in groveling awe. Whenever the dog trotted past the pigpen on some errand, the pig grinned, grunted, and squealed in an attempt to catch the dog's eye and curry his favor. Normally the busy dog ignored such toadying, but one day as the alert collie went high-stepping by, he did turn his head to woof condescendingly in the direction of the fawning pig.

Well, wonder of wonders, the pig immediately answered in what was an admittedly porcine but nonetheless recognizable imitation of Basil's bark.

The pig's unexpected utterance prompted the dog to add to his itinerary periodic stops at the red pighouse where, having established that the pig was closely watching, he would rotate his head as if to ask a question, then carefully bark, once. The pig in turn would hold his head up and sideways, tightly close his eyes in concentration, and yap or yuff (the sound could be variously described) in reply, if not with success, at least with conviction.

Whether Basil considered the pig's continued efforts to produce canine vocalizations as a wry source of fun, or the dog was making a serious attempt at cross-species communication, became a point of some discussion. Grandpa, who thought Basil possessed of a sense of humor, maintained that the dog was giving the pig barking lessons as a way of ridiculing the preposterous assumption that a pig could reach the status of dog. Uncle August, on the other hand, saw the dog as a natural-born teacher, with the pig his talented pupil. There was evidence in favor of this argument, for after a while the pig did appear to be making progress. On summer evenings, you could hear him in his pighouse, practicing.

Grandma gave credit for neither sense of humor nor proto-linguistic effort. In her curmudgeonly opinion, the whole nonsensical affair could be dismissed quite simply: the two animals got along only because they had no competitive food interests. "If both of them liked ham bones, things would be different," she told a bewildered Uncle August and an appalled Grandpa. Uncle August told Grandma she lacked even a remote appreciation of the phenomenon they were witnessing. Worse, her choice of the term, "ham bones," to make her point was, simply put, cruelly insensitive to the pig.

Grandpa added that he found Grandma devoid of charitable inclination toward the two creatures. To this Grandma readily agreed. Grandma preferred plants to animals and always kept out of the barn.

High adventure for the pig consisted of digging out of this pen and, once beyond the confines, to transgress much farther than the usual errant pig. Herein lay the deeper reason that Grandma regarded him with jaundiced eye and curled lip. Upon digging himself free, the pig would scamper about the farm, searching for attention and scattering any lounging cats in the process. By and large somebody was about, so he got a pat, a handout, and a lug back to his pen.

That is, if Basil the collie hadn't come on him first, in which case the pig, not daring even a yap, was sternly escorted home. But there were those occasions when the porker found no one to shake down, and when Basil was off working somewhere. Then Mr. Pig took the backup option of a culinary trip to Grandma's garden, in which a cornucopia of delicacies was available, including not only the fullest range of herbs plus a plethora of plump, succulent vegetables, but also great stands of the most thoroughly edible flowers. After the second of these pig forays, Grandma declared that should the animal trespass against her garden one more time, he would be coming to Sunday dinner by way of a large serving platter.

Such dark talk caused the young Junior great emotional consternation, for he dearly loved the pig, as the pig did him. During their hours together, Junior never failed to speak respectfully and kindly to the animal. The boy had fantasies of taking Dill to school that fall, to show off his tricks and accomplishments, a plan he discussed several times with the attentive pig.

Junior told Grandma that in order to save her garden from further plunder, he would gladly take the pig off her hands, giving it a loving home. Uncle August was somewhat lukewarmly in favor but Aunt Melodie firmly vetoed the offer. In the first place, they had no suitable pig quarters available. More importantly, Aunt Melodie had vegetables and flowers of her own to consider. By way of allaying Junior's fears for the pig's longer term, Grandpa said he would come up with a way of keeping him where he belonged, well away from Grandma's cooking fires.

On a bright Sunday in late summer, Grandma and Grandpa had the family over for a sweet corn picnic. Uncle Carl and Aunt Mabel drove over; there was Uncle August and Aunt Melodie with Emma and Junior, as well as Second Cousin LeRoy, Aunt Olivia, and their kids. The plan was to partake of the season's first sweet corn, after a round of general visiting. During the course of a hotly contested horseshoe match between Grandpa and Uncle Carl on one side against Uncle August and Second Cousin LeRoy on the other, the spotted pig got out. Attracted by the commotion coming from the direction of the horseshoe pits, the pig sprinted toward the game by way of the backyard. Squealing gleefully, he breezed past Grandma, Aunt Melodie, and Aunt Olivia, who were on their knees digging up liriope. The pig continued his raucous gallop on through Grandpa and Uncle Carl's horseshoe pit, then disappeared behind the barn.

Grandma, Aunt Melodie, and Aunt Olivia, armed

with brooms, scurried hysterically toward the garden where they figured to intercept the pig if a raid were intended. Of course an animal as smart as Dill would naturally anticipate such an obvious reaction. Instead of heading toward Grandma's garden as he came around the barn, he ran straight away from the buildings, sailing joyfully through the kids' softball game (Aunt Mabel was umping) in the west pasture.

At a safe distance out, among the gawking cows, the pig stopped to catch his breath.

The moment Second Cousin LeRoy had seen Dill spring by, he dropped his horseshoe, located a sheep crook, and lit out after the pig. The kids joined their ample relative when he too, following the pig, bounded unceremoniously through their ball game. Basil, who had been trying to sleep under a bush behind home plate, got up to trot along behind, with yawning enthusiasm. The well-trained Border collie would cut off the pig in short order, when the loose animal was eventually obliged to run back down the pasture fence line toward the farmyard.

With Second Cousin LeRoy in the lead, a laughing reaper swinging the sheep crook like a great scythe, followed by the leaping kids, and tailed by the drowsy dog, the dancing parade flowed through the sun and wind of the brilliant pasture in a cacophony of squealing, the calling of "peeg-peeg-peeg," and drowsy barking.

The gamboling pig had no difficulty staying safely ahead of his pursuers, all the way to the fence in the direction of the Creek. There, Dill unexpectedly turned north. Unfortunately, Basil had already reversed direction back to the south in preparation for an easy interception. Again the pig had foreseen a move; he raced up the fence line to the high corner of the pasture, paused for a moment to pitch a derisive squeal in the direction of Second Cousin LeRoy and his followers, then entered the great cornfield. Everyone stopped when he vanished among the dark rows.

"Let's not go running though those sharp corn leaves," said Second Cousin LeRoy. "Let him come out on his own."

"Ignore him; he'll come out eventually. Then the dog can catch him," Uncle August called out to them.

"Just keep it away from my garden," squawked Grandma, parking her broom.

By now Basil had corrected his miscalculation and had nearly topped the upper end of the pasture, intent on following the pig into the cornfield. Grandpa whistled him up. The dog stopped at the command to leave off. He looked back at Grandpa. You could see he wondered why the chase was called off. Grandpa had to whistle again before the dog started back down the hill, head lowered in a disgruntled pout, as if to say he could have flushed the loose pig, but orders were orders.

After an animated review of events, the men returned to their horseshoes, the kids plus Aunt Mabel to their ball game, and the ladies to their liriope. No one remembered scores or whose turn it was; Grandma couldn't locate the trowel she had been using. After a while, the women went into the house to get the meal started. A half-hour later they were all sitting around the picnic table when Emma spied the pig standing at the edge of the cornfield.

"He'll come closer if we don't look at him," said Uncle Carl. "Then Basil can round him up."

Basil showed that he was still annoyed with the pig's having outfoxed him. He lay beside the table with a bone hanging from the corner of his mouth, growling to himself. His head was stretched out between his paws. He couldn't start after the pig until he heard the word from Grandpa.

As they watched without letting on, the pig strolled well out into the pasture, wanting to be seen. No one paid attention.

"Pass the chicken, please," said Junior.

"Do have some more potato salad, Second Cousin LeRoy," offered Grandma.

"This is truly wonderful sweet corn," said Aunt Olivia, taking a second ear.

Everybody agreed. They went right on eating and talking, following the spotted pig out of the corners of their eyes. The pig very deliberately moved to the middle of the pasture. Still there was no reaction from the crowd at the table. The pig squealed. No one even glanced in his direction. He sat up tall on his backside, like a squirrel — the picnickers kept on talking about food. The pig went down on all fours and walked in a backward circle, oinking. There was no comment from the table. Throughout this charade the dog chewed furiously on his bone, with smoldering, half-closed eyes focused on the strutting pig. Second helpings were begun. The family complimented Grandma on her sliced cucumbers with vinegar.

Dill squealed again, but to no effect. There was only eating and chatting.

The dog labored even more furiously at his bone. The pig danced forward with abandon, recklessly tossing its head from side to side. They ate on, looking everywhere but at him. The pig swayed even closer; it was now two-thirds of the way across the pasture. The dog began to moan in frustration.

"Another minute, Basil," Grandpa whispered, leaning toward the dog.

Abruptly the pig stopped and stared hard at them. He had heard Grandpa speak to the dog. Was it Grandpa's conspiratorial tone that he had detected? The pig raised his nose to them, grunted, then high-tailed it away and back into the towering cornfield.

"What happened?" asked Aunt Melodie.

"He knows that we know," someone said.

They ate slowly, watching the edge of the green cornfield. The pig did not reappear. The consensus grew that he was taking a nap in the corn. He usually slept in the afternoons. He would come out sooner or later. Right now he found it too warm to run.

Vigilance gave way to talk of dessert, which was pleasantly underway when the dog sat up with a jerk. He started barking in the direction of Grandma's garden.

"Why, that pig animal's snuck back into my garden," Grandma screamed, reaching for her broom.

"Get him, Basil," ordered Grandpa. The dog launched himself toward the garden and the pig's comeuppance.

Dill was about to partake of a row of carrots, beginning with the tops, when he sensed the dog's approaching rush. The pig spun on his hooves to head back toward the pasture. But now it was the dog who anticipated the pig.

Without breaking stride or speed, the collie turned well out ahead, to cut him off. In response, the pig doubled back toward the yard, only to come face-to-face with Second Cousin LeRoy sweeping his great sheep crook, the entire howling family fanning out behind him. In desperation Dill sprinted for the milk house. If it were open, he could get into the barn, run through the stables, and escape out the end of the barn facing the back forty. To his dismay, the milk house door was closed tight. He was cornered. He knew it, and the dog knew it, as Basil closed in.

The dog pulled up nose to nose with the stymied pig, who stood glowering and panting. In a moment someone would grab him up, maybe even hogtie him, for a haul back to his pen. The dog rocked from side to side, daring the pig to try an end run.

But the resourceful pig had enjoyed his caper far too much to see it finish with indignity. With the dog poised in front of him, and as the raucous human hoard approached, in its center Grandpa, holding open a large gunny sack, the pig gathered strength, stretched its neck full out, and gave forth a formidable grunt, sounding so much like a bark that the amazed Basil backed away two steps, in awe. With this opening, the pig dashed around the dog, through the legs of the approaching battalion, and sped once more for the cornfield, into which he dove with yet one more satisfied squeal. The dog looked, Grandpa looked, Second Cousin LeRoy looked, Grandma looked. They all just looked.

As evening softened to twilight, they gathered on the lawn, resting on blankets, to listen to the whippoor-wills, to the crickets, to the many strange calls from the oncoming night. They spoke of one thing and another, of the fine weather, of the promising season, of those events, marvelous and ordinary, that defined their lives. It had been a day all right, a day of good food, of unfin-ished games, of memorable times. It had been a day they would recall when they came together again, a day to talk of in the winters and summers to come. And, they all agreed, this day belonged to the pig.

Quiet talk gave way to yawns, to thoughts of a peaceful rest; but there was no hurry yet, no rush at all to leave the good company, nor the sweet grass. Beetles buzzed. A barn owl called. Cow bells chimed faintly as the hired man walked the drowsy herd to fresh clo-ver. Over the stillness of the fields the golden sun be-gan to fade.

As they lingered, they saw in the pasture, touched by the lowering shafts of gentle light, the spotted pig, trotting head up toward his pighouse.

"There he goes," whispered Aunt Melodie.

"Isn't he the sassy one," said Aunt Mabel.

"Homeward to pen and swill," chuckled Uncle August.

"He showed us one thing, for sure," said Grandpa with great seriousness.

"What's that, Will?" asked Uncle Carl. The others wondered too.

"The value of a second language," answered Grandpa.

Gypsy Baby

There was talk of Gypsies at Brother Bob's store: a small caravan of them had camped on the State land downstream from the Mill Pond. The camp was off and above the county trunk by maybe a quarter mile, on a piece of high ground overlooking the Creek. To get up there, the Gypsies had crossed the Mill Pond bridge, then had driven up and around the abandoned mill to the high ground.

This elevated location gave them a clear view of the road and bridge, so they would know if somebody were going to visit them, or bother them. There were a good twenty in the band — fat ones, skinny ones, old, young, all shapes and sizes.

The darkened toddlers went around naked. There was also a blonde white girl with them. She was maybe eighteen or so. She was pregnant. The group at the store reckoned the girl came from the Monroe area, down toward the Illinois border, or close to it. They'd heard Gypsies had camped there over the winter. The betting was that she had gotten herself pregnant by a Gypsy boyfriend, then sent away from her house by her old man.

The consensus was to keep an eye on the Gypsies,

and leave a dog out at night. They advised Brother Bob not to allow more than two at a time into the store. If you let a lot of them in, a couple of them would keep you busy while the rest robbed you blind. Brother Bob nodded his agreement. All the same, Eris Droster declared he planned to hire a crew of them when his beans came in; those people could work steady, morning to night, in the hot sun. They could really pick beans. But you had to watch them; if you didn't, you might find yourself shy some poultry. You had to tell them right off not to come near the buildings, to stay just in the fields.

"It looks like the girl might have her baby soon," Grandpa mentioned.

"Big as a house," said someone in the group.

If you walked up the Windsor Road, up toward the cemetery, to the white schoolhouse, you could see the whole Gypsy camp. They lived in decorated little wagons with tiny chimneys. The wagons had miniature windows, and sharply peaked roofs. The wagons looked like cheerful little houses with rubber tires.

Every inch of them was completely painted, even the springs, in vivid colors: blues, yellows, greens, reds, with black shapes and swirls added here and there, which some one said were hex signs. Rickety cars were parked beside the half-dozen wagons. The camp was formed in a circle, surrounding an area of perhaps a quarter acre in size. An orange fire burned day and night in the middle of the encircled wagons. Twice a day, morning and afternoon, some of the Gypsy women went out to gather firewood in the lower woods of Big Hill. Water came from the Creek. The Gypsies had set up a couple of unpainted outhouses a little way from the circle, downhill from the camp.

The day after the Gypsies arrived, Grandpa took Emma and Junior for a walk up to the schoolhouse, to sit under the trees and watch. They were quite close to the camp.

"I'll bet they can see us too," Emma said.

"They can," agreed Grandpa.

While they sat there, they saw the blonde white girl ease herself down the steps of a wagon. It was easy to notice the wagon — its steps were painted crimson red. The girl walked awkwardly, her legs apart as she moved, toward the Creek. She was carrying a metal pail. When she reached the Creek, she pushed herself through the marsh grass that lined the bank to get out onto a rock resting in the steady current. There she dipped the pail full of water, then began trudging back up toward the wagon. Her stomach stuck way out. It was obvious that lugging the heavy pail was an effort for her — on the way back she put it down twice, to rest. Grandpa and the kids saw that most of the Gypsies were sitting around on old chairs and benches, in front of the other wagons, or by the fire. None of them got up to help her. The girl emptied the pail into a tub in front of her wagon, then made another trip down to the Creek and back. After that, she sat for a while on the red steps.

She eventually pushed herself up and walked to the central fire, from the top of which she fetched one

of the large kettles there. She went back to the tub and poured in hot water from the kettle. After she had returned the kettle to the fire, she ducked into her wagon. She was out quite soon with an armload of clothing that she dropped into the tub. She poured in some soap powder from a tin she had brought out with the clothing. She churned the clothes for a few minutes with what looked like an ax handle, wrung them out, and placed them in a large metal pan with handles. She took this load down to the Creek for a rinse. Back up from the Creek, she hung her wash on a row of pegs on the side of her wagon.

While she was working, a man came out of the wagon, looked at the girl, then settled down on the red steps. As the girl finished hanging the last article of clothing, he said something to her. She walked toward the wagon. He stood to let her get up the red steps and inside. She emerged a minute later with a decorated tin that she handed to him. At first neither Grandpa nor the children were sure what the tin was for. The Gypsy man was doing something with the contents, but they were just a little too far off to see what. After they saw the man bring a cigarette to his mouth and light it, and when they saw the smoke, they realized that the blonde girl had brought him tobacco. The man stayed on the red steps for some time, smoking. The girl sat on a step below his, leaning against his legs. It was hard to tell if the man and the girl were talking, although he kept a hand on her shoulder.

The next morning the blonde girl and a skinny, wild-haired Gypsy kid no older than seven or eight turned up begging on the front steps of the store. Each had a metal cup that they held out toward people who were stopping for groceries and whatnot. The pair must have got there pretty early because the first two of Brother Bob's Saturday customers had to walk past them, avoiding their eyes, to get inside. After a bit Brother Bob came out and shooed them off. When he did, they walked across the road to sit on the edge of the ditch, trying to figure out what to do next. When it was clear they had no chance of a handout, they started walking slowly back toward their camp.

First Widow Lawrence, who lived kitty-corner across the intersection from the store, had been watching the goings-on from her kitchen window. When the two beggars turned back, she came out and gave them each some change. Then she walked over to the store.

"Why'd you give them money?" Big Mrs. Hoogewind asked while she was waiting for Brother Bob to slice her a pound of bologna.

"Well, you can be sure if they go back to that camp empty-handed, they'll get roughed up," the widow answered. "I don't expect they have an easy life, poor things."

On Friday two of the Gypsy men came into Brother Bob's store. The men asked if they could sit on his steps and hire out their people for bean picking. They also wanted to put up a handwritten notice on the telephone pole in front of his building. Brother Bob gave them the go-ahead.

"We got fourteen pickers. We get six cents a pound," the younger of the two Gypsy men told Brother Bob. It was in the younger man's wagon that the blonde girl lived. The man had striking blue eyes, made more noticeable by his dark eyelashes and perfect black eyebrows. He was fairly tall, and quite muscular — not at all fat. Women would find him attractive. He was definitely in charge.

When the local beans started coming in, all able-bodied Gypsies had been hired out to pick, so the camp was quiet during the day, except for a handful of very young children and a couple of old women watching them. Emma went up to the schoolhouse everyday, where she sat on the steps and watched the Gypsy camp, hoping to see the blonde girl. The girl seldom came out of the wagon; if she did, it was only to go to an outhouse, or to sit on the wagon steps for a few minutes. Emma gave the girl a wave once, while the girl was sitting on the red steps. The girl stared at Emma for a long moment, across the empty field that separated them, but didn't wave back. Every so often, one of the old women went over to the girl's wagon, to see if the girl was all right, Emma guessed.

A week later the young Gypsy man who had organized the bean hiring rushed into the store. Grandpa was there, buying a wood rasp. When Grandpa saw the man was upset, he told Brother Bob to take care of him first.

"Is there a doctor anywhere around here?" the Gypsy asked in a rush.

Brother Bob spread out his hands, to ask why.

"My woman's having trouble with the baby," he answered.

Brother Bob gestured toward the telephone on the wall. He wrote a number on a piece of butcher paper and handed it to the Gypsy.

The operator put the man through to Doc Drake in DeForest. The Gypsy was very clear as he explained the situation to the doctor on the other end — he was calling from the Token Creek Store, his camp was close by, the woman was in great pain. The baby had started coming out and then stopped. The arm was out, that was all. She had been in labor since just after midnight. She kept vomiting and screaming that something was wrong. She had begun to bleed around the baby. The women midwives who were attending her were getting worried, and couldn't figure out what to do.

The man paused for a moment while the doctor asked some questions, which the man answered either yes or no. The last question upset the Gypsy.

"We're here because we're picking beans," he responded. After another moment, he pronounced a fuming thank you and rang off. Grandpa and Brother Bob looked at him, waiting.

"He's going to come. I'm supposed to meet him here."

Grandpa said it might take the doctor an hour to get to them. Could his wife wait that long? The man didn't know for sure, but he didn't think so. Things were bad.

"Look. I can come and see if I can help. I was in an ambulance corps when I was overseas. I've delivered babies," Grandpa said.

The man had started to leave to wait outside. He turned and looked hard at Grandpa, sizing him up. Finally he nodded. He and Grandpa left together. When Grandpa followed the Gypsy to his car, the man asked Grandpa if he didn't want to take his own.

"I'll ride with you. Yours is running," Grandpa answered.

The Gypsy advanced the spark and throttle of his Ford so quickly that Grandpa nearly fell out as the car lurched onto the road. The Gypsy didn't let off during the entire dash to the camp, clattering so fast over the wooden bridge across the Mill Pond dam that planks jumped in and out of their tracks as the car passed over.

A dark-eyed Gypsy woman was sitting on the red steps of the wagon when the man and Grandpa pulled up. The woman stood to let the two men pass. She said nothing as Grandpa climbed into the little wagon. He had to bend down to get through the low door.

"She's there," the man said, pointing to a dark area in the wagon.

Grandpa couldn't see things right away — it took a moment to become accustomed to the low light, and to the smell. The interior of the wagon was minuscule, not much larger than one of his calf pens, Grandpa thought. On one side of the narrow central aisle were shelves holding cooking utensils — pans, metal plates, different sized containers with handles, and various tools that looked like they were used for metal work-ing. There were other tools that Grandpa didn't recognize. The tools and other pieces were fastened down, probably so they would stay put while the wagon was being pulled down a road.

At the end of the wagon, on the same side as the tools, was an area that looked like a sink, where a pail of water sat. Grandpa noted a metal dipper hanging on the outside of the pail.

"Good," he said to himself. He could wash. He would get someone to fetch hot water from the fire in the middle of the camp.

On the other side of the stifling wagon, opposite the utensil shelves and sink, were closets. Between the closets was a narrow bed, folded down from the wall. She was in this bunk bed, on her back. There was some sort of sheet draped over her stomach. Her legs were spread, dangling at the knees over the end of the bunk. The sheets under her were soaked with a stench of body fluids and blood. Her head was turned to one side, facing the outside of the bed. She had a roll of colored cloth in her mouth, but she was not biting down on it. He smelled her vomit. Its rancid foulness mingled with the musty stink of the dim wagon. As he looked, Grandpa thought she might have been unconscious, but as he began to see better, he could tell her glassy eyes were looking at him, or trying to. Then he saw the baby's arm, hanging from her.

Two Gypsy women in long skirts were sitting beside the bed on stools, close around the girl's head. One of them, the younger, was wiping strings of tangled hair back from the girl's forehead, using a rag. The other, a leather-faced old woman with jewelry on her arms, was holding a small bowl of something that was smoking and producing an unpleasant odor — an acrid, weedy smell. The old woman was mumbling and waving the smoke toward the girl's face, as well as inhaling it herself each time she waved her hand over the bowl. Suddenly, the girl began to writhe; she coughed the cloth roll from her mouth and cried out, but weakly, Grandpa thought. The older Gypsy woman, the one with the bowl, said something to the Gypsy man in another language.

"What did she say?" Grandpa asked, still trying to take stock of the situation.

"She said they're both going to die, that it can't be helped. The baby won't come out."

"Can they get us some hot water?" Grandpa asked him.

The Gypsy man said something to the women, again in their language. The older woman stood and glared at Grandpa, but remained close by the girl, holding the bowl. The Gypsy man repeated the order, angrily. The younger attendant stood and began leaving, squeezing past Grandpa and the Gypsy man.

The older woman grimaced and said something sharp to the Gypsy man, but she did begin moving out of the wagon.

"I need to wash my hands," Grandpa said. He had already rolled up his sleeves. The girl moaned loudly. The man gestured toward the sink. Grandpa edged by the bunk; the man came after him and poured water over Grandpa's hands and arms.

"Do you have soap?"

The man reached down a tin from a shelf; it was borax powder. The Gypsy poured some into Grandpa's cupped hands. In spite of the coolness of the water it lathered up enough.

"Listen," Grandpa said. "That baby is only partway born, and it's stuck. It must be too big for her, and it's sitting kitty-corner. The arm's outside, but the head could be turned back and wedged, like this." He mimicked the baby's likely position. The Gypsy man understood.

"We've got to reach in and turn the baby if we can, so that his arm goes back in enough, maybe all the way back in, so it has a chance to come out head first. It might be dead by now. Its neck could be broken. But

we've got to get it out or she'll die. There's blood built
up behind him."

The man nodded again.

"We need to get some clean cloth of some kind to
put under her."

The man reached over the half-conscious girl, into
a closet above the bed. He took out several lengths of
grayish cloth. Grandpa began pulling the blood-and
fluid-soaked material out from under the girl, dropping
it on the floor. With the Gypsy rolling her gently to one
side and then the other, they tucked dry sections of the
cloth under her.

"Okay. Now we've got to get her knees up. You
may have to hold her legs apart, and keep her knees
bent up. I've got to stand between them. You stand
beside her, here." The Gypsy put his hands under the
girl's knees and lifted them.

"You might have to hold her down too," Grandpa
added as he moved into position.

It was the baby's left arm and hand that were pro-
truding. The palm of the little hand was down. That
could mean the head was turned back to the left. As
carefully as he knew how, Grandpa eased the fingers
of his right hand along the baby's arm, following it past
the woman's vagina. He didn't feel a head, so he must
be touching the baby's left shoulder. More blood started
oozing out. He got the fingers of his left hand partway
in, on the other side. He felt something and stopped for
a second. The head was there all right, bent way back.
"Easy now, easy," he told himself. He started turning
the baby, turning ever so slowly, trying not to go too
fast, ever so gently turning the tiny body, coaxing it,
trying to twist it back in.

The girl screamed and made an attempt to kick.
The Gypsy held her legs. She tried to sit up. The man
eased her down with his forearm. The girl's screaming
was smothered with what sounded like retching — she
was vomiting again. Grandpa kept turning or trying to

turn the child. The blood was getting worse.

"Stroke it," Grandpa said to himself, "like you're giving a massage." He was remembering what the army doctor had told them, and what he had seen. Was it turning? He thought so. Yes, it was turning, he could feel it move. Yes, it was. The girl was gurgling and moaning.

"Turn her head so she doesn't choke," he told the Gypsy. The Gypsy reached up and gently turned the girl's burning cheek to the side.

Grandpa felt heat on his legs. Blood was running off the bed and onto him, and onto the floor. She was hemorrhaging badly. Sweat kept running into his eyes. He wiped it away as best he could with the back of his arm. But, the baby was turning. It was. The arm was almost back in. He kept palpating, stroking, massaging, trying to ease the tiny body around ... turning ... never too much pressure, just enough. Keep it going, keep it going. Suddenly it turned very quickly and the arm was gone, back in. Grandpa pulled his hands back. As he did, the top of the baby's head appeared. It was coming out, blood and all.

The light from the doorway dimmed as Doctor Drake stooped in. He paused for a moment, to adjust to the obscurity and wretched air. He began rolling up his sleeves.

"I'm here," he announced.

"The sink's over there." Grandpa gestured with his elbow toward the washing area. The Gypsy man eased away from the convulsing girl to help the doctor wash. He poured water directly from the pail when Doc Drake held out his hands. The doctor was looking at the girl.

"I had to put the arm back in. Just the arm was sticking out when I got here. Now it's all coming out right, I think," Grandpa said. "But she's bleeding too much." Tears of sweat and frustration were on Grandpa's face.

'Thanks, Will. Let me look now," the doctor said gently.

The baby was halfway out. Doctor Drake put his hand and forearm under it, to cradle it. With the other hand he was guiding it as it moved smoothly from the mother, who was alternately moaning and crying out in anguish.

Then the baby was out. The doctor grabbed it by the feet and held it upside down. It began wailing and gasping as he flipped it over. He slapped the bottom just the same.

"It's alive," he said.

But the girl was bleeding too heavily to spend more time on the baby. He gestured to Grandpa.

"Here. Hold him while I cut the cord."

He did. More blood flowed. Grandpa moved away with the baby.

"Get some of those women to clean it up," the doctor ordered. "I've got to try to help this girl."

She was beyond help. Her hemorrhaging was now so profuse that blood was running everywhere in the wagon. The bed was soaked with it. The three men were standing in it, sliding in it. The Gypsy man shouted something toward the door of the wagon. A woman appeared. She reached in with both arms, taking the bloody and yowling baby from Grandpa.

"Damn, damn," the doctor muttered as he used packing cloth to take up the rush of blood. "Damn it to hell, where's the placenta?" he raged. He was sponging furiously, but losing ground. The mother was moaning and trying to push herself up by the elbows. Grandpa was dizzy from the heat and the fetid air.

"Get the baby," Grandpa said to the Gypsy husband, whose gaze was fixed on the girl. The doctor nodded his assent. The dazed Gypsy went to the door and called out. A moment later the old woman who had taken the baby reappeared. She held it up. The child was partially cleaned. They had started to swaddle

it. The doctor motioned her in. The baby was squall-
ing. The doctor took the baby and removed the cloth
the woman had put around it.

'Take him. Put him on her," the doctor told the
Gypsy man, as he pulled off the sheet covering the girl.

The girl was conscious enough to realize that the
man had laid the baby on her. She feebly reached for it,
resting her hands on its tiny shoulders, flexing her fingers over it. The baby continued to yowl, even when its
mouth touched one of her nipples. The men stood
watching. The mother's fingers twitched over the baby,
trying to stay with it.

But, gradually, gradually, the girl's hands slipped
from the child and, fading downward, came haltingly
to rest, quieted and still, on the blood-soaked sheets of
her tiny bed.

The doctor looked at her for a moment, then put
his hand on the girl's glistening neck, to search for a
pulse. He frowned as he moved his hand around. Finally, he picked up the wailing baby and passed it to
the father, who handed it out to the old woman.

"I'm sorry," the doctor said to the Gypsy man.

Grandpa went outside to sit down on the running
board of Doctor Drake's car. He was aware of the reek
of the wagon still in his nostrils, and on his clothing.
He pulled off his shoes. They had blood in them. Doc
Drake came out after a few minutes and sat down beside Grandpa. Like Grandpa's, his clothing was
drenched with sweat and blood. All the Gypsy camp
was standing around them, looking at the exhausted
men. At a command from the old woman, two younger
women came forward, each carrying a basin of water.
Doc Drake and Grandpa got up and followed them to
a bench in front of the fire. The women put the basins
down and helped the men wash. A Gypsy man handed
them drying cloths. When he had dried himself as best
he could, Doc Drake went back to his car and took out
a satchel.

"Damned placenta," he muttered as he rummaged through papers in the satchel. He found what he wanted and walked over to Grandpa, who was finishing drying his arms and hands. The doctor gestured for another cloth.

When it was handed to him, he took it and wiped some blood from Grandpa's cheek. The Gypsy man was standing there too, soaked and grim. He had come out of the wagon to stand near the doctor, but not facing him.

"I need some information, to write up a birth certificate ... and a death certificate," the doctor said in a tired voice. The Gypsy turned toward the doctor and shrugged. Whatever.

The doctor asked the required questions. It turned out the girl was from Illinois. She had been with the Gypsy band for a couple of years. Her name was Karina. Nobody knew her maiden name, but that didn't matter because it also turned out she and the Gypsy man were married. Doc Drake wasn't sure what being married by Gypsy law meant — he decided not to make too fine a point of it.

She was a missus. That's all that was necessary. Last name: Gitano. The Gypsy wanted to know if they could bury her in the Token Creek cemetery. Doc Drake said that was best, as long as she was in a casket.

"You want to name the baby now? I'm supposed to record it, if I can."

The Gypsy looked at Grandpa. Grandpa met his eyes. Grandpa was aware of the hush around him. Out of the quiet he heard the fading screech of a hawk, soaring upwards, above them. The Gypsy continued to stare at Grandpa.

"What's your name?" the Gypsy asked after a moment.

"William. William Armstrong," Grandpa answered.

The Gypsy paused. He turned toward Doctor

Drake. After a few seconds, he gestured toward Grandpa. Doctor Drake bit his lip, showing he understood.

Grandpa looked at the people standing around, watching. None made a sound. Grandpa looked back at the Gypsy headman. Grandpa nodded to him.

"His last name is Gitano," the Gypsy said loudly.

Doctor Drake wrote down "Gitano, William."

That evening, at dusk, the coffin of Karina Gitano, age about nineteen years, who had died in childbirth, was carried from the Gypsy camp to the Token Creek cemetery. Her rough wooden bier was held on the shoulders of four Gypsy men. The Gypsy chief, the husband, followed directly behind. After him trooped the rest of the band, including the leather-faced old woman holding the baby.

From the steps of the white schoolhouse, a few people from the village watched the burial rite. Besides the Gypsies, the graveside ceremony was attended by Grandpa and Doc Drake. Grandpa was there because he had been asked to be, by the Gypsy headman. Doctor Drake was there because the county coroner had told him to be, to be sure the girl got put away right. The Gypsy chief and the leather-faced old woman officiated.

As soon as the humming and chanting was over, and the coffin lowered into the ground and covered, the Gypsies walked back in a silent file toward their camp. It was clear they intended to leave. They had let the central fire dwindle. They had been picking up and putting things into their wagons. Doc Drake predicted they would be gone by morning light.

* * *

An unusual smell woke Grandpa long before the following dawn. The odor blowing into his open window at first made him fear one of his buildings was on fire. When he got outside however, he realized that what he smelled was smoke trailing downwind from the direction of Token Creek. In fact, he could see flames in the distance, on the hillside at the Gypsy camp. The flames were quite high — a wagon was burning, by the way it looked.

At the same time, down in the village of Token Creek, Brother Bob, in his rooms above his store, was also awakened by the unpleasant smell blowing in his open window. Like Grandpa, his first thought was that a nearby building had caught fire. But, when he had pulled on some cloths, and had run downstairs onto the store's porch, he too could see flames in the direction of the Gypsy camp. It looked like one of the wagons was burning. While he was standing there, Grandpa drove up.

"We better go up there," Grandpa called to him. Brother Bob nodded vigorously and scrambled into the car.

The blaze was high enough to light the surface of the wooden bridge as the two men drove over it. Grandpa stopped his car just past the end of the bridge.

They would walk up.

The Gypsies must have broken camp right after dark. As Grandpa and Brother Bob got closer, they saw no other wagons except the one burning. It was a good bet that the Gypsies had set the fire, Grandpa was beginning to think. They hurried into the abandoned camp, toward the fire and sticky smoke.

As the two got closer, the smell became stronger. It was revolting, like burning hair. Grandpa recognized the wagon by its blood-red steps. It took him another moment to understand.

"We had better go telephone Doc Drake again," Grandpa said, drawing Brother Bob back.

Brother Bob lifted his shoulders and spread his hands, asking for an explanation. He didn't know what Grandpa was getting at.

"We're seeing her real funeral this time," Grandpa said. "It's a pyre."

Then Brother Bob understood.

Note: *To understand why Doctor Drake was at first worried, then upset, about the absent placenta, its structure and function need to be explained. The placenta is a web-like vascular structure, joined to the uterine wall; the placenta brings the blood supply from the mother to the fetus by way of the umbilical cord. When a doctor or midwife cuts the umbilical cord of a newborn, the cord not only empties itself of blood, but the end joined to the mother also empties the placenta. Normally, when the cord is cut there is a momentary surge of blood from the mother; this increased outflow of blood from the placenta empties it, causing it to collapse so that it is expelled. The discharged placenta is part of the afterbirth. With the placenta detached from the uterus and out of the womb, the uterine wall can clamp down and stop pumping blood. In this case, the placenta did not come out after the baby was born and the structure must have remained attached or grown onto the girl's uterus, continuing to draw blood from her body. That's probably why the girl hemorrhaged to death.*

Fox and Goose

Oh, the fox went out on a chilly night,
And he prayed for the moon to give him light,
For he'd many a mile to go that night...
(English folk song)

Big Hill stood north of Token Creek. The hill was an elongated monadnock, rising abruptly out of the earth and fields along the Creek's flood plain, overlooking the Mill Pond, and the rich land around. Big Hill was close to a mile long from northwest to southeast — a half mile wide in the other direction.

It was high as glacial hills went, nearly a hundred feet, measured from the mill yard at the bottom to its tree-topped crest. The core was granite, slabs and boulders of which were exposed in a rocky band almost completely surrounding the hill. This rugged belt separated the old landmark into upper and lower zones, where there were hardwood stands. But on the harsher middle slope, only scrub oak, hazelnut, and gooseberry maintained a hold on the patches of earth that were scattered among the great white rocks. It was among these stones and scrub that Grandpa discovered the pair of fox.

He came across the animals quite by accident; he had walked out on his porch one lilac-scented dawn, to inspect the greening countryside with his army binoculars. While he was scanning the steep midsection of Big Hill he spotted them, sunning themselves on a boulder. The mouth of their den was visible below them, behind a clump of gooseberry, close to the great rock on which they were dozing. He wondered if there were pups.

There were. On a Sunday morning two weeks later he watched a hesitant pack of downy little ones creep from the den, led from behind the now leafy gooseberry bush by the orange-red parents. Grandpa speculated on how the fox and his wife fed themselves and their little ones. No doubt the family was living on the area's many rabbits and pheasants, and field mice. Grandpa had heard no reports of missing poultry from area farms. In fact, no fox alarm had been sounded for some time. His first reaction was to keep his discovery to himself.

He knew well that fox were the sworn enemy of all farmers, yet he saw no point in putting the animals in danger if they were causing no harm. He consulted with Uncle August, just to be sure.

Uncle August hadn't experienced fox problems for a long while, nor had anyone else that he knew of. It was agreed that they would leave things as they were, for the time being. Uncle August became interested in the fox himself, and began keeping track of their comings and goings. He even walked over to Grandpa and Grandma's house from time to time, to watch the fox family with Grandpa, bringing his own field glasses.

Grandpa and Grandma's farm was a half-mile down the road from Uncle August and Aunt Melodie's. Grandpa's pastures bordered the fallow land and back woods belonging to Uncle August. Grandpa and

Grandma's rich acres were home to eight black and white milking Holsteins, two heifers, a team of hefty, dapple-gray work horses, a strawberry roan mare named Truth, a dozen sheep counting the spring lambs, a Border collie named Basil, Dill the spotted pig, and twenty or so Leghorn chickens. There were also two recent arrivals: a black and green crossbred duck with a white mask, part Muscovy, part domestic, plus a large, bad-natured, gray gander goose, a French breed of some sort. The duck and goose had come to the farm in the company of a temporary hired man, taken on at spring planting when the regular hired man, Old Tillman, went out of commission with a broken arm.

The two birds were confined to a makeshift pen, furnished with a lean-to shelter. The temporary hired man had set up these quarters for them next to his own, his being the converted machine shed on the hay field side of the barn. The shed was hidden from the house and yard because of the interposing barn, so no one saw much of the duck and goose during their early residency. The temporary hired man fed and watered them himself, and kept them under control. In the late summer Old Tillman was able to return to his duties, so the temporary hired man was paid off as had been agreed. He immediately departed for destinations unknown. Surprisingly, he left behind both the red-eyed goose and its short-legged, sidekick duck.

No one was sure what to do about the abandoned duck and goose.

Grandpa thought that their pen was pretty small. He considered building a larger one, but wondered if the two orphans should be penned in at all. They were big birds who needed room for exercise. He decided to try giving them the run of the farm, so they could forage for at least part of their keep. They would roost in their pen, with the gate left open so they could come and go.

Unfortunately, Grandpa could not have anticipated what troublemakers the two free-ranging fowl would turn out to be.

Their first escapade involved Dill the pig. Dill lived in an extensive pig yard, complete with soupy mud-wallow downhill from the barnyard. The third morning of their liberation, the drake and the gander brazenly entered the pig's grounds, where they found and began circling the affable porker. The duck edged around him, quacking belligerently and menacing with extended black wings. The big goose circled with equal belligerence, wings adroop, and with its long neck run out, hissing nastily. The spotted pig's initial reaction tended toward amused curiosity until, his attention momentarily directed toward the noisy duck, the gander snuck up from behind and clamped its formidable bill onto the pig's curly tail. Dill hotly turned on the biting bird, snatched it by its long neck, and dragged it down to his oozing wallow for a going-over. The pig hauled the choking goose out to the middle of his wallow, where he repeatedly dunked the flapping interloper until it was nearly drowned. When the pig eventually did leave off, the bird's overly preened feathers were covered and caked with black muck from one end to the other. The gander staggered off to the pasture, where it spent the remains of the day in the little pond there, laboriously washing and cleaning itself. From time to time, as the goose worked, it snapped at the duck, who had run off but had now returned to swim and paddle merrily around the pond, its incessant quacking strongly resembling derisive laughter.

A week later the duck and the goose went after larger but less clever game.

They had waddled out to the pasture for a dip in the little watering pond, followed by a round of leopard frog-hunting. The Holstein cows, who were also there, standing around and having a drink, gawked contentedly at the two busy birds whose foraging brought them closer and closer to the herd.

When practically nose to nose with the ogling bovines, the duck and the goose suddenly rushed at them, flapping their wings and making a frightening racket. The bewildered Holsteins clumped off in a panic, running out to the middle of the big pasture. When they realized there were not pursued, they stopped and looked back.

Meanwhile, the duck and the goose quickly settled down in the grass, giving the impression of sleeping. Driven by curiosity, the cows inevitably wandered back toward the pond, noses out and large eyes rolling at the duck and goose, not quite understanding why there had been such a fuss. The goose and the duck, watching through half-closed eyelids, waited until the cattle came very close, then leaped up and ran at them again. This time the cows really bolted, mooing and bellowing as they again fled from their tormentors.

Basil the dog heard the row and went to investigate. He arrived on the scene just as the cows were in full stampede, with the duck and goose in hot pursuit. The collie had been trained to never make milk cows run. First he turned the herd back toward the pond and slowed them down. He then cut between the frightened cows and the flapping birds, the latter of which he nipped all the way back to their shed-side pen. There the stymied vandals immediately took refuge. They spent the next two days hanging fairly close to their old pen. If they saw the dog, even at a distance, or suddenly got it into their heads that he might be around, they rushed into the protection of the lean-to.

The truce was temporary. Three mornings later, the gander, with the duck egging him on, started bullying the chickens. The gander would raise its big wings above its head, extend it neck, and feign at the hens, as if it were about to crash through the chicken yard fence. The dim-witted chickens thought the goose was on the verge of attack, not understanding that their wire fence kept him out as well as them in. Cackling with fright, they scurried into the hen house where egg laying slacked off considerably due to all the tension. The harassment continued unnoticed for nearly a week, until Grandma began complaining of a dramatic drop in egg production.

Grandpa looked into the matter. Right after morning milking, he hid himself in the sweet corn patch near the chicken house. When the two shifty birds slunk down to the chicken yard for another round of terror, Grandpa burst from the corn patch and caught them red-handed. They tried to escape to the pasture but with the help of the dog, Grandpa chased them down and stuffed them into a feed bag. He took them to the woodshed and emptied them in for a lockup. This punishment was an inconvenience for Grandpa, however. He was obliged to feed and water the birds as long as they were shut in. He released the prisoners after a week — he had enough to do without catering. He began to hope those fox up on Big Hill would come down and carry off the two miscreants.

"Maybe I should take them up to the fox myself," Grandpa said to Grandma. He had been watching the fox family since spring, through the summer, and now into fall. The pups were nearly grown and would be on their own before winter.

Within a few days, the duck and goose were right back persecuting the chickens, but at odd hours, when neither person nor dog was close by. They also made sure to employ quick, hit-and-run attacks, to avoid detection. But, a few days into these tactics, they were caught again when the goose got hung up in the chicken wire. It happened while Dill the pig was taking a post-breakfast nap in the October sun, stretched out on the browning grass by the south side of his pig house. He was enjoying the quiet that had descended on the farm as things wound down with the onset of fall.

The dozing pig was suddenly awakened by a rhubarb coming from the direction of the chicken coop. He joined Grandpa and the dog as they ran to investigate. Of course the goose and the crossbred duck were the cause of the commotion, with the major racket being generated by the goose. In the process of rushing at the frightened chickens, it had managed to get its head stuck in the mesh of the chicken yard fence. Now it was boisterously struggling to pull itself free, while the duck stood by, not knowing what else to do except quack at full volume. Grandpa had had enough.

"It's time you two were penned up again, permanently," he told them when he and his escorts arrived at the chicken yard.

He untangled the goose and popped it into a gunnysack. While he was dealing with the goose, the dog grabbed the duck by the neck. They carried the protesting captives back to the woodshed for another lockup, this time a short one. After the birds were securely in, Grandpa drove off in his pickup truck, the dog and the pig riding in back, to buy a roll of wire fencing from Brother Bob down at the Token Creek store. Back home, he worked until supper time driving fence posts and hanging wire, constructing an expansion of the original pen that was attached to the machine shed. He let Old Tillman do the milking by himself.

Before he went in to eat, Grandpa lugged the two delinquents, each in a gunnysack, down to the new enclosure he had built. He dumped them in and locked the gate.

At supper, Grandpa and Grandma talked things over. Grandpa said it was no longer reasonable to maintain the trouble-making duck and goose, if the temporary hired man didn't come back soon and claim them. The birds were by rights his, even though he had left them behind without a word of warning, nor even mentioning them when he took his severance pay. Did Grandma think the man would come back? Grandma thought the honest thing would be to keep the duck and goose for a little while longer, until the remaining October fieldwork was done. If by then the man didn't show up, they'd consider the birds as theirs to eat. In the meantime, they'd keep them inside the enlarged pen. Grandma said she would feed and water them, since she knew Grandpa had had his fill of them. Grandpa liked her proposal, and agreed to it.

"Hello jailbirds," Grandma said to the birds the next morning. Grandma had brought their ration of grain and water. The sulking pair glared at her from behind the new wire fence. When she entered the pen with their water and food, the goose made a motion to nip at her. She stared him down.

II.

On a hushed, clear night, just a few days later, a massive full moon, the kind they call a hunter's moon, emerged above the southwest horizon. The flooding moonbeams soon reached the rocky cliffs of Big Hill. There, the resident reynard and vixen awoke, stretched, and checked their pups. The little ones were sound asleep. The two adult fox quietly left their den and set out south and west. They traveled for some time in that direction, until they were more than two-thirds of the way along Big Hill. They then turned south and down.

They descended out of the rocky area of the hill and entered the lower hardwoods, eventually passing through them and reaching the bogs bordering the Creek. They stopped for a drink, listened for a moment, then were ready to continue.

Moonlight was flickering on the dancing flow of the Creek as the animals crossed, nearly a mile downstream from the Mill Pond. Splashing out of the slow current, they negotiated a swale of rustling cattails, which gave way to a narrow stand of coarse marsh grass as they moved toward the embankment of the county trunk road. They climbed the embankment and hid themselves below the shoulder of the road, in a stand of thistle. They crouched there for perhaps a half-hour, waiting until the moon had risen higher and its brilliant light could tell them if there was movement along the open track of gravel. When the moon was higher, they saw that the road was quiet and empty.

The hunters sprinted across the dusty gravel road and into the woods on the other side. They were now behind Uncle August and Aunt Melodie's land. In the woods the going was easy; the park-like landscape was clear of brush, and by now so brightly lighted by the great moon, that the rapid pair might have thought there was a radiant dawn coming just ahead of them, rather than the long country night. They soon emerged from the woods, arriving at a barbed wire fence that marked the north side of Grandpa's pastures. The fox paused there, at the edge of the sea of silvery grass of the wide pasture land, watching, with their ears alert. They raised their noses into the soft air, in search of any warning it might carry.

There were no sounds of danger; the air was free and crisp, yet the breeze was behind them — they would need to go farther. The fox were quickly up and moving again. They slipped noiselessly down the weed-grown fence line, until they were well past the farm, and downwind from it. The wide circuit had taken them a mile from their hillside lair, but now their approach could be into the breeze. The light wind would bring them the scent of dangers, and guide them to the location of the things they sought. The route also had put the great white barn between themselves and the sleeping farmhouse, where mortal danger dwelled. They rested again, crouched in the trembling grass at the side of the brilliant field, again testing the chilly air, listening, and watching.

The two fox now leapt into a noiseless burst across the south pasture. They raced directly toward the shed

that stood out like a dark beacon in the stark luster of
the towering moon. As the fox drew closer, toward the
shed and the pen that was fixed to it, they saw the lat-
ticework of new wire that sparkled, weblike, in the incredible moonlight.

Without pausing at the new fence, the fox dug their
way under, making hardly more than a rustle as they
worked expertly through the dark, rich earth. Within a
few short minutes, they were under the barrier and
moving toward the lean-to where the duck and the
goose slept, head under wing.

The dozing prey did not awaken until the fox were
into the little shelter and upon them. The fowl reacted
immediately, vigorously, terror lending strength to their
resistance. They twisted and struggled, thrashed,
kicked, flapped, bit, and beat with their wings. They
called out when they could. The relentless teeth of the
attackers would catch a feathered throat, lose hold, take
hold again, would be beaten off, but would return
again, with fiendish will and grasping energy. The fox
were working and fighting to take a sure hold, to cut
off breath, and life, before the birds' strident calls might
summon help.

The goose was able to bite its attacker above the
eye. The fox jerked back in pain, allowing the goose to
flee out of the lean-to. But it only flew hard against the
sturdy, shining fence. It rolled backwards and the fox
pounced again, leaping on the big gander's back and
pressing the bird down into the dusty grass of the pen.
The duck too, fought hard and long, hammering at the
vixen with it dark wings, striking with its bill, rolling
and writhing, even as the she-fox bit so hard down upon
a thigh that its jaws broke though bones and flesh.

Lighted by the giant moon, the churning battle
raged and spun, but moved steadily, and inexorably,
and in deadly favor, to the fox.

The dog awoke first. Strange cries had flown in
through the open window of the kitchen where he slept.

The sounds pulled him quickly out of his slumber; he was immediately alert and on his guard. Totally quiet, he listened without breathing, moving his head carefully from side to side, attempting to catch a sound wave or pick up a scent. He remained attuned, stone still. There was indeed something out there; there was something afoot. He detected it, off behind the barn. Then he heard the pig grunt, from his pighouse; in a second the pig grunted again. There came a spurt of frantic quacking, gone almost as quickly as it had come. Basil began barking towards Grandpa and Grandma's bedroom door. He heard Grandpa throw off his blankets and jump out of bed.

"What is it, Will?" Grandma whispered.

"I think we've got fox visitors," Grandpa answered, also in a whisper. He was already buckling his trouser belt.

"Light a lamp, please," he said to his wife. "Quickly, Kate. I need to get the shotgun." He could hear Basil alternately barking and listening.

"Hold on boy, we're going out," Grandpa called. He got his shoes on and came out of the bedroom. He rushed to get his shotgun.

Grandpa and the dog strode across the yard and toward the shed on the opposite side of the barn. Other animals were stirring in the barn and around the farm. A horse whinnied; there was clucking from the hen house; Dill was grunting steadily.

The farmyard was so wonderfully illuminated by the wide, radiating moon, standing full overhead, that Grandpa put down his lantern when they reached the pigpen. He lifted the gate as he went by, so Dill could join him and the dog.

By the time they came around the back of the barn, the female fox had already dragged the weakened and broken duck under the fence and was outside the pen with it. She was holding the bird in her teeth, shaking it, and waiting for the male fox to follow with the goose, which he had halfway out of the enclosure.

Grandpa saw what was happening as he ran forward, but he was not close enough for an accurate shot, nor would he have chanced one — the dog and the pig had run on ahead of him, into the line of fire.

"Basil, Dill. Sit!" he ordered, and the dog and the pig stopped, but too close to the vixen and the dying duck. A shot was still too risky.

He saw that the duck was weakly beating its wings. Its dulled eyes were only half open. The reynard was now emerging from beneath the fence, dragging the gray goose by the neck. The pig and the dog were too close, and they were preparing to attack the fox. Grandpa had to get them back.

"Dill, Basil. Over here, by me. Heel!" he called.

Basil and Dill began their retreat. They kept their eyes on the two fox as they did. Basil was growling deep in his throat. The pig was squealing steadily, almost as loudly as the dog was growling. The two animals reached Grandpa, and stopped, one on each side of him. The fox were facing them, one holding the dying goose, the other the weakly flopping duck. The dog and the pig became quiet, as if braced for the coming shots. The burning eyes of the two fox were fixed on Grandpa.

Grandpa did not move. Every detail of the duck, the goose, and the two raiders seemed present and clarified in the stark moonlight. Feather and fur stood out sharply and defined. The spectral light of the moon glimmered and danced in the glowing eyes of the fox. And yet Grandpa had not raised the gun.

The two fox did not move.

Still Grandpa hesitated. He released the safety of his heavy gun, but he did not bring it to his shoulder. Other than the diminished hissing of the dying goose, and the occasional, soft thump of the duck's wings, there was only the tiny, intermittent rustle of the breeze, passing over the swaying grass of the field.

Now the fox were backing away, eyes always held fast onto the three enemies before them. Grandpa saw the duck shudder. The goose continued its faint hiss, but its wings hardly beat now. Its legs moved and jerked, as if it were trying to run, but it could not kick now, nor strike. Its fiery eyes had closed.

The dog and the pig waited, in the dazzling moonlight, expecting the crash of exploding shells. Yet there was no roar from the shotgun, no shock of a discharge. The fox backed off farther, holding their near-dead prey, burning eyes on Grandpa. Grandpa stood without moving.

Suddenly the fox wheeled, each throwing a bird over its back, and were off. As they streaked away through the silver-white grass, their feet raised flecks of moonlit dew that flew up, and sparkled around them, in a diminishing trail of tiny stars.

Grandpa remained still for a long moment. He then softly clicked his gun back to safe, and placed the stock on the ground. The dog and the pig sat without moving, still obedient, watching the fox dissolving away across the ghostly field, away toward Big Hill, lighted and shining in the moonlit distance.

* * *

The morning after the fox had come and gone, Grandpa stepped out onto his front porch, looking about his peaceful October farmyard. He took up his binoculars and studied Big Hill. Then he put down the glasses and looked again at the farm around him. He saw, once again, that a silence had descended, and again he had not been ready for it, and for the sudden freedom that the closing season brought with it.

Autumns were difficult for Grandpa. Seemingly without warning the ceaseless activity, the daylight-to-dark hours, the flow of tasks and projects that had begun with the spring and carried through the wonderful summer and into fall, all abruptly stopped, and came to completion. He loved the spring, the summer, the warm months of planting and growing, and of harvesting. Spring was his favorite time, the season of new animals, of warming fields, of crops to put in. Spring brought fences to mend, gardens to start, repairs, improvements, expansions, and plans. Then came the summer with the cultivating, the hoeing, the calves to wean, the mowing of the first sweet hay, animals to tend, more cultivating, more haying, more feeding, and healing. There followed the ripening and the gathering, the pickling, the digging, and harvesting. It would never end, it had seemed, every moment was so filled. And this year there had been those strange birds, the quandary of the fox on the hill, and their beauty.

But almost as quickly as winter had turned to spring, and to summer, it was there and gone, and here arrived the change to fall and then fall itself, here again came that bright morning when he walked outside, as he was doing now, to realize that the stock had been sold, and the corn brought in, and the hay stowed, that the threshing had been done, and the fall plowing finished. Now, the barn was prepared, and the fences were checked; he had walked the bounds.

The cycle was slowing. There was time to linger, to pause in the stillness, before going down to the chores. There was time. He could watch for a spell in the glowing October sunshine, listening to murmurs where there had once been a din.

Grandpa sat down on the porch steps. A melancholy moved through him. He realized that, once again, he had failed to prepare himself for this unforewarned hush, for this forgotten privilege of rest, for this peace.

He watched, and listened. The brightness of the quiet day was growing, and he felt the sun on his face. He shaded his eyes in its splendid light, hearing crickets singing of its warmth, yet detecting too, in their cheerful song, a lament for the end of summer. He heard the sigh of the windmill as it began to turn toward a shift in the wind.

He sat, and watched. Then, out of the dazzling glare and the black shades of the lane, he felt that someone was approaching, coming down and toward him.

Grandpa couldn't make out the figure, with the fierce light behind it, but the shadow moved steadily closer, expanding, and becoming taller. In another moment Uncle August emerged from the brightness. He smiled when he saw Grandpa. Grandpa smiled too.

From the kitchen, Grandma heard Uncle August's cheerful "Good morning." She took down another cup from the shelf, and brought it outside with the coffeepot. The men accepted the cups with thanks, and Grandma filled them. She put down the pot on the table beside Grandpa's field glasses and sat beside her husband. Uncle August sat down too. They were quiet for a time.

Then Grandpa told Uncle August what had happened overnight, about the fox and their raid, about the duck and the goose. Had he done the right thing?, he wondered.

Uncle August thought for a moment, then said he thought he had. The farm was well rid of the nasty goose and the brazen duck. Yes, Uncle August said, there was no harm done. He would likely have done the same.

Grandma too expressed the same conclusion.

She too reassured Grandpa. He should feel no remorse, she said. He had reacted with his best instincts, when he confronted the two fox. He had been watching them, with his field glasses, for nearly six months now.

"I went out this morning myself, too," Uncle August said. "I watched them for a while, through my field glasses. I could make out the feathers."

"Maybe I would have shot if I thought the birds could have been saved," Grandpa decided, after a few minutes.

"I think I would have seen it the same way you did, Will," August said.

"Right," Grandpa said.

Then he added, "We will have to tell people."

"We're obliged to, I'm afraid," agreed Uncle August.

Grandpa stood. He went to the table where he had put down his binoculars. He lifted them to his eyes and trained them on the hillside. He located the fox where he expected them, resting on the great white boulder above their den. Beneath them, the nearly grown pups were chewing on the bones of the previous night's meal. Grandpa handed the glasses to Uncle August.

After Uncle August had a turn, they left for Bother Bob's store, to announce the fox.

Prohibition

Rile spotted the disabled car as he topped the last hill coming west into Token Creek. It was a big car, in the ditch, with the back end sticking up. They were probably driving too fast on the loose gravel and lost control on the downgrade. They're lucky they didn't roll over, he thought. The accident must have just happened — he could see people climbing out of the car and clambering to get to the flatter ground behind it.

Rile downshifted his truck. He pulled off the road as he got closer and eased to a stop. He left his big International idling, set the brakes, and swung down onto the grassy shoulder.

"Anybody hurt?" he called as he walked toward them. There were three men, in suits. Not from around here, Rile could see.

"Nah, we're all right," one of the men answered. "Can you get us out?"

Rile looked things over from a few yards away. The ground was level enough to back the truck close to the car. He walked down to it. Its front end was pretty well down the bank. It was a Buick.

"Skidded on that damned gravel," the same man

said, moving closer to Rile.

Nope, these men were definitely not from around here, Rile decided for the second time. The man who did all the talking had a funny accent. It wasn't foreign, but he talked with a sneer. From Chicago — tough guys from Chicago. The man smelled of alcohol too. Hoodlums ... bootleggers.

"I've got a tow chain in the back of the truck," Rile answered. "Well give it a try." He decided not to ask questions. He went back to his truck.

The tow chain was in a toolbox welded to the running board, on the passenger side. Rile snaked it out onto the ground. He closed the toolbox lid and hooked one end to the tow bar of the truck, then began dragging the rest of the heavy chain toward the car. None of the men offered to help. Two of them were standing near the car, cigarettes in their mouths, watching Rile work. The third, the one who had talked to Rile, had walked off a ways to urinate. He was holding onto his hat with one hand, to keep the spring wind from blowing it off.

Rile knelt down and hooked the end of the chain around the rear axle of the big car.

"I'll move the truck so I can pull her straight out," Rile said. One of the two men nodded.

Rile climbed up into the cab of his truck and maneuvered the big vehicle so the back was toward the car. The man who had walked off came over, still buttoning his fly.

"After I get the chain taut you'll need to push on the car to take some of the strain off. You'll want to steer your car too, through the window. We got to keep the front wheels straight so they'll roll, and not drag," Rile told him.

"Gotcha," the man said, but didn't move toward the car. He gestured with a sideways wave of his head to the other two men. They dropped their cigarettes and got ready. One of them reached into the open win-

dow to hold the steering wheel.

"I'll direct you,' the man beside the truck said.

Rile shifted the truck into low and let it gradually take up the slack in the chain. He felt the engine strain slightly when the chain stiffened out.

"Tell them to push," Rile called to the man, above the noise of the engine.

The man gestured to the men. Rile eased the truck forward. The car followed up and out of the ditch. It was far enough up on the shoulder to back the rest of the way out under its own power, so Rile stopped and motioned to the man.

But when the man in charge tried the starter, there was just a click. The motor didn't even turn over.

"Look, there's a garage about three-quarters of a mile from here. I'll get you turned around so I can tow you there," Rile offered. The man in charge nodded.

After some re-hitching and maneuvering, Rile got the car facing east, toward Token Creek. He pulled the truck around in front of the car and attached the chain to the front axle.

"I'll ride with you," the man told Rile. "Mink, you steer the car," he called to the two men.

"Be ready to brake if I slow down," Rile told the man named Mink. "I'll wave with my arm if you need to get ready." Rile didn't want him plowing into the back end of the truck.

When everybody was ready, they started out. Rile was eventually able to shift up to second but he kept his speed down.

While they were moving along, the man asked if there was a local sheriff or constable. Rile wasn't sure why the man would ask such a question, or if he should answer it, so he just shrugged.

"Just curious," the man said. "I thought I might have to report the accident, that's all."

Rile told him it wasn't necessary. There had been nobody hurt, and no damage that he could be see, except the car wouldn't start. Just a wire pulled loose or something. It couldn't be much. Besides, they didn't have a constable. There was a part-time sheriff up in DeForest. There wasn't much need of a sheriff or a constable around here. The man said he could understand that.

When they pulled up in front of the Token Creek

garage, Ruben Rodefeld came out, wiping his hands with a rag. Rile did the talking. Ruben went back into the Garage and got a flashlight. He looked under the hood for a minute.

Then he lay down on his back and pulled himself under the front end of the car.

"Starter cable's yanked loose," he said from underneath.

Rile knew it wouldn't take long to fix that. He explained things to the man from Chicago while Ruben was getting out from under the car.

"Probably got pulled when you bottomed out," Ruben said. "I'll get her back together in two shakes of a lamb's tail."

The man laughed when he heard the expression.

"We're headed for the Dells," he said.

"You'll need to drive back to 51 and head north," Rile told him, pointing back down the road they had just come in on. "West from here, then turn right," Rile continued. He wasn't going to ask why they'd gotten off the highway in the first place, even if these kind of people being in the area didn't make sense.

Ruben came out of the garage with some tools. He slid himself under the car again. After five minutes of grunting and mumbling, he climbed out.

"See if she'll start now," Ruben told the man in charge.

The car turned over and started easily. The man drove the car over to the gas pump and got out.

"We'll take a fill-up too," he said.

Ruben cranked the pump and began gassing the car. The man in charge walked back over to Rile, who had gathered up the tow chain and was laying it back in the toolbox on the truck.

"What do you get for the tow job?" the man asked.

"That's all right. The county expects me to give people a hand if they have trouble," Rile answered.

The man seemed surprised.

"I didn't get your name," he said to Rile.

"Rile."

"Rile what?"

"Rile Armstrong."

"My name's Carney. You live around here, Rile?"

"Up the road a couple of miles." He indicted the Windsor Road, running north from the nearby intersection.

"What's a couple of miles? Two, three?"

"Just a little over two."

"They pay you okay, Rile?"

Rile shrugged. He didn't want to talk to this character if he could avoid it. He wasn't doing very well at it, he thought to himself. The man was persistent, and stood waiting for a response.

"You handle that truck well. Been doing it long?"

"Couple, three years." This guy was pushy.

"What do they pay you? Fifty, sixty a month?"

"Something like that."

"Look, Rile. Here's twenty bucks. Take it and don't say no. You did us a service. Here, c'mon. Take it."

Rile took the bill and nodded his thanks.

"Appreciate it," mumbled Rile. He nodded to the other two men, who were standing close by, watching the transaction. They moved their heads slightly, acknowledging Rile's gesture.

The man joined the other two by the car. He asked Ruben the charges, for the repair and the gasoline. Ruben told him and the man pulled out more bills from his pocket.

"Keep the change," he said to Ruben, and Ruben thanked him.

As Rile turned his truck out of the Token Creek Garage's lot, he looked in the side mirror. He saw the men climbing into their car.

"Goons," he said, out loud.

A week and a half later, Rile was dumping gravel for a culvert repair south of Token Creek when he saw the big Buick coming. When the car eased up behind, Rile saw that the man named Carney was riding in the front seat. The driver was one of the men who had been with Carney when Rile had helped them. There was also a man in the back seat, but Rile couldn't see his face.

Carney waved to Rile when he got out of the car. "Hey, Rile. How're you doing?" he called.

Rile nodded to him and raised his hand, indicating to wait a minute. He was raising the truck bed and gravel had begun to flow out. The man named Carney grinned and stood watching. When Rile had finished and lowered the bed, he went up to the truck and turned off the engine. He walked back to find out what Carney wanted

"Betcha didn't think you'd see me again, right?" Carney said, extending his hand.

"No, I guess not," Rile answered. He reluctantly took the man's hand.

"Look, Rile. I told my boss what happened the week before last. I told him you helped us out. He wants to meet you. Come on over to the car and say hello. His name's Mr. Brozzo. That's what people call him, Mr. Brozzo. No nicknames."

Rile didn't guess he had the option of refusing. He followed Carney toward the black car. Carney opened the back door for him.

"Go ahead, Bud. Jump in," Carney told him.

"I'm a little dirty," Rile said.

"No problem. Just slide in," said the man in the back seat. His voice sounded like Carney's, a little hoarse. Carney was already getting in the front of the car. Rile edged in beside the boss, Mr. Brozzo.

Carney made the introductions.

"Mr. Brozzo. This is the guy I was telling you about. His name's Rile Armstrong. He knows how to handle a truck. He got us out of trouble."

Rile nodded to Mr. Brozzo, who held out his hand.

Rile took it. Mr. Brozzo had a pockmarked face.

"So Rile. You helped out my man Carney, here."

"I gave him a tow — part of my job."

"Carney said he gave you twenty bucks for helping him, and you didn't even want to take it."

"That's right," said Rile. He wondered if they had come to get the money back.

The boss reached forward with his hand out. Carney handed back two twenty dollar bills. Mr. Brozzo took it, and held it out to Rile.

"For what you did; I don't think Carney paid you enough. He should have given you this much."

"No, now. That's all right. I didn't expect anything. This is too much money. I'm supposed to give people a hand. It's part of the job." Rile held up his hands in a gesture of refusal. Mr. Brozzo frowned.

"Take it, Rile. You helped us out — you get paid," Carney said. "I should have given you more right away."

Rile wasn't sure what to do. He was still holding his hands up in front of himself, still refusing. He glanced at the unpleasant-looking man beside him, then looked down. Rile lowered his hands. Quite abruptly, the man began talking.

"What I'm telling you, Rile, is that you can earn this much every month, plus what Carney gave you the other day. You can make sixty bucks cash, just to help us out again, and only once a month. Here's the deal: we need a good truck driver like you once in a while. The sort of man who knows how to move trucks without having an accident. We need somebody to drive a truck for a few miles, no more than a day's work, and on Saturday."

Rile looked at the man, but didn't respond.

"What you'd do is pick up a truck in a town a little ways from here, Beloit say, and take it up to the Dells. Easy enough. How far would you say that was?"

"That's quite a drive," Rile mumbled.

"How far?" Mr. Brozzo asked again.

"Maybe a hundred miles."

"Not so far, after all." Mr. Brozzo said. "What you do is pick up a truck, drive it for a ways, then drop it off. We pay your salary of sixty bucks, for one trip a month, plus expenses. Easiest thing in the world, and once a month, no more. You take the train to Beloit, get the truck, drive it to the Dells, then take the train home from there. Twelve, fourteen hours at the most, from start to finish. We've worked it out. Good pay for good work."

"What's in the truck?" Rile wanted to know.

Carney now spoke:

"C'mon Rile. You figure it out. This is Prohibition. Just a little joy for the folks up north."

Rile was looking for a way to put them off, and to get out of there.

"I ought to ask my wife first. See what she says."

"What's the little woman's name, Rile?" Mr. Brozzo asked. His voice was softer than a moment ago. He laid a hand on Rile's shoulder.

"Leah."

The boss studied Rile for a few seconds, smiling very slightly.

"I think that's the right thing to do, Rile — be careful and get some advice. I like that. I talk to my wife when I have to decide on a new deal. Nice name, Leah."

Rile acknowledged the compliment, if it was one.

"We just need to know before the end of the month," Mr. Brozzo added.

"Sure hope it's in the affirmative," said Carney. His tone too was more friendly.

"Anyway, I want you to keep this money," said Mr. Brozzo. He held the bills practically under Rile's nose. "We owe you."

Rile saw himself slowly extend a hand and take it. Mr. Brozzo smiled. Carney got out of the car. He opened the door for Rile.

"Thanks," said Rile to the boss.

"Well stop around the end of next week, when we come back through," Carney said to Rile as he got out of the back seat. "We'll see what you want to do."

Rile began to walk toward his truck. Carney was walking with him.

"Once a month. It's a good deal," Carney said.

"I suppose," Rile conceded.

The driver of the car tapped the horn. Rile and Carney turned around.

The driver motioned for Carney to come back. He pointed to the back seat with his thumb.

"Wait a minute," Carney told Rile. Rile waited.

Carney walked to the car and leaned in the back window. Mr. Brozzo said something to him. Carney nodded his head, then walked back to Rile.

"The boss would just as soon you not tell anybody about our offer, except your wife, naturally. And, ask her to keep it under her hat too. Okay? Keep it between us, so to speak."

"All right," Rile told him.

Carney returned to the car and got in the front seat. The driver started the car and backed it up nearly off the road. He then swung around and headed back the way they had come. Rile stood watching for a few minutes, then got in the truck and rumbled off.

Rile drove slowly toward the County garage, thinking. The fact was that he made fifty-five dollars a month. They got by, but things were always tight.

Another sixty dollars a month would more than double their income. If they stuck with it for a while, they could think about some improvements to the house, like a real bathroom, and a better furnace. Leah would like a new washing machine. He could do something for little Emma, too. She was really smart. Why, she had walked when she was only ten months old. And here she was talking a blue streak, and not even a year and a half old.

Leah said she was almost trained too.

Still, he didn't like the idea of getting involved with these birds. They were tough guys. How long was this Prohibition going to go on anyway? And that driver — he looked like he would just as soon shoot you as look at you. Rile doubted Leah would go along with it. Maybe he should ask August his opinion.

No, he'd better not. They told him not to bring anybody else in on it.

Rile was right about Leah's opinion. She acknowledged that they sure could use that kind of money, but when she understood what Rile would be doing, she said she hoped he wouldn't. It didn't sound at all safe. What if he got stopped and arrested? He'd lose his job, and then they'd really be up the creek.

Then she decided to tell him her secret. He would notice pretty soon anyway, because it had happened two months ago: there was another one on the way. Rile was pleased, but after a while, he started thinking about a new baby meaning more expenses, so he told her he had an idea. Suppose he did it for a few months, until say, the new baby was born. Then he'd give it up. They could get ahead some, with the extra money coming in. Let's say he'd give it a year, then quit. That would be enough, he thought. Leah wanted to sleep on it.

In the morning she still wasn't sure. She wanted Rile to decide — he knew more about it than she did. He had seen the men. Maybe it would be safe. Rile said the men would be back in a week or so. He'd get some more information before he'd commit himself one way or the other. He'd find out if it was safe, and if he was at all likely to get caught.

The Thursday of the following week, late in the day after little Emma had been put to bed, Rile and Leah were sitting on their front steps when a car rolled down their driveway. It was the big Buick. Rile stood up and looked at Leah. She got up and walked onto the porch and sat down on a chair. The man Carney wasn't in the front seat, but the driver was the same. Rile couldn't see if there was anyone in the back seat until the car stopped. Then he saw that Mr. Brozzo was there all right. Rile walked over to the car. Rile asked the two men if they wanted some coffee or a drink of water. Mr. Brozzo said he was fine.

"But my man here sure would like to use your outhouse."

"Sure. It's around the back," Rile said to the driver. The man got out and walked toward the back yard. He looked at Leah as he passed the porch.

Mr. Brozzo leaned over and pushed open the rear door of the car behind the driver's side. He beckoned Rile to get in. Rile got in.

Had Rile thought over the offer? He had — he had some questions. Sure, shoot. He was worried about getting caught. Not likely — the loads would be disguised very well. The beer and whiskey would be loaded on first; then they'd stack four or five rows of canned goods behind them, right to the back of the truck, and right up to the ceiling. Everything would be tied down. If Rile got stopped, they'd have to unload almost the whole truck to find anything. Also, there'd be a different truck every trip, and he would have a different route each time. There wouldn't be any trouble from the cops in Beloit, nor up in the Dells.

That part was all taken care of. If one of the local sheriffs in between was smart enough to think the truck was carrying booze, he'd be very surprised. They looked like a pretty limited bunch to him. Besides, he'd been doing this for a while and had looked things over pretty well. It was okay.

How would he get paid? The money and instructions would be mailed to him before he went to Beloit. Where in Beloit would he have to go? If Rile accepted, then they'd tell him. It would always be the same place unless they told him different. The same held for the

Dells. He'd go to a certain garage and that would be that. He would then just take the train home. They'd send him a map every time. Everything would be written down — train schedules, addresses, the roads to take, directions, what to say if he was stopped, everything.

Rile sat thinking. He looked forward and out of the front window of the car and saw Leah sitting on the porch, watching the car. She probably couldn't see his face, there in the dark interior.

Was it the money, Mr. Brozzo asked. That wasn't it. He was scared. He and his wife were scared. It sounded too dangerous.

"Look, Rile. I think you're the man for the job, somebody who's careful and uses his head. That's what we need, somebody who won't rush and do something foolish. Tell you what, Ill make it seventy a trip, plus expenses. That's my final offer. Seventy plus train fare and gas money, even a little for lunch. That means I'm putting way over a hundred into this little deal, just to get you. It's once a month, payment in advance. I'd say that's not bad. Can you afford to say no?"

Rile wanted to talk to his wife again. Sure, go ahead. Take your time.

Mr. Brozzo looked through the car window toward Leah, sitting on the porch. She was clearly anxious.

"That her there?"

"Yes."

"A good-looking blonde," he said, and broke into a smile.

As Rile got out of the car, the driver came back around the house. He nodded to Rile.

Leah was equivocal. "I don't know, Rile. That man looks like a bad one," she whispered. She was referring to the driver. "These aren't very nice people."

"I'll tell him it's only until next summer, just until we get on our feet."

"It's just once a month, isn't that right?" she asked

again.

"I'll make sure."

Rile went back to the car. He told Mr. Brozzo until next summer. It was a deal. And no more than once a month? Once a month was all they needed; that was plenty. Rile said all right then, he'd do it. Mr. Brozzo shook his hand. The driver turned around and said, "Hey, nice going, Bud."

What else then?, Rile asked. Mr. Brozzo tapped the driver on the shoulder and held out his hand. The man produced a large envelope and handed it back. Mr. Brozzo in turn handed it to Rile.

"Open it," he said to Rile.

Rile opened it. Just as Mr. Brozzo said, everything was written down. In fact, it was typed. Rile found a hundred dollars in twenties. Salary plus expenses, Mr. Brozzo pointed out. There were train schedules from the Windsor station, maps. It was very thorough. The instructions indicated he would be going the weekend after next.

"Okay," said Rile, after looking everything over. "I can handle this."

"I know you can Rile. We'll be in touch with you. You'll hear from us once a month, in plenty of time to know what to do. You can figure on the second Saturday of the month, unless you hear otherwise. You have any problems or questions, tell the people in the Dells. You'll see. It'll work very nice."

Rile thanked him and started getting out of the car.

"You know. I think I will take that glass of water," Mr. Brozzo said to him.

"Sure," said Rile. He went to the house to pump the water. He looked at Leah as he walked up the steps.

"Just until next summer." he said to her as he walked past. She looked away.

Rile brought the glass of water to the car. Mr. Brozzo reached out the window and took it.

"Tasted good," he said when he handed back the empty glass.

The driver started the car. Then Rile remembered something he had intended to ask.

"I forgot. Where's Carney?"

"He up and went to work for somebody else," Mr. Brozzo answered.

Rile watched the Buick roll down the driveway. He wondered why Carney had decided to jump ship.

* * *

The system did work. On the second Saturday of that same May month, Rile caught the four-thirty morning train from Windsor. He arrived in Beloit at nine o'clock on the dot. He went to an address within walking distance of the train station, picked up the truck, and made it to the Dells in a little over four hours. He had followed the driving directions carefully: 81 west out of Beloit, through Monroe to 78 at a little crossroads called Argyle, then 78 north up to 12 and Sauk City. Rile wondered if the route was chosen to keep him away from Madison. It was all country driving. He stopped once, for gas, in Sauk City, right after he crossed the river. He took 12 into the Dells. When he got there and found the garage, they were waiting for him. They took the truck from there.

The garage man in charge drove him to the train station. He asked Rile a couple of questions and seemed satisfied with the answers. Before Rile knew it, he was on the five o'clock train out of the Dells.

Leah and Emma met him at the Windsor station and he was home by a quarter after eight, right at sunset. A long day, but he had made more in that one day than he would all month. He was pleased and Leah seemed relieved that it had been so easy. He had been on edge during the whole trip, he told her, from the time he had left home (she said she had noticed), but nothing out of the ordinary happened. Rile said he would take a lunch pail along next time so he could eat in the truck. There was no sense spending money on restaurant food on the road.

The following week Leah drove Rile to work at the Highway Department garage so she could have the car. She needed to drive to the DeForest bank to open two savings accounts — one for Rile and herself, the other in the name of Emma Armstrong. When the new baby arrived, he or she would have an account, too. After the next trip, they would think about something for Leah.

The second trip turned out to be like the first, easy and uneventful. A package with the directions and money inside had appeared in Rile and Leah's mailbox at the beginning of June, two weeks before Rile was to leave. The directions were clear and precise. On the day of the trip, the trains were on time and the weather was good. Things went off without a hitch. Good money for a good day's work.

The directions for the third trip contained a change in his route. Rile was to take 51 to Madison, then 51 from there to pick up Highway 12. He was a little surprised that they didn't keep him to the back roads as they had for the first two times, but he guessed they knew what they were doing. Besides, there was nothing unusual about seeing trucks on the road, so he stopped thinking about it and started planning for the new bathroom he was excited about. Taking 51 brought him within 10 miles of home. He almost took a side trip there for lunch but decided it wouldn't be a good idea if people who knew him saw him.

There had also been a note in the third package. It had said: "Keep up the good work, Rile." It was signed "R.B." Rile wondered what the R. stood for.

As the monthly trips continued, the pickup spot in Beloit was altered between the garage that he could walk to from the station and another place, a warehouse that was on the edge of town. A car was waiting for him the first time the change took place. The driver told him that if he wasn't there to meet him when he got in, Rile should go to the original place. Rile actually began to enjoy the trips. The train ride was always a little exciting and he saw the same conductor, who recognized him and said hello after the second trip. The whole thing was kind of thrilling, all in all. In turned out that gas cost Rile less by about five dollars than his advance for expenses. He asked the man in the Dells if he should send back the extra money. "Keep the change," the guy said.

For the sixth trip, the one in October, Rile was instructed to take the original route again. He did. The November route was different yet again, a combination of the one going through Madison and the one farther west, jogging over to Mount Horeb and then north as usual. The November trip was different in another way too: when Rile got off the train at the Beloit station, the Buick driver for Mr. Brozzo was there to meet him, not with the Buick, but with the truck. Rile asked what was up.

"I'm riding shotgun this trip," was the answer he got. The man had a small suitcase with him. Rile asked if he was going to stay over in the Dells.

The man laughed and said, "That's right, Bud," and laughed again.

Rile climbed behind the wheel of the truck and they started out. The man put the suitcase on the seat beside him.

The man hardly talked. He smoked a lot and looked out the window. He even reached out a half dozen times and turned the rear view mirror so he could see behind them. Rile had to ask him to readjust the mirror after each time the man had changed the mirror. As they drove along, the man made an occasional disparaging remark about the empty countryside and all the hicks in it. Rile tried to make conversation.

"What's Mr. Brozzo's first name?" he asked.

"Who wants to know?"

"I do. I got a note from him signed 'R.B.' I was just wondering."

"I think it's Rofelo, but nobody calls him that. Just Mr. Brozzo."

What kind of a name is Rofelo?, Rile wondered. He didn't like it. He tried to talk again, but the man simply ignored him. When they were just outside Madison, he told Rile to pull over so he could urinate. Back in the truck, he smoked a couple more cigarettes, had a coughing fit, then moved the suitcase onto the floor, put his feet over it, and went to sleep. He didn't wake up until Rile stopped for gas, not far from the Dells. He looked around and said he was hungry. They found a restaurant and had a sandwich and coffee, neither man saying another word to each other. Rile had to pay for the food when the man just got up after they had finished eating and walked out of the restaurant. As soon as they were on the road again, the man put his head back and slept some more. He woke up as they pulled into the garage at the Dells.

"Finally I can get a drink," the man said, and jumped out of the truck. He walked over to the straw boss, who was putting on his coat, ready to drive Rile to the train station. The two men spoke for a couple of minutes. Then his rider came back to the truck and took out his suitcase.

"Thanks for the ride, Bud," he said to Rile. He took the suitcase and patted it affectionately. Then he looked at Rile and laughed. On the way to the station, Rile asked the straw boss what was going on.

"Why?"

"I had an escort this trip."

"They heard somebody might try to horn in — try to take over the action."

"So he really was riding shotgun,' Rile said.

"Yup. He sure was."

Rile decided that this was his last trip. He asked the straw boss how he could get in touch with Mr.

Brozzo.

"Through me," was the answer. "You got a problem?"

"I need to talk to him, that's all."

"What about?"

Rile didn't answer. The straw boss waited for a minute. When he saw Rile wasn't going to tell him anything, he said he'd pass the word.

"I'd appreciate it," Rile told him.

When Leah met Rile at the station, she saw he was bothered by something. He told her he was just tired. He had decided not to tell her about the hoodlum who had ridden along with him. She would have been very frightened and wouldn't have let him go the next time. He would tell her after he quit. Maybe he'd never tell her.

By the time a week had passed, Rile began to expect to hear from Mr. Brozzo. He kept a lookout for the big Buick while he was out working with the state truck.

Every evening he expected it to roll down his and Leah's driveway. He started waking up at night, to listen, hoping they might stop by, even if it was late. But Rile neither heard nor saw anything of Mr. Brozzo, or any of his men.

The package came as usual a few days later. The directions and maps for the next trip, plus the money was in it, just as before. Rile looked for a note from Mr. Brozzo but there was none. He looked several times. Rile looked over the directions and the map. He saw that he was to take the route he had taken when he first started. He wanted to send the package back, money and all, but there was no return address, just the Chicago postmark. He would have to make this last trip. He'd tell them at the Dells that he was quitting, like it or not.

The road out of Beloit west to Monroe was gravel in those days. The pavement ended at the Beloit city limits. The road passed though Monroe, where it was the main drag. The five blocks in Monroe were paved, but it reverted to gravel once you were outside of town. This drive west, from Beloit to the Argyle turnoff, was the slowest part of the trip. The road was rough and narrow, and there were a lot of one-lane bridges. Usually there weren't many cars or trucks on the road, especially this time of the year. His trip that day was even slower than usual because a cold drizzle was falling, keeping his speed down. It was dismal and hard to see. He was looking forward to the turnoff onto 78, which was paved all the way to 12 and to Sauk City. Once on 78, he would make better time.

He was about five miles out of Monroe when he noticed headlights in his mirror. In a few minutes the vehicle, which was a car, caught up with him, flashing its lights. Rile slowed down and edged the truck onto the shoulder to let it pass. As it pulled up beside him he saw it was a big car. It was a Packard, not a Buick, but it was probably Mr. Brozzo, Rile thought. He brought the truck to a stop. The car stopped a few feet ahead of him. Rile got out of the truck and started walking toward the car. Three men got out, buttoning their coats. He recognized that the man who got out of the back was Carney, not Mr. Brozzo.

One of the other men looked familiar, but Rile couldn't place him. Rile stopped walking and waited for them to come to him. Carney and the familiar man stopped in front of Rile, the other one just kept on going to Rile's truck.

"Hey, Rile. How're you doing?" Carney asked. "We meet again."

"Hello."

"We'll take her from here," Carney said. His voice was not pleasant.

"What's the matter?" Rile asked, confused.

"Nothing to worry about Rile. We're taking the truck, that's all. Giving you some time off." Carney had the sneer in his voice that Rile remembered.

Rile heard the engine of his truck race. He turned around. They were taking it.

"Got anything in the truck, Rile?"

"My lunch pail," Rile told him.

"Go get it," he was ordered.

Rile went back to the truck. The man now at the wheel handed it down to him. As Rile turned toward Carney and the man with him, he heard the truck start moving. It was being turned around to head back toward Beloit.

"I thought you weren't working for Mr. Brozzo anymore," Rile said.

Carney looked at Rile for a minute.

"I ain't. I work for myself now. These are my guys. I guess you didn't understand — we're taking the truck for ourselves. You remember Mink here, right?" Carney gestured toward his companion who was lighting a cigarette.

Rile nodded. He understood. It looked like he was in for a long walk.

"Now Rile. I don't want you to take this personally, but there's something we need to do," Carney said. The man, Mink, smiled.

Rile stood still. Mink stepped forward and held out his hand.

Rile got out his wallet and handed it over. Mink removed the cash and returned the wallet to Rile. Rile nearly fainted in relief. He had been sure they were going to kill him right there. Mink stepped back and turned toward the car.

But Carney didn't move. He saw something he didn't like.

"Rile, you've pissed all over yourself," Carney growled.

Rile realized he had lost control; he had been so frightened. The whole front and legs of his trousers were soaked. He felt the heat on his shins.

Mink turned around and walked back. He was

annoyed to have been bothered. Mink looked at Rile
and the wet across his front.

"Disgusting," he snarled.

Rile stood facing them, humiliated and becoming
very frightened again. Carney called to Mink.

"Get off the road," Mink said to Rile with a jerk of
his head toward the shoulder. Rile stepped off the road.

"Farther," Carney said, to Mink, not to Rile.

Mink made the same gesture to Rile. Rile moved
down toward the water-filled ditch. He stopped near
the side, very close to the cold water. He looked up at
the two men on the road.

Mink began shooting while Rile was standing there,
facing upwards. As the last shot slammed into him,
Rile slumped down and slid on the wet, brown grass,
part way into the shallow water of the ditch. Mink let
himself down the embankment and shoved Rile the rest
of the way in, with his foot.

It wasn't until the following Tuesday that a passing road crew found Rile's body. One of the crew had
spotted the lunch pail on the side of the road and went
down to pick it up. While he was looking at the lunch
pail, he noticed the partially submerged corpse. Long
before that, Leah had become so frantic that she had
gone to the police in Madison and reported her missing
husband. The police started contacting other police
departments in the counties through which Rile might
have passed on his way to the Dells. The Green County
police telephoned to report the body, which had been
identified from the wallet. They figured it was a
highjacking. He had been shot a half-dozen times in
the chest and stomach.

* * *

Leah rode with August and Melodie to the cemetery. It was a clear day, but cold. In the car, on the
way, she began to feel contractions. She didn't tell August and Melodie — she wanted to stay. They were
lowering Rile's coffin into the frozen bleakness when

she had to ask for help. August and Melodie walked her to the car and drove to the store. August telephoned Doc Drake, who told him he would be there as fast as he could. They drove to August and Melodie's house, where Leah and Emma had been staying since Rile had been killed.

The baby was born in the early afternoon. It was a boy. He seemed healthy, but Leah was not doing well. She was so despondent that she had to be coaxed to nurse. Once she started though, she seemed to gather some energy and perk up. She named the baby Rile Junior.

By the end of the week, ice was forming on the Mill Pond. There was a light snow on the ground. Leah and the two children were still staying with August and Melodie. The baby was quiet and didn't cry at all. It just made little noises when it was hungry. Doc Drake came by to check it, and to talk to Leah.

He told her the baby was doing fine; it was very healthy. He told her she had her hands full now, but she had plenty of support.

Emma hung around Leah and the baby a lot, watching him and asking to help. She told Leah she wanted to change his diapers every day. At supper one evening, Emma asked after her father. They told her that he'd be gone for a good while. Emma accepted that. She didn't ask again.

The next day August told Melodie he thought Leah might pull out of it. Melodie agreed — Leah was up early that morning, for the first time since she had learned Rile had died. She had even come out into the kitchen and helped. Leah had asked if Melodie would mind watching the children later, so she could go up to her house.

Late in the morning, after Leah had finished nursing the baby until he fell asleep, she said goodbye to Emma. She was going to drive up to the house, she said. She'd be gone for a good while.

"I can drive you, if you aren't up to it," Melodie offered.

"I'll manage, thanks," Leah said. She put on her coat.

"Don't rush, Leah. There's plenty of time to move back." Melodie felt that Leah's going up to the house might be all right, if it helped her. But she was welcome to stay with them as long as she had to.

Leah hugged her hard and left.

They found Leah near the dam, under the ice. She had drifted down there from the upper end of the pond, where she had gone in, up where the Creek flowed in and there was still open water. They could see her through the new ice.

Her arms were spread, and her hair was fanned out, waving in the slight current. Even though there was ice over her, it was fairly thin — it hadn't been cold for very long. They were able to cut through without too much trouble, and pull her out. Almost everyone was there to watch.

When August got back home from the Mill Pond, he found Melodie feeding the baby with a bottle. Emma was sitting at Melodie's feet, on the floor, playing with some old hats. She had one of them on.

"He didn't fuss at all when I gave him a bottle,' Melodie whispered, looking at August.

Emma paused in her game, listening to the two adults.

August nodded gently. He took out his handkerchief and carefully dabbed Melodie's face.

"You're getting him wet," he said. His voice was soft.

"Sorry."

"They'll be easy,' he said.

He stood for another moment, then sat down on the floor, beside Emma and at Melodie's feet. Emma handed him a hat and waited. Melodie reached down with her free hand and helped him put it on.

Sledding

The Burke Road changed its name when it reached the country trunk at Token Creek. On the north side, after it crossed, it became the Windsor Road.

This Windsor Road was not a wide road. Even in summer, wagons or cars could pass each other only if right wheels were edged onto a shoulder. In winter, with the heavy snows, the Windsor Road was reduced to a narrow, single lane, in places where highway crews ran out of space to push snow, as they tried to keep a route open. You found these snow-cliffed bottlenecks on open hillsides, like the one just above and north of Token Creek. In such areas, constant drifting added so much more to snow already fallen or falling that, as winter progressed, there was less and less room for the plows to push it aside.

Drivers did their best under such conditions. People drove slowly. If two vehicles appeared unexpectedly in front of one another, inside one of the narrow, hill passages, the drivers both came to a quick stop. One would then back his machine to a wider area to allow the other to pass. Or, he reversed into a nearby farm lane — into the school house driveway, if the travelers happened to meet near the Token Creek school, which was part way up the Windsor Road hill. The cemetery entrance was also used, if there had been a reason to plow it open.

Still, there were occasional mishaps, on the order of bumper knockings or minor jolts, before there was time to stop. These little accidents couldn't be said to be the fault of one or the other driver — you just couldn't see far enough ahead to avoid them. In bad weather, nobody could be expected to know what was coming around one of those blind curves. In recent memory, fortunately, there had been no incidents where lasting injuries had been suffered.

The Windsor Road hill outside Token Creek was a popular sledding hill. A sled works poorly in winter fields or pastures where the snow is deep and soft. Thin sled runners need a firm surface, solid enough for speed. Sledders looked for hillside roads where traffic had packed the accumulating layers of unrelenting white into hard, parallel tracks. If you lived around or in Token Creek, you went sledding on the Windsor Road hill.

A system had been worked out for keeping traffic from starting up the hill when sledders were on their way down. An adult remained by the stone bridge at the foot of the hill while the youngsters walked up.

When the group reached the top and was ready to start down, one of the children waved a red handkerchief at the guard by the bridge. He or she would then stop the occasional automobile or truck, or even a horse and sleigh if one was out, and hold them until the kids came down. It took sledders only a few minutes to reach the bottom, so no traveler ever waited too long. The last sled down sported the red flag, indicating the road was now clear. When the red flag arrived, a driver could move up the hill without fear of meeting a descending sled.

Because of the length of the hill, nearly half a mile, a typical day's sledding consisted of not many more than a handful of trips from the crest to the bridge.

With considerably more time spent trekking up than sliding down, a passing glance at sledding activity out on the Windsor Road on a winter weekend, or on a holiday, would have shown a patient adult or two waiting at the bridge, plus a group of children in the process of slowly hauling their Flexible Flyers up the long slope. The relatively short time taken for gleefully skidding downward, compared to the long time traipsing and dragging upward was a topic of discussion one Sunday afternoon in a frigid January.

"There should be a way to get back up the hill faster," complained August Armstrong, the oldest of the three. He and his two companions, Karl Armstrong and LeRoy Armstrong (who was actually his second cousin) had been out sledding on the Windsor Road since early afternoon, but three hours later they were dragging their way up for only a sixth run.

"I'll bet we could get Dad to pull us up with one of the horses," eleven-year-old Karl declared. "He told me that's what his dad did, when he was a kid."

"After we come down again, would you ask him?" Second Cousin LeRoy wanted to know. William Armstrong, Karl's father and August's half-brother, was the guard at the bridge that day.

It was four o'clock and getting close to getting dark

when the three boys, ruddy-faced from the cold, walked toward the Token Creek store to warm up. William Armstrong was with them. The day's sledding was over.

"Did Grandpa George really used to pull your sleds up the hill with a horse?" August asked.

That was right, William said. He remembered his father bringing out one or another of the workhorses, to give him and his friends a pull from the bridge up to the top of the Windsor Road hill. It gave them a lot more turns sledding down the hill. His father said it was good for the horses, too. It gave them exercise during the inactive winter months.

The boys asked William if he would do it for them. He said he was willing to give it a try. It seemed safe enough. The boys cheered and became very excited and animated.

When they arrived at the store, they headed for the wood stove, peeling off coats and gloves as they did. There were quite a few people in the store, not buying anything much, but talking and hanging around. Brother Bob always served up hot chocolate for the sledding parties, so people usually stayed around for a while after they had come in. Second Cousin LeRoy's father, Vernon Armstrong, was sitting next to the heat, waiting to fetch his son. Vernon asked how the sledding had been as the boys rushed to the stove.

"Dad says he's going to get out one of the horses to tow us up. We're going to do it next Saturday!" Karl said.

"When we have the horse pulling us up, we can slide down a lot more times," Second Cousin LeRoy told everyone.

There followed quite a bit of discussion about winters past, when horses had often been used to tow trains of sleds. Most who grew up in the area remembered horses being out and busy on sledding days. Vernon, who didn't own a horse anymore, but kept a Model T, suggested a car might be just as good as a horse for pulling up sleds, maybe even better.

"With a car, we wouldn't have to worry about being pulled over the top of any mess left behind," August quipped.

The group laughed. He did have a point, though. In any event, whether a car or horse was doing the towing, they could use the same system for signaling.

They could tie the sleds in a train, pull them up, then let them take off. The car or horse driver could bring down the red flag.

"We sure will be able to do a lot more runs," Karl said.

"Well, I don't mind using my horse," William told them. "Besides, horses don't get stuck in the snow."

"I doubt the Ford would have a problem with chains on," his Cousin Vernon answered.

"Why don't we try both?" asked Karl, by way of suggestion.

This was sensible. Of course, it was just as likely one or the other would do the job. William said that next weekend he could bring down one of his team, hitched to his sleigh, unless the weather was bad. Cousin Vernon said he would drive down with the Model T, depending on the weather. It was a good compromise, and it sounded like it would be fun to see which was better, car or horse.

The following Saturday was bright and gusty. You had to squint to look into the fields, with the sunlight reflecting off the snow. The temperature hovered right around twenty-five; not bad. The wind was a nuisance though, on and off bringing bursts of powdery snow across paths that had been cleared, and making you turn your head away when a sudden gust hit.

People had heard about William and Vernon's sled pulling. The event had the makings of a contest, so when William, August, and Karl arrived at the store, in a sleigh pulled by one of William's big Percherons, a dozen onlookers came outside to inspect the rig, and to admire the muscular dapple gray.

Cousin Vernon arrived a few minutes later in his Ford. His son LeRoy was riding in the rumble seat. The boy waved at the welcoming crowd. Vernon had fitted chains onto the rear wheels of his car, giving it excellent traction on the snow-covered roads. When Vernon chugged up to the store, the noisy engine caused William's horse to shy. The big animal began high stepping sideways, trying to get away from the rattling machine. It would have turned over the sleigh had William not been able to grab the bridle and calm the high-strung beast while Vernon turned off the car's nasal popping.

With the horse settled, they discussed their project. There were seven children and four sleds. Either the horse and sleigh or the car could take everyone in one load. They also had to consider the horse's fear of the car's noise. The arrangements decided on were that Vernon would remain at the store while William tied the sleds to the back of the open sleigh, then set off for the stone bridge and up the hill. When William was well on his way, Vernon would start his car and drive down to the bridge. He'd wait there until he saw the signal from the top; then he would hold traffic until the sleds arrived, and of course the sleigh that followed, with the red flag. When William reached the bridge, he'd keep right on going to the store. That would get the horse away from the car, so when Vernon started it and left with the sleds, the animal wouldn't act up again. When he saw Vernon leave with the sleds, William would go down to the bridge and wait for the signal to stop traffic. They would alternate like that until everyone had had enough.

The first group left in a flurry of hand waving and cheers from the bystanders and participants. Since there were more sledders than sleds and William didn't want too big a load behind the sleigh, three of the children rode in the sleigh. Four rode behind, each on a sled, steering with their feet. William asked the passengers in his sleigh to keep a careful lookout behind, in case the trailing riders had difficulty keeping their little train from fishtailing. William decided to walk the horse; he didn't want to cause any accidents.

Even with the horse only walking, the caravan reached the top of the hill in what seemed like so little time compared to before. Everyone knew there would be a lot of sledding that day.

The first round went off without a hitch — the sledders raced down, William followed with the horse and empty sleigh, this time at a canter speed, and the flag was passed. When William had driven out of range of the loud engine, Vernon began tying the sleds to the Model T, then cranked up and set out, up the Windsor Road hill. Like William, he asked those who rode with him to keep a sharp eye behind for trouble. Unlike William, however, the Model T went faster than William had allowed the horse to move. It went so much faster, in fact, that Karl Armstrong, who was in the sled directly behind the car, started waving his arms. Vernon stopped to see what was the matter. Karl explained that the chained wheels of the car were throwing up chunks of hard snow that were flying back on him and his friends. Vernon said he couldn't run the engine any slower, or it would stall. They decided that the best solution was to have the sledders change positions on the sleds, lying on their stomachs instead of sitting up. By riding like that, most of the chunks of snow would fly over them, or hit them on their backs, rather than in their faces. By lying on their sleds rather than sitting on them, the children's heads were at a level below the rear bumper of the high-backed Ford.

They started out again. The change did seem to help some. A few pieces of packed snow dropped on their backs, but the group accepted the annoyance as part of the game, and the party glided up the hill behind Vernon's banging Model T.

As Vernon's car and the sled train entered the narrowed part of the road that curved between the highest mounds of blowing snow, a heavy milk truck from the DeForest Dairy started down the long hill, toward Token Creek. The truck and Vernon's Model T met in the blind curve. Vernon didn't see the truck coming down, nor did the milk truck driver see the car coming up the road, until the two were no more than a few feet apart. Both drivers braked strongly to avoid a collision, but both vehicles were still moving when they hit each other.

The heavier truck not only halted the forward motion of the lighter car, but it jolted it hard backward for a good yard before both car and truck came to a dead stop.

It appears that it was this backward motion of the car that killed Karl Armstrong. The momentum of the boy's smoothly gliding sled plus the force of the three sleds hitting him from behind carried Karl beneath the rear bumper of the Ford, slamming his head against the Model T's large differential housing.

When the car lurched backwards from being hit by the truck, Karl's head was forced under the differential. His skull was crushed by the weight of the car.

Vernon and the truck driver frantically jacked up the rear of the car to free Karl. The boy was limp and lifeless when they pulled him out. As quickly as they could, they loaded him into the Model T. Vernon couldn't turn the car around, so he got everyone in front of his car and he began backing down the hill. He turned around in the school house driveway, then drove at nearly full throttle down toward the bridge.

The group at the bottom realized that something was wrong when they saw the Model T descending rapidly. Vernon stopped at the bridge. William reached the car first and saw his son sprawled motionless over the front seat.

Vernon tried to tell William what had happened. William waved him quiet. They had to get him to Doc Drake in DeForest.

"Tell me on the way," William said as he climbed into the car and gathered the unconscious boy onto his lap. They roared off, past the rearing horse and the shocked crowd.

An hour later, Doctor Drake pronounced Karl dead of multiple skull fractures and profuse cerebral hemorrhage.

* * *

A thick snow was falling as the funeral procession left the Token Creek Church. It had been snowing since before dawn. The wind was straight out of the north, and biting. You would have thought it was too cold to snow, but it did anyway.

After the graveside service, after the other family members and the mourners had left, William and his wife Kate still stayed on, with August, and William's sister Mabel, just sitting in the car, not able to leave. The minister came over and stood outside their closed car window for a few minutes, staring. He wanted to say something but he didn't, or couldn't. Finally he walked to his own car, started it, and drove off.

They watched as the grave was filled in. The men worked fast — wanting to be done and out of the cold wind and snow.

After a while Kate said, "It's getting cold, Will."

He nodded. The men were pretty much finished filling the little grave.

William opened his car door and went around to the front to crank the engine. It started with difficulty.

William drove out of the cemetery and turned south down the hill. They had traveled only a few yards when William saw another car coming up the road from Token Creek. William stopped, and reversed back into the cemetery entrance. They waited there until the other car had passed by.

The Token Creek
Land Company

On a freezing, dour, snow-blown Thursday afternoon in an early February, in the winter
later remembered as the bad winter, a well-dressed
young couple, she complete with an impressive fur hat
and black gloves, he in a vested, dark wool suit, his
handsome face topped off with a well-trimmed mus-
tache, drove a newish Packard slowly between the high
walls of plowed snow lining the road through Token
Creek. Seeing a Mobilgas sign rising out of the raging
flurries and great mountains of graded snow, the man
eased up to the pumps of the Token Creek Garage. From
inside, Ruben Rodefeld made out the big car through
the haze of his frost-glazed front window. He set aside
the carburetor he was rebuilding, bundled himself in
his thick coat, laced his heavy boots, lowered his ear
flaps, adjusted his gloves, and trudged out to wait on
his customers. When Ruben came to the car, the man
got out, pulling himself into a long coat as he did. He
also put on a scarf, a big hat, and black leather gloves.
He asked for a fill-up of high test. As the mechanic
pumped the gas, the gentleman pointed out that it sure
was drifting and hard to see.

"You ought to have chains on these roads," answered Ruben.

"We have these new kind of tires. They're called snow tires," the man pointed out. "They're sure selling in Chicago. They're real good in snow, and you can drive them on pavement without doing any damage. They say they're good in mud, too."

Ruben had a look; like little tractor tires, only for a car. Funny-looking things. All the same, they seemed to be getting the man's Packard where he wanted it to go. He had heard about these mud and snow tires from the Goodyear representative. He and his partner hadn't ordered any as yet, though.

Maybe they would. But chains were what people were used to. All the same, these tires might be a good idea; not having to put them on and take them off like you did chains.

The gentleman with the Packard kept talking about the wild weather and all the snow. Ruben said that Wisconsin did have its winters, and of course as soon as it stopped snowing, it got so cold you could hardly step outdoors.

The man walked inside the station with Ruben to pay for the gas. He found the office area and counter orderly. While Ruben was ringing up, the gentleman took note that the garage was well painted and clean. The flying red horse sign looked new. There were two cars in the bays for repairs, with someone working under one of them. There was another car sitting outside, in the plowed lot. The man learned from Ruben that the Token Creek Garage was the only one within fifteen miles — a going concern.

The man asked where he and his wife might find local lodging. Ruben directed him to First Widow Lawrence's, kitty-corner across from the store, on the Windsor Road. It was the brown house with the big porch half way around it. The man asked Ruben his name, and told him he had a fine looking establishment.

The gentleman's name was Graff. He and Ruben shook hands when the gentleman left.

The couple drove over to First Widow Lawrence's house. First Widow Lawrence was outside shoveling a path from her porch to the newly plowed driveway when the couple drove up. They spoke to her, were invited in, and found the house charming. They rented the room with the bath.

The gentleman and the lady were from Florida, First Widow Lawrence was to inform the curious and the meddlesome gathered around the stove at Brother Bob's store, early the next morning. Her guests were real estate agents selling vacation lots on the oceanfront down there. The couple was nice, very nice.

Ruben, who had rushed over when he saw First Widow Lawrence walking toward the store, agreed — he and the man had talked when the couple got gas. Why, the man told First Widow Lawrence her room and board was too low, insisting he and his wife either pay more or at least he be allowed to carry in wood, just to be sure First Widow Lawrence got her money's worth. First Widow Lawrence told the gentleman bringing in wood was just fine, if he insisted. After dinner the lady had right away helped with the dishes. Later on, all three of them took coffee in the living room and had a very interesting chat about the Florida climate. The three of them just talked and talked all evening long, with the man tending the fire. He even banked the stoves for the night when they were ready for bed.

And this morning, when First Widow Lawrence inspected their room, while the gentleman and his wife were downstairs eating breakfast, she found the bed made and things very tidy. First Widow Lawrence had also seen a lot of official-looking papers, nicely fanned out on the writing desk, with seals and signatures on them, plus colored maps, not to mention a stack of impressive photographs of Florida, with palm trees and all. The couple hoped to come over to the store on Sat-

urday to speak to whoever might be interested in buying a seafront lot on the Atlantic coast, near a town
called Boca Raton. First Widow Lawrence said the
gentleman and lady had sent her, on their behalf, to
obtain the proprietor's permission before they would
come over. Brother Bob shrugged his shoulders and
nodded. Sure they could come over. Good for business.

First Widow Lawrence had other, more personal
information about the couple. Boca Raton was the area
of Florida where they had lived since they had left Wisconsin. Originally, they were from Milwaukee. They
had grown up there and had been married there, but
family obligations had taken them to Florida.

When they settled in Florida, there was plenty of
land available, so they had bought up several coastal
lots for investment. Now they wanted to get their money
out of them because they had held onto them for coming on seven years.

But the major reason for selling was they needed
the money to send a niece to college. The niece was the
woman's sister's child; they had raised her after the
mother had drowned and the despairing father disappeared. Brother Bob looked up Boca Raton in an atlas;
there it was, just south of Palm Beach, right on the ocean.

The agents arrived at Brother Bob's store on Saturday morning promptly at nine. They were pleased to
find Brother Bob had cleared a long table in the back
room so they could set out their papers and photographs. First Widow Lawrence was with the couple, to
help with introductions. Brother Bob had fired up the
spare wood stove early, so the room was comfortably
warm. He also had a pot of coffee going, to sustain the
agents as they dealt with the expected crowd.

Not that there would likely be buyers for the lots.
The Depression had a hard grip on the cold land. There
weren't many in Token Creek — let alone that end of
Dane County — with money for fancy properties down

in Florida. Still, there would be a good many who would brave the weather to keep up with what was going on, or seek the honor of talking to the attractive couple. And most everyone would want to take an envious look at those photographs of a place that was warm in the winter.

The lots were a full acre in size. The plot maps showed them to be almost square, slightly wider on the waterside than on the shoreward side where the access road ran. Each piece of land had over 220 feet frontage on the water.

You could put a single trailer on your lot — that was the law. But if you did, you had to build within five years. Such regulations were to keep trailer parks from sprouting up. The taxes amounted to $65.00 a year, which is where they had been since the couple bought the lots. The taxes would probably go up in the next ten or so years, when the local government realized how valuable the properties were. That was a sure sign of a good investment. The first year's taxes were included in the purchase price. The man and his wife were originally from Milwaukee, they reminded everyone. He was a Wisconsin notary. Nice, polite people, all in all. They knew a lot about farming. The gentleman was particularly impressed at how well kept the farms around Token Creek were. He hadn't seen any buildings or barns that needed paint. He complimented Mr. Yon Hamsum on the size of his house. So did the lady.

The couple was going to hold onto two lots for themselves, to build a house on one day. An acre lot, on the water, cost $590.00 with all the paperwork, including the deed transfers in Florida, notary fee, and as mentioned, the first year's Boca Raton taxes. With entire farms around Token Creek going for $15.00 an acre, and that was high, most people were incredulous at the $590.00 for a single acre, waving off even consideration of such nonsense. But, then, the land was right on the Atlantic Ocean don't forget, so of course it was expensive by our standards.

You could sit under the shade of a palm tree on any one of the lots, and all day long too, just watching the ocean. If you felt like it, you could walk into the surf and cool off — even have a dip before lunch. Florida was a paradise, like the place you hoped to go for life in the sweet by-and-by. Right now you could bet it was 75 degrees down there, with oranges and lemons growing right in people's backyards.

And talk about fishing. Why, it was the best in the world. To save costs, Mr. and Mrs. Graff handled everything right then and there, since he was a Wisconsin notary and both were licensed real estate agents. They showed their licenses and certificates first thing, each placed in very nice frames that they set right up on the table. They didn't want there to be any question whatsoever about credentials.

There was a lot of looking at photographs, and wishing, but nobody seemed warmed up to the idea of buying more than a thousand miles away. Prospects looked as bleak as the dreary countryside in the raw February weather. Toward noon, Mrs. Graff took the initiative.

"Have you gentlemen considered a joint venture?" she asked Able Greun and Ruben Rodefeld, the owners of the Token Creek Garage, who had been sitting around for nearly an hour admiring the Florida photographs, not to mention competing for conversation with the good-looking lady real estate agent. They had their young helper, Albert Tippergore, over at the garage pumping gas and holding down the fort.

"By golly, no. But that's a pretty good idea, when you come to think of it; of course, that's what you do with ideas — think 'em," chuckled Ruben, whose face turned seven shades of red when the pretty Mrs. Graff smiled ever so warmly at him. She appreciated humor.

"What I mean is, Mr. Rodefeld and Mr. Greun, several people together could purchase a lot. It could be a group vacation retreat as well as a group investment."

It was amazing how she remembered exactly who someone was, once introduced. She had met perhaps twenty people within the first half-hour of coming in and yet was able to call each by name, when she talked to them again, without having to ask at all who somebody was. Mr. Graff showed the same talent, especially with the women.

"Well, maybe some other people would come in with us. What do you think, Able?"

"Who'd run the garage if we went off to Florida?" Able asked his partner.

"Why, one of us would go at a time, maybe with some of the other co-owners."

Ruben shrugged, rolling his eyes to indicate to the lady agent that he was surprised Able hadn't thought of such an obvious possibility.

"Now, you, sir, have just had a very good idea," said the charming lady, lightly putting her hand on his arm. She was impressed with such quick reasoning.

The gist of this conversation soon got around, sparking some serious talk of going in together on a lot. At half-past twelve, the couple returned to First Widow Lawrence's for lunch. Several people stayed on, considering the idea of a group purchase. Ruben and Able went over to their gas station to check on activities; they talked things over while they ate.

The real estate agents returned at two o'clock for an afternoon session. Ruben Rodefeld and Able Greun were waiting for them. The two mechanics declared they would each put up a hundred dollars toward a lot if there were others willing to do the same.

"Oh, that's marvelous, Mr. Rodefeld and Mr. Greun. I can see you recognize a good investment when you see one," said the lady real estate agent, shaking their hands.

"I'll bet that's how you got into the garage business. You saw an opportunity and you made a wise decision," continued Mr. Graff as he too congratulated them.

"Well, I figure if we can afford it, we better go after it," said Able Greun, standing tall.

"That leaves not quite four hundred dollars to raise from other investors," said Mr. Graff. "I hope there are others as smart as yourselves. You'll never go wrong with land in Florida."

Mr. Graff explained how a group of people could buy a lot. They just had to write up an agreement of partnership, and call the partnership something or other. For instance, you could call it The Token Creek Winter Vacation Society. There would have to be officers, like a president, plus a treasurer and a secretary. It could be done; it was very straightforward. He knew how to do all the paperwork. But, by the end of the day, although a good number of people had looked and talked, no one beyond Ruben and Able came forward with even the makings of an offer.

Shortly before four-thirty the couple started gathering up the paraphernalia. It was already getting dark. Brother Bob's thermometer showed two degrees — even the short walk to First Widow Lawrence's would be a frigid one. The couple promised to be back on Monday morning, but not for the whole day. By then, if there were no other parties willing to go in with Ruben and Able, they might head north to Green Bay, in spite of the weather, to try their luck up there. They had fellow real estate agents in Green Bay, who could doubtless direct them to buyers. The couple inquired about a church for the next day, eventually deciding on the one at Token Creek, which was the closest. Not that it would matter about which church, as far as they were concerned. Let us not forget we are all one here under God's great roof.

That evening as she served dinner to her guests, First Widow Lawrence gained sufficient control over the butterflies in her stomach to declare she was interested in participating in the joint purchase. Mrs. Graff stood up and hugged her — she was so pleased for First Widow Lawrence. After telling her how pleased he was, Mr. Graff suggested First Widow Lawrence inform Mr. Rodefeld and Mr. Greun of her courageous decision. The two bachelors would be relieved to know they weren't alone.

After dinner, Mrs. Graff insisted she wash the dishes so Mr. Graff could drive First Widow Charlotte Lawrence up to Ruben and Able's. He needed to warm up his car, anyway. First Widow Lawrence had never ridden in a Packard before.

The next day, during the service at the Token Creek Church, as the chilled congregation was intoning the twenty-third Psalm ("...He maketh me to lie down in green pastures, He leadeth me beside the still waters...."), Mrs. Knut Yon Hamsum looked at her husband and nodded. They had been awake half the night considering. She had made up her mind. It was decided.

The sermon that morning was based on a passage from Ecclesiastes:

> *I returned, and saw under the sun,*
> *That the race is not to the swift,*
> *Nor the battle to the strong,*
> *Neither yet bread to the wise,*
> *Nor yet riches to men of understanding,*
> *Nor yet favor to the men of skill;*
> *But time and chance happeneth to them all.*

After the service, Mr. and Mrs. Yon Hamsum found the young couple in the church vestibule, chatting with the minister. The Yon Hamsums managed to get the couple's attention, and got them back into the sanctuary. Mr. and Mrs. Yon Hamsum declared they wanted to go in with the others. Mrs. Graff was so pleased for the Yon Hamsums that she hugged Mrs. Yon Hamsum.

Mr. Graff shook Mr. Yon Hamsum's hand.

"We've worked hard all our lives. There aren't children, so we can spend a little, I guess," said Alice Yon Hamsum.

"You should do something for yourselves. You deserve it," said the lady, with frank sincerity.

"Next winter you will go to Florida," said Mr. Graff. "No more freezing Februarys."

Mrs. Graff suggested an immediate meeting of all the interested parties at First Widow Lawrence's. Ruben and Able weren't at church; they were probably working on somebody or other's car down at the garage. Why didn't everyone drive back there to inform the two men about the new investors? Mrs. and Mrs. Graff, with First Widow Lawrence in the front seat of the impressive Packard, followed the Yon Hamsum's little truck back to the Token Creek Garage.

They found the two mechanics trying to start a Model A. Both were certainly willing to leave off the cranking and tinkering to discuss real estate investing; just let them clean themselves up a little bit first, then they'd be over to First Widow Lawrence's. First Widow Lawrence said she would have lunch ready by the time they got there.

An hour later Mr. Graff called to order the investment group's first meeting. The members were topping off lunch with a round of First Widow Lawrence's pie and coffee, in her warm kitchen.

"At the moment, you have Mr. Rodefeld and Mr. Greun who have agreed to invest one hundred dollars each, for a total of two hundred dollars; Mrs. Lawrence has agreed to put up one hundred fifty dollars; the Yon Hamsums wish to invest one hundred dollars. That comes to four hundred fifty dollars. One more investor could be enough. Do you know of anyone else who might want to join you?'

"The person who can afford it, is that Brother Bob. He's always at the store bringing in money. Let him spend some of it for a change," declared First Widow Lawrence.

"I could talk to him," offered Ruben Rodefeld.

"He's pretty tight. I doubt you'll get anywhere with him," said Able Greun. "How about Big Stella Hoogewind?"

"She can afford it too," said First Widow Lawrence.

"I'm sorry to interrupt this meeting," said Mr. Graff, laying a warm hand on First Widow Lawrence's arm, "but I have to say this apple pie is wonderful, Mrs. Lawrence. Truly wonderful." There was a chorus of agreement.

"What kind of apples do you use, dear?" asked Mrs. Graff.

"Jonathans. I keep them in the root cellar. I think I should talk to Stella Hoogewind. Does anyone object?"

Ruben Rodefeld was surprised that, on her own, Big Stella Hoogewind hadn't considered buying in. She was always trying to get involved in things.

First Widow Lawrence nodded her agreement.

Mrs. Graff said she had met Mrs. Hoogewind at the store and had found her a very, very interesting person. Then Able Greun told how Big Mrs. Hoogewind was set for life because she still owned and had the income from her late husband's hardware and feed store over in Deerfield. Somebody ran it for her. She could buy a piece of Florida all on her own.

"I do like the lady," decided Mrs. Graff.

"I could go see her after I do the dishes," said First Widow Lawrence.

"Now dear, don't be silly; Mr. Graff and I will clean up," said the lady real estate agent. "You should go over and speak to Mrs. Hoogewind, just to see if she might be interested."

So while the real estate agents plus the remaining investors cleared the table and began washing dishes, First Widow Lawrence, along with Ruben Rodefeld driving the garage tow truck, left to visit the comfortable widow, Big Stella Hoogewind. Within a half-hour they were back, bringing along the loquacious Mrs. Hoogewind, the last investor. But unless she was willing to invest one hundred forty dollars, or the others upped the ante, they would need yet another person to go in with them. But just as Big Mrs. Hoogewind was about to announce that she was ready to meet the needs of the group — after all, she could afford it — Mr. Graff provided a far better solution:

"There are five of you willing to put up one hundred dollars plus Mrs. Lawrence who would like to contribute one hundred fifty. So you have five hundred fifty dollars. The cost of the lot you picked out, which is in the best location of them all, was supposed to be five hundred ninety dollars. Now it doesn't look like you're going to find anyone else to go in with you, so I'm willing, or Mrs. Graff and I are willing — Bonnie and I talked it over together last night, in bed — we're willing to take five hundred fifty dollars for the property. What I mean is, if you each contribute ten dollars more, except our wonderful hostess, Mrs. Lawrence, who can reduce her offer, you'll all be putting in the same amount.

"That means nobody will have controlling interest — which is democratic, so to speak. So there you are. You can have the lot for five hundred fifty dollars."

The group couldn't thank him, and his wife, enough. First Widow Lawrence kept shaking his hand as tears welled up in her eyes. Big Mrs. Hoogewind said over and over how pleased she was that the group asked her to join in. Mrs. Lawrence brought out a bottle of plum brandy and they all had a glass.

"If we buy the land now, I mean tomorrow, after we all get to the bank and draw out the money, could we go down there this winter?" Big Mrs. Hoogewind asked.

"Why, of course," answered Mrs. Graff. "It will

be yours as soon as you all sign the papers. The deed will be registered in your name in about two weeks. We will be sure to mail the paperwork to the Boca Raton court house right away, special delivery, but the mail each way will take a week or two, plus the courthouse will take a few days. If you want to, you can take the deed to Florida yourself and save time," she teased.

"Well, you know; I just might do that," laughed First Widow Lawrence.

"And I'll go with you," said Big Stella Hoogewind.

Mr. Graff made the paperwork easy for them. First, he drew up what he called a partnership agreement, in which the parties named Able Greun, Ruben Rodefeld, Charlotte Lawrence, Knut and Alice Chalmers Yon Hamsum, and Stella Hedwig Hoogewind, had come together in common interest to form the Token Creek Land Company (the name they decided on), for the purposes of buying and selling of land designated for the common enjoyment and profit of the limited shareholders. Equal access, joint property rights, the ability of one party, i.e. shareholder, to purchase the share or shares of another shareholder, and all other such good and right aspects of their joint investment applied to any properties, structures, or rights of way purchased or to be purchased by and for the aforementioned persons and parties.

The partnership agreement was signed with alacrity. It was notarized with solemn dignity. The Token Creek Land Company had been created.

Mr. Graff had provided a copy of the agreement for everyone, so there was a great deal of passing of a pen back and forth while the signing went on. When they were all done signing the documents, Mrs. Graff cheerfully handed one to each investor.

Next came the actual purchase of the land, by the partnership. Of course, the purchase would only be finalized when payment was made. Nevertheless, all the preliminaries could be taken care of that day.

"He's done this many times before," Mrs. Graff assured them.

The first document was the bill of sale between the Graffs and the partnership. The bill of sale was actually a kind of contract, Mrs. Graff explained: the parties entered into a mutually satisfactory agreement whereby the parties of the first part, Mr. and Mrs. Clyde Graff, agreed, for the sum of five hundred fifty dollars, to sell, release, and surrender, to the party of the second part, that being the Token Creek Land Company, all rights and access to the property being known and designated as lot number seven, comprising one full acre, and whose dimensions were more or less two hundred twenty-four by two hundred twenty-four feet, located on the plat known as Brooklyn's Dune, Palm Beach County, Boca Raton, in the state of Florida, recorded in the Palm Beach County plat book W.P.C. 4/31. A survey map of the parcel, dated in December of the previous year, and thus only two months old, showed the location of boundaries, markers, and other necessary and prominent features. The map was to be included as an attachment to the contract and the deed, when the latter were signed over to the Token Creek Land Company.

"We can't sign anything else until payment is made. If we all signed now, you'd get a free lot," joked Mr. Graff.

"We're all going to the bank first thing in the morning," said First Widow Lawrence.

Late Monday morning, when First Widow Lawrence, Big Mrs. Stella Hoogewind, and the Yon Hamsums had returned from the bank, and when Ruben Rodefeld and Able Greun had brought over their cash contribution from the garage safe, the bill of sale was signed, the deed transfers signed, the documents were notarized, the money handed over, and the receipts distributed.

It was now totally official.

During the celebration lunch that followed, at First Widow Lawrence's, the agents brought up the unpleasant but necessary subject that they said they had been avoiding, but couldn't any longer: they really needed to get started for Green Bay. The weather had cleared and the roads seemed to be pretty well plowed. Their announcement put only a temporary damper on the party, for everyone understood.

Within a half-hour, the couple had gathered up clothing, packed, sorted and put away the business materials, and had everything in the car. It was fortunate the entire investment group was there to say goodbye, to give them some small gifts of appreciation. Mrs. Lawrence found a jar of watermelon pickles, and she absolutely refused payment for their room and board. Ruben and Able went over to their garage and brought back a free set of tire chains, just in case those fancy snow tires weren't enough; the Yon Hamsums managed to get home and back with two jars of gooseberry jam, and Big Mrs. Hoogewind fetched a brightly colored, knitted car blanket for Mrs. Graff — to keep her legs from getting cold on the long trip, although the heater in the big Packard was said to be adequate for any weather.

Hadn't the last four days been a whirlwind? So much had happened. Finally, they could wait no longer. They should get on the road if they wanted to reach at least Fond du Lac before dark, yet wishing they could stay for a while longer. Everyone had been so kind. But they would meet again, in Florida, as neighbors. For now, the gentleman and the lady needed to get their work done so they could be back home by March to plant their garden. That was practically around the corner. Could you imagine planting a garden in March?

The investors escorted the couple to the car. Mr. Graff started it and got out. The women hugged Mrs. Graff — the men shook her hand. Everyone shook hands. They thanked Mr. Graff and he thanked them.

Mr. Graff opened the Packard's door for Mrs. Graff
to get in. He then walked around the front of the car to
get behind the wheel, but he returned to the group and
shook hands, one more time, with all of them. At last,
he went to the driver's side and put himself in. Slowly,
the sedan, with the handsome couple safely inside,
moved off. The man and the lady waved and waved.

The group of investors waved back, saddened to
see them go, to have to say goodbye to such impressive
and respectful people, but at the same time filled with
new anticipation. Each was elated, thinking of the adventure they had begun. Each investor had experienced a sense of liberation from the discontent of the
static, formless winter.

Now the tedium of snow, of ice, of shoveling, of
the dimly lit and short days, of the drudgery of maintaining fires, of the cheerless anxiety of being shut in,
day after day, would no longer weigh on them. The
desolation would seem less, would be less — they would
now meet at each other's houses, visit, conduct business. They would greet each other as fellow business
partners; they would discuss the future, talk about warm
days and tall palm trees, of sunny skies and blue water.
There could be plans made.

There were trips to arrange, transactions to carry
out. Just think — they might even make the trip to
Florida all together one day, taking the limited train from
Chicago, sleeping on a Pullman, eating in the dining
car where there were flowers on every table, where a
ready Negro steward always smiled at them, welcoming them each morning, noon, and night with food
cooked to order, as they watched the countryside blur
by, rolling southward to warm freedom.

The investors lingered at the end of Mrs. Lawrence's
driveway, in the bitter, sharp wind, watching the dark
Packard flow away, down the snow-covered road. They
watched it roll past the frozen Mill Pond, work its way
along the icy bogs, then move past the hushed woods

and white fields. They watched the car head west, seeing it soon become no more than a black object upon the pure whiteness, and then disappear around the far curve of the county road. And thus began the promising life of the Token Creek Land Company.

The Stranger

Our revels are now ended.

1. Prelude

New Year's eve that year came on a Saturday that promised snow. The radio predicted ten inches by morning, with blowing and drifting. Aunt Melodie said this sounded as if they meant a blizzard. After breakfast, Uncle August and Junior went out to do some chores. Emma went along to gather eggs. She could feel that snow was on the way: the temperature was holding right at freezing, and the air was percolating with a rise in humidity that comes ahead of a snowstorm.

The weather vane on the barn put the wind out of the northeast. It was an easy wind though, not strong or gusty, just steady — a little raw perhaps, but pleasant too, with the moisture in it. The clouds were still high and not too dark; the high overcast allowed a skimpy patch of light to show where the sun was. When the clouds became lower, and grayer, and thicker, when there was less light, that was when the snow would start.

Junior remarked how quiet it was. He spoke in a whisper as he said this. He was right. Even the sparrows living under the eaves of the chicken house were nearly silent. There were faint crow calls on and off, from up in the woods somewhere.

Emma didn't stay in the kitchen after she had brought in the eggs. She was intending to, but Aunt Melodie told her it wasn't necessary; there wasn't that much to do now. Emma decided to spend the rest of the morning going over the last chapter of the textbook she used. She went upstairs to her room and settled at her desk. She looked at the book for a moment, then opened it. By the beginning of the chapter's third page, she realized that she wasn't reading with interest, but only picking out a few words in a paragraph before dragging on to the next one. She supposed she was taking in the gist of the material, but she wasn't holding on to the details. She wasn't up to details just now.

She gave up and closed the book. She went to the bookcase, stared at it for a while, then picked out one of her old art history books that Aunt Melodie still kept there. Emma went to the bed and stretched out; she propped herself up with pillows, and started over, looking at the reproductions but not able to bother with the text. Pictures were about all she could manage on a day like this. She guessed that she was too distracted by the thought of the snowstorm to concentrate on anything.

She considered going downstairs to hang around the kitchen with Aunt Melodie, but Aunt Melodie had been gently emphatic about not needing help. Aunt Melodie hadn't said it, but it was evident she wanted to be by herself, not talking. Her aunt had seemed subdued — perhaps apprehensive about the coming bad weather. Emma supposed they all were apprehensive. No one wanted more snow, nor to miss the family New Year's party because they couldn't travel.

When Uncle August and Junior came in from the chores, Junior went up to his room too. He wanted to go over some notes from one of his classes. Uncle August settled in the living room, with a magazine rather than a book. He found himself reading without interest. He got up every few minutes to walk over to the bay window to check the weather, and the darkening sky. Aunt Melodie came in and sat on the window seat. She had a sweater on. She was leafing through a new book. When Uncle August came over to the window to look out, he put his hand on her shoulder, saying how nice it was that the kids were home. Aunt Melodie nodded and smiled. She looked at him for a moment, then returned to her book. It had nice illustrations, she said to Uncle August.

Aunt Melodie and Uncle August usually talked a lot when they were together — about what one of them was reading, or the news, or about some event in the area. This morning they were almost glum. They both were expecting the coming storm. They peered out the window more than anything else, and felt the minutes drag along. But nothing changed over the morning: the clouds stayed up; the wind even dropped a little, and it stayed fairly bright. Uncle August began to wonder if the snow would hold off for a while, or pass father south. Aunt Melodie said she hoped so, but she knew it could change awfully fast, once it made up its mind.

Just before one o'clock Emma came down to announce she was going for a walk. She waved off Uncle
August when he offered to go along. She bundled up
and said she'd be back in a little while. She didn't stay
out even that long — she turned back after going only
halfway to the mailbox. Back inside and unwrapped,
she suggested lunch. Aunt Melodie perked up and said
that was a good idea, and went into the kitchen to make
sandwiches and to heat up some soup. Emma said she
would help. Uncle August went upstairs to get Junior.

After they ate, Uncle August and Junior cleared
and washed so Aunt Melodie and Emma could get
started on the pies. Junior and Uncle August helped
peel the apples. They were taking apple pies and a hot
dish to Grandma and Grandpa's that evening. Aunt
Melodie had made the hot dish the day before; it would
just have to be heated up when they got to the party.

After they'd finished with the apples, Uncle August went out to the machine shed to grease the hy-
draulic plow on the Farmall tractor. It looked like
they'd need it for digging out again by tomorrow morning. Junior returned to his room to take a nap, or at
least to relax, knowing they'd be up late that night.

As soon as the pies were in the oven, Emma went
back upstairs. Aunt Melodie stayed in the kitchen, starting her new book and waiting for the pies to bake. When
Emma got back to her room, she looked around, wondering what to do. She straightened up the desk. She
took off her shoes, thinking about getting undressed for
a bath. She saw the art book she had left on her bed
and returned it to the bookshelf. After that, she took
out her clothing for the evening, but instead of taking a
bath, decided to stretch out on the bed again with the
textbook. She felt chilly and covered herself with a blanket. As she tried to read she kept nodding off. Eventually she put the book on the night table and let herself
fall asleep.

When Emma woke it was later in the afternoon. An aroma of the pies had flowed up the stairs and into her room. They were still cooling in the kitchen, she assumed. She got up and looked outside. There weren't even flurries. Good. She opened the curtains as far as she could to let in more light, but ended up turning on the lamps. She took a warm bath, brushed out her hair, and dressed in a skirt and blouse for the party. On the way downstairs she knocked on Junior's door and asked if he was coming down. He must have been sleeping, because he sounded groggy when he answered that he was. He'd be down in a bit, he said, after he took a quick bath.

In the living room, Emma turned on the floor lamps. She hadn't seen Uncle August stretched out on the couch. The lights woke him; she apologized for startling him. It was all right he said, and sat up. He went to the window. The thermometer was still reading thirty-two but there wasn't even a stray flake coming down. Aunt Melodie and then Junior wandered in a few minutes later. The pies had turned out well, Aunt Melodie said. She'd put up a pot of coffee, if anyone wanted some. Seeing Emma and Junior looking at each other in dismay, she added that the pies were for the party. Sorry, no previews. Junior said he hadn't gotten too far with his work, when Uncle August asked. Emma said she hadn't with hers either.

II. Interlude

As they turned into Grandpa and Grandma's drive, the car's headlights swept over withered, yellowish cornstalks in the big field by the road. A great many of them, most of them, were lying on the frozen ground, like old bones, broken and shattered by the winter storms. A gaunt few were still upright, but they wouldn't survive much longer. In the spring they would be turned under with the first plowing, returned to the earth.

Emma said it looked like they were near the last to arrive: Second Cousin LeRoy and Aunt Ollie's car was already there; so was Carl and Mabel's. Grandma and Grandpa must have invited Big Mrs. Hoogewind — her car was parked close to the house. She would have brought along First Widow Lawrence. The Yon Hamsum's pickup was closer to the road. They didn't see Brother Bob's Studebaker, which wasn't surprising — he was often late to get-togethers if customers lingered in his store. All the vehicles were parked facing the road, ready to escape quickly if the snow began and got heavy.

Uncle August drove around and past the house. He parked facing down the drive as the others had done. There were still no snow flurries. As they walked to the house, they were beginning to hope the snow might come late enough to let them stay until midnight. Grandpa opened the door as they reached the top of the porch steps. He had been watching for them.

When Grandpa saw Emma and Junior, he said, "You two get more grown up every time I see you."

Emma and Junior had been taller than Grandpa for a long time now, so he meant more mature. He was proud of them. He announced them as the two professors when they entered the bright living room.

There was a general hubbub of hellos. Emma and Junior took the time to speak to one after another of the friends and relatives. Grandma stood beside Grandpa. She didn't say much. Emma noticed that Grandma looked a bit unkempt, and distracted, as if she hadn't started getting ready until the last minute. When Junior gave her a hug, she called him by the wrong name. It wasn't just that she used the wrong name that was troublesome — it was the name she used. She had said, Karl. Did she mean the Wyoming Carl, Mabel's husband, who was there in the room, or did she mean the other Uncle Karl? Aunt Melodie offered to brush

Grandma's hair for her, so the two of them left the room and went upstairs. Junior asked Grandpa how Grandma was doing. Uncle August was listening. Grandpa told him that Grandma got mixed up sometimes but she was doing well enough.

When Grandma and Aunt Melodie returned from upstairs, Grandpa said he thought it was high time for some music.

"Will you play something for us, mother?" he asked Grandma.

"I can't just now," she answered, looking at him carefully.

So Uncle August was persuaded to sit down at the piano. He started easily and played well, as he always did. He knew a great many tunes and songs, without needing sheet music to remember them. He even played some classical pieces. He bridged smoothly from waltzes, to ragtime, or to his beloved Mozart, without a pause in the flow, easily changing key. He added little fanfares as he drifted from one melody to another. He played more slowly than Emma remembered. He had mentioned that his hands were stiffer from arthritis this year. That must have been why the music was slightly more melancholy than she was used to from him. It was pleasant all the same. Second Cousin LeRoy and Aunt Ollie walked over to the piano to watch and listen. After all these years, they still held hands.

Mabel and Carl were sitting at the card table, with the Yon Hamsums, all listening to Uncle August. First Widow Lawrence and Big Mrs. Stella Hoogewind had gone into the dining room to find table cloths and to get out Grandma's silver. The two widows paused for a few minutes when Uncle August started playing. Then they went back to setting the big table, and humming along with the tunes, smiling at each other. They sang the snatches of a chorus of one of the songs they knew, and then laughed.

Emma and Junior sat down with Grandpa and

Grandma, and Aunt Melodie, on the couch. After they listened for a while, Aunt Melodie and Grandpa excused themselves and left for the kitchen. Emma and Junior both thought that their departure was a signal to start bringing out the food, so they got up to follow along and help. Aunt Melodie said she just wanted to talk to Grandpa. Would they mind staying with Grandma? They'd put things out a little later, after everybody had visited a bit more, and had had some punch or whatnot.

"Anyway, Brother Bob's not here yet. Let's wait for him," she said.

The kids sat down again, to chat with Grandma. Emma noticed the photographs in frames on the end table. There were seven, the same as she remembered. Three were of Emma and Junior; one was a black and white, of them standing on Grandma and Grandpa's porch. It dated from their grade school days. The other two were individual, cap-and-gown college graduation shots, in color. There was a medium-sized studio photograph of Uncle August and Aunt Melodie, dating from about fifteen years earlier, as near as Emma could recall. Uncle August and Aunt Melodie had given a copy to everyone because it had turned out so well. There was a small wedding photograph of Second Cousin LeRoy and Aunt Olivia, who had been married by a judge.

There was another from six years ago. It was of Grandma and Grandpa, taken on their fiftieth anniversary celebration at Uncle August and Aunt Melodie's house. The picture was not a formal one — it was a very good snapshot of the two of them sitting together on the porch swing, just before the party. Grandpa was wearing a dark blue suit, with a white shirt and dark red tie. The dark suit and tie emphasized his white hair. It seemed as starkly white as the shirt. He was looking at the camera with a wry smile on his pleasant, tanned face, as if he were about to wink at whoever was taking the picture. Grandma was in a beige dress with a white lace collar. Her hair, unlike Grandpa's, was more gray than white. She was flushed, with a surprised look on her face, although you could see the beginnings of a smile coming on. She had her hand on Grandpa's arm.

The last photograph, the oldest and largest, was silver-framed, and one which Emma had admired many times. It was Grandpa and Grandma's wedding photograph, in black and white but retouched to add color to their cheeks and lips, and eyes. It was quite formal, taken close up, just of their heads and shoulders. There was excellent quality of detail; you could see the warp and weave of the fine clothes they wore. The photograph had not been taken on the same day as their marriage, but, as the story went, a few days later in Milwaukee, where they had gone for a few days, after the wedding. Grandpa and Grandma looked so startlingly young in the picture that Emma had often thought they were really not the same people as her grandparents, which was a silly thing even to imagine. Of course it was unquestionably Grandma and Grandpa. Even now Grandpa had the same full head of hair as he had had then, only now it was snow white instead of brown going on blond. The ironic smile was there too, predicting a sense of humor and his familiar good nature.

And the same aspect of mild surprise, or perhaps bewilderment, was on young Grandma's lovely face. The same expression could be seen in the much later anniversary photograph. It might be called a look of delight, as if she had at that very moment made some new discovery. It was an engaging look, bordering on the mischievous or even flirtatious. They had been a very handsome couple, striking perhaps. Grandma had been a real beauty. Funny; when Emma thought about it, Grandma was younger in the marriage photograph than she, Emma, was now. People married earlier in those days.

Emma turned toward Grandma, sitting on the couch. Junior was asking her about the old farm, and all the animals they used to have. Grandma said she couldn't recall their names, but there had been a lot of them, and they certainly had kept Grandpa and that what's-his-name hired man pretty busy.

"What ever happened to Old Tillman?" Junior wondered, referring to the long-gone hired man. "Did he really get angry and leave when you sold the stock and the machinery?"

"I don't remember now. I think he went to live with a sister somewhere."

"He was from Iowa, wasn't he?" Emma asked.

"I don't remember for certain, dear," she sighed. "He lived here so long that we were his family." She paused for a few seconds, smiling at them. "And what have you two been doing for fun these days?" she asked.

"Just relaxing. I'm rewriting something, or trying to. Junior says he's preparing the last part of his pig course. It's nice to be home."

"So busy," said Grandma, shaking her head. "My land."

Aunt Melodie and Grandpa came back from the kitchen. Grandpa looked grim. He walked straight over to the front window. He pulled aside one of the drapes a little, to look out. Junior started to make space for Aunt Melodie, but she sat down on the edge of the couch to be close to Grandma. Aunt Melodie took Grandma's hands in hers.

"Oh, Melodie. It's so good you could come by," Grandma said disconsolately. Her voice trembled as she spoke. Tears were welling up in her eyes. She moved her head slightly from side to side as she stared at Aunt Melodie.

"It's good to see you too, Grandma," Aunt Melodie told her. "Is everything all right?"

"Every time there's snow, it makes me think of poor

Karl, lying out there freezing. When we buried him, it was snowing so hard. Oh my." She pointed to Junior's photograph.

Aunt Melodie rubbed Grandma's hands, telling her she mustn't let herself dwell on such things. Emma and Junior both realized that Grandma must have been thinking of Karl when she had called Junior by the wrong name. It was said Junior looked very much like Karl. The talk of snow, and seeing the photograph, and then Junior, must have started Grandma thinking about her long-dead son. He'd been dead for well over forty years. They buried him in the little cemetery, during a snowstorm . Emma and Junior knew the story.

Aunt Melodie was telling Grandma that it had been a very long time ago, now. Karl had been gone for many years. Grandma should try to put it out of her mind. She should try not to dwell on it.

"I suppose not," Grandma whimpered. She sat quietly for a few moments. Aunt Melodie offered her a handkerchief. She took it and wiped her eyes. Emma and Junior weren't sure what to say. Grandma sighed and smiled at the children. She seemed to be getting a hold of herself. She looked around the busy room, still smiling. Her eyes fell on Grandpa, who was still at the other end of the living room, holding aside a drape, peering outside and into the driveway. Uncle August was playing softly on the piano. Emma was trying to remember the name of the tune. She looked at Junior, who shrugged slightly. He couldn't recall either.

Grandma looked at Grandpa again, then leaned closer to Aunt Melodie.

"I have to talk to you and the children," Grandma whispered huskily.

Just then there was a racket of stomping feet outside the front door. Grandpa was already walking toward it.

"Well, guess who's finally here?" he exclaimed. He opened the door, letting in a rush of cold air as Brother

Bob scurried inside. He carried a large, cured ham under his arm. Grandpa quickly closed the door. Grandma moved herself forward on the couch, but couldn't quite push up to stand. She sat on the edge of the couch with her lips slightly parted, her eyes following Brother Bob.

"I should help," she said, steadying herself.

"We're not going to eat for a while yet. Let's just visit," Junior said to her, coaxing her to sit back. Junior waved to Brother Bob, who winked at him, while removing his coat.

"Brother Bob's brought a ham," Grandpa told everyone.

"Well, he did bring himself," said Uncle August, over the light notes of the piano. There was some chuckling around the room. Brother Bob held up the ham above his head, and turned in a circle, showing it off. He then bowed to Uncle August.

"Robert, thank you. You can take it right to the dining room. Just put it on the sideboard," Aunt Melodie said to him. "We'll slice it in a few minutes."

When Brother Bob returned from the dining room, he came over to the couch to greet Grandma.

"Oh my goodness. Hello there," Grandma said to him, trying to stand, but again giving up when she couldn't quite make it. She kept holding on to Brother Bob's hand. He bent down and kissed her wrinkled cheek.

"Good to see you, Bob," Emma said, as she took her turn to hug him.

After a moment, Brother Bob gestured a temporary goodbye and went to the card table, to greet Carl and Mabel, and the Yon Hamsums. Second Cousin LeRoy and Aunt Olivia left the piano, and went over to say hello to him. Uncle August started playing, *For He's a Jolly Good Fellow*. Aunt Melodie thought about leaving Grandma, but first she wanted to know what it was that Grandma had to confide in her and the children.

"Oh my. Well, I don't remember now. Isn't that funny? What was it?" Grandma wondered.

"It will come to you in a minute," Aunt Melodie assured her.

Aunt Melodie told Emma and Junior that she'd stay with Grandma if they wanted to get something to drink, and to talk to the others. They said that would be nice; one of them would come back in a few minutes and relieve Aunt Melodie. They went to join the group at the card table. Uncle Carl was pleased to see them. He wanted to hear about the University and what graduate work was like these days. Emma talked about the writing course she was teaching.

"And you have your own courses and seminars to worry about too," declared Aunt Mabel.

"It's not so bad," Emma said. "The professors help a lot."

"I hear Junior is teaching about pigs,' Second Cousin LeRoy offered.

Junior nodded, but he said it was the professor who did the lecturing. Junior just held a class for the under-graduates, where they could ask questions plus get some hands-on experience with the animals.

"How'd you get so interested in pigs, of all things?" Alice Chalmers Yon Hamsum asked.

"Well, I learned so much from Dill, Grandpa's old pig, that it just seemed natural to study them, I guess."

"The never-to-be-forgotten Dill," Emma laughed.

Then Grandpa told the story of how, when Junior was in the third grade, Junior had persuaded him to loan out Dill for the demonstration part of a school speech. Junior was supposed to give a talk on farm animals, so he wanted to make it realistic. Well, it seemed the pig took an immediate dislike to the teacher, old Miss Liptrap.

"When Junior and Dill walked up to the front of the class for the speech, next to the teacher's desk, the

pig started squealing at the top of his lungs at Miss
Liptrap. Then he started toward her. When Miss
Liptrap yelled for Junior to get the pig out of there, Dill
ran at her and she had to stand on a chair, until Junior
got him under control. She wouldn't let Junior back in
school until he took the pig home, even when Junior
offered to lock him in the school woodshed for the rest
of the day."

"Dill was a good judge of character," Junior
giggled.

"He lived a good life, did that pig," said Uncle
August, playing the piano softly so he could follow the
conversation.

"They all did. All our animals," Grandpa said. "I
hated to see them go."

"Who are you renting the land to, Grandpa?"
Emma asked.

"To the oldest Hoogewind boy, the one they call
Rocky. He rents from August too."

"He has for quite some time now, since this fit of
people retiring started spreading all over the county,"
August added, still playing the piano.

"He's done well for himself. He works three
farms," Uncle Carl noted.

"Just corn and hay though, and that he sells. No
livestock except beef, and he sells them in the fall, so he
can cook in a restaurant in Madison," Second Cousin
LeRoy pointed out.

The implication could have been that young
Hoogewind was less a farmer than a cook, or was
obliged to be, to make ends meet.

Aunt Melodie announced that they might want to
eat dinner soon, in case it started snowing, and they
would have to ring in the New Year a little early. It did
look like it was starting, Grandpa told them, looking
out the window. He said he could see flurries in the
yard light. Several of them looked, and agreed.

But while they were eating, the snow let off almost altogether, so they relaxed and planned on cheering for the New Year at the right time after all.

Grandpa was always expected to make an after-dinner speech when the family had a gathering. They hadn't all been together for some time, so for the past few days he had been thinking about all the things he wanted to say. He usually told a funny story or two, to warm up, like the one he had just told about Junior and the pig. After his stories, he usually said something thoughtful, then offered a toast.

There were so many stories. He had definitely planned to tell about the seven cats who all had kittens at the same time, so that overnight they had found themselves with more than fifty cats on the farm. Then he'd talk about something more serious. He intended to mention that he and Grandma were now in their fifty-sixth year of marriage, and how they hoped to see everyone for more holidays to come. He'd mention how proud they all were of the next generation, of Emma and Junior, of LeRoy and Olivia's children who, it was too bad, couldn't be here with them tonight. He would mention them in the toast. After his speech, they'd talk and tease each other just a little. But he was so troubled by the conversation in the kitchen with Melodie, earlier in the evening, that he wasn't sure if he would talk much about time passing and people getting on, getting old. He knew that Grandma wasn't doing as well as she should, but he wanted to take care of her, even if Melodie questioned his ability to do that.

He was staring in front of himself, at his pie, mulling his quandary, when someone started tapping a glass with a spoon. In a couple of seconds the whole bunch was doing it, tapping glasses and looking at him with bright smiles. Even Grandma was tapping away joyfully, and laughing as she looked at him. Uncle August gave him the eye and nodded slightly. Grandpa smiled and nodded back. Well, he had to do it. As he stood, the tapping stopped and there was a clatter of applause.

He looked at them kindly, with his warm and familiar smile. They quieted down.

"I had thought I might wait until we were a little farther along with dessert for my few little words, but it looks like you want to hear something, even if we are in the middle of Melodie's pie. I hope that doesn't mean I'm going to miss seconds, while you've got me distracted into talking. So reserve a piece for me now, please."

He paused, and they chuckled and smiled at him.

"It looks like we're going to have more snow, again, whether we want any more or not. August told me he greased his plow today. Maybe if I grease his palm, he'll plow us out too, after the storm."

"I'll take your second piece of pie as a down payment," Uncle August quipped.

Grandpa paused, looking surprised. He stroked his chin thoughtfully. "All things considered, I think Id rather shovel myself out," he decided. "There are some things that you just can't give up."

"I would have made the same choice myself," Second Cousin LeRoy said, laughing.

Then Grandpa gave his speech. He talked about the farm, where he and Grandma had lived since they had been married. He said their life there had been wonderful, and plentiful. It had been sad sometimes, to be sure, but funny sometimes too. He told the seven cats and all-the-kittens-in-one-night story, and how after the forty-nine-plus new kittens had been weaned, he and Grandma, with help from all the relatives who could join them, spent nearly a month hunting up homes for the cats; he had gone to every neighbor and acquaintance in the county, sometimes more than once because they had so many cats to keep track of, and neighbors too. Why, the descendants of those darn cats and kittens still roamed barns and corncribs as far away as Deerfield, and even up to Merrimac, in search of mice and timid dogs. All those cats from one little farm. My land.

And what a beehive that farm had been. What a treasure. It was a place where so much seemed to have been happening, all at once lots of times! It was a place where there swirled a never-ending series of situations and events, some serious, but a lot just plain ridiculous, at least in retrospect. The place had been a little universe all to itself.

So there they were. They had gotten so occupied, dealing with the goings-on and the pace of things, that time got away from them. He guessed they had been so busy watching and being part of the shenanigans that, before they knew it, here they were with children grown up. Now it seemed people were going into an epidemic of retirement, with fields rented out and somebody else's machinery in the sheds.

Well, let's hope that someday the farm will return to its former life. Who knows? Maybe Junior, or Emma, might decide to come back with a wife, or a husband, one of these days, and then things could get started again. There'd be a pig in Dill's old pighouse, and horses in the barn, and cows out there by the pasture pond. There'd be chickens running around and sheep in the sheepfold. And he'd sure like to see another dog like dear old Basil, who knew what you wanted before you even told him. Sometimes he even knew before you did. You just looked out into the pasture, and he'd go and bring the cows in, or maybe you'd nod in the direction of the mailbox, and an hour later, when he heard the mailman coming up the road, he'd trot out to meet him and pick up the mail. What a time they'd had, what a grand and marvelous time.

And that's the way it had been, that's the way it was right now. He proposed they raise their glasses, to drink to the farm, to the family, to this New Year and what it brings, by golly. Let them toast all the wonderful times they'd had; let them remember how the farm had brought them together so often, for so many years.

Let's hope it would continue to do that for years to come.

"Hear, hear," they said.

When they stood to raise their glasses, Brother Bob, to bring back a little levity, and to make a pun in the only way he could, with a gesture, raised his eyeglasses rather than his glass.

III. Finale

They stayed at the table after they finished dessert, talking and waiting for midnight to come. Emma and Junior made a few trips to the kitchen, with dishes and silverware to wash. They even did do a little washing up, as much as their aunts would permit. Aunt Melodie sat by Grandma, keeping her busy so she wouldn't start trying to pick up. They had some more coffee, and chatted about one thing and another. Then Grandma remembered what she wanted to say to Aunt Melodie and the children.

"I have to talk to you and the children," she whispered to Aunt Melodie.

"We can go to the living room," Aunt Melodie suggested.

As she and Grandma stood up, Emma and Junior came back from the kitchen for another load of dishes.

"Grandma has a secret for us," Aunt Melodie told them. "Just for us."

She laughed and raised her eyebrows as she made this announcement, as if the secret were probably some confidence about a gift, or to reveal a little surprise when midnight came. The four of them walked into the living room, to the couch. They could hear a murmur of conversation from the dining room, but they couldn't make out what anyone was saying. They could share Grandma's secret here, without being overheard.

"What do you want to tell us, Grandma?" Aunt Melodie asked. She was serious now.

Grandma hesitated. She glanced around the room,

then looked back toward Melodie and the two young people.

"There's a strange man in the house," she said. "In my house."

They didn't understand. What did she mean?

"I mean, the stranger. He's living here. He's right here, now. Oh, he's very nice, and I enjoy his company." She smiled, looking at them cheerfully.

"Can you show him to us?" Junior asked. He was totally confounded. Grandma sat, hesitating.

"Can you point him out?" Emma gently asked.

"There he is." Grandma gestured toward Grandpa, whom they could see, at the head of the table, in the dining room. "That old one."

"Grandma, that man over there, that stranger; he's your husband, William." Aunt Melodie said quietly.

"Oh no, he is not." Grandma laughed, but there was impatience in her voice too. "I know my husband." She pointed toward the dining room again. "That is not him. That is not my husband, not at all."

"Grandma, listen to me, please. You've known that man there for a long time. You're married to him. That's Grandpa. He's your husband."

"No, he is not. This is my husband, right here," she said with annoyance. She was pointing to the wedding photograph on the end table. She stood and took up the old photograph.

"This is my husband," she said, tapping with her finger on the image of Grandpa on the silver-framed picture. "I don't know who that man over there is. He is very nice, to be sure, that one. He even cooks and does housework, but this is my husband, right here." She tapped on the picture again, then put it down.

The four of them were quiet for a moment.

"Grandma. Let's go back. It's going to be midnight soon," Emma said.

They returned to the dining room together, to ring in another year.

IV. Reprise: The Dead

On the second floor of Grandpa and Grandma's
farmhouse, Uncle August's former room had, for some
time, functioned as a spare room. There was still a bed
and a dresser there, and a lamp on the bedside table,
and a braided rug on the wooden floor. A soft arm-
chair was placed next to the south window. Grandma
and Grandpa kept the bed made and ready, should the
old room become the temporary layover for family, or
for friends, as it had so often done after Uncle August
had left. But, no visitors had stayed in the room for a
long time now.

A few minutes after midnight, Emma climbed the
stairs to sit in the room, wanting to be alone for a while.
She had been deeply affected by Grandma's strange
confusion. She was unsure how she felt. She wanted
to laugh or weep at the same time. When she entered
the darkened room, she found Junior kneeling in the
big chair by the window, with his arms over its back.
He was looking outside toward the yard lights near the
buildings. He told Emma that he had heard Uncle
August talking to Grandpa about selling the land, about
moving Grandma to where she could get professional
care. Emma stood beside the chair, and looked out too.

The lights of the yard fell on dense lines of snow,
on receding layers of silver-white streaks and flakes,
blurred in their rapid descent. Emma and Junior could
hear the faint rustle of their fall, their slight, windblown
brushing on the cold window panes. The air was getting thicker and heavier with snow even as they
watched. Very soon they would not be able to see past
the space that had once been the garden. They could
still see the silent white barn, and the old pighouse, even
the outline of the empty sheep shed, but behind these
old structures were only veils of white, covering the farther blackness. Beyond the empty buildings, they could

see no more of the pastures, nor the lanes, nor the fences, nor the fields of fallen corn. Beyond, there stood only profound darkness.

Emma remained beside her brother, watching the thickly falling snow, listening to its ceaseless tapping. Uncle August and Aunt Melodie would want to leave soon, for the trip home, before the roads got worse.

The radio had been right. Snow was falling over the whole southern half of the state, falling on the marshes and bogs, on fences and lanes, on the miles of silent land. Quieting snow, covering grasses, falling upon the little woods behind the schoolhouse, and on the hushed graves of the cemetery close by. It fell on the new graves, and on the old, on those whose stones were leaning and sinking, that had begun to decay and crumble. Snow was falling relentlessly on all the markers, on the grand and the simple, on the graves of grandparents, of parents, of children and of children's children. Snow was falling on the cold grave of Karl Armstrong, on Rile's, on Leah's. It would not be long before their names, then even the little monuments themselves, would be overcome by another shroud of ceaselessly accumulating white. The deepening snow would soon hide them, extinguish them inch by inch, change them, until the inscriptions were covered and their dates and spans made indistinguishable. Then these chill headstones, row on row, would lose their separateness, to become as one, as the night and the snow progressed.

Yes, the radio had been right. Snow had come, and was falling on the cattail swamp, on the old mill, on the bridges and quiet roads, on the treasured land, on the icebound Mill Pond, and falling softly upon the cold meanders of the quiet, ever-flowing Token Creek.

Aunt Mabel

Give me thy hand, thou fair and gentle creature. I am a friend and come not to punish thee. Be of good cheer! Thou shalt sleep peacefully in my arms.
— Matthius Claudius: *Death and the Maiden*

Swann, Mabel Armstrong

Madison — Mabel Armstrong Swann, age 91, died on Monday, January 13, 1992, at a local nursing home. She was born on May 1, 1900, the daughter of George and Turena Armstrong. She was a charter member of the Token Creek Church. Survivors include three daughters, Rachel (Leon) Reed, Pauline (Richard) Oliverson, and Esther (Rile) Peterson, all of Madison; five grandchildren, April Ann (Harry) Lawrence, Sara (Glen) Tillman, Leah (Rocky) Marion, Karen Lee, all from Madison, and Dr. David Erwin (Susan) of Mount Washington, Maryland; six great-grandchildren, and several nieces and nephews including the authors Emma Armstrong Reed, and Rile J. Armstrong of New York City. She was preceded in death by her husband, Carl, on February 28, 1978, and earlier by her parents, a sister, and two brothers. Funeral services will be held at 2:00 p.m. on Saturday, January 18, 1992, at the HOWARD and PHILLIP FUNERAL HOME, 3725 East Washington Avenue, with the Reverend William G. Peterson officiating. Burial will be at THE TOKEN CREEK CEMETERY, on the Windsor Road north of the village of Token Creek. Friends may call from 12:30 until 2:00 p.m. on Saturday at the funeral home.

About the Author

Erwin Riedner grew up in Wisconsin. He attended the Token Creek Elementary school, a one-room schoolhouse in those days, and now long closed.

Erwin is a graduate of the University of Wisconsin where he majored in French and in Anthropology. He holds a master's degree in literature and languages from the University of Michigan, and a doctorate in audiology and public health from the Johns Hopkins University in Baltimore, where he was once on the faculty.

Erwin has been teaching, carrying on research, and publishing in audiology for the past 25 years. He has been writing fiction for the past seven.

The stories in *Token Creek* are based on tales he has heard, his childhood experiences in Wisconsin, and on memories of the tiny crossroads hamlet of Token Creek, in Dane County in southern Wisconsin. Erwin is currently at work on a second collection of short stories about New York City.

Besides writing, Erwin's hobbies are reading, sailing, and gardening. Erwin and his wife Susan have lived in the Mount Washington area of Baltimore since 1975. They have three grown children Rachel, April, and Sara. A new son-in-law, Harry Gamble, April's husband, has recently joined the family. The whole bunch loves to tell a good story.